7/14

Seeing

AMERICA

Seeing AMERICA

NANCY CROCKER

MEDALLION
P R E S S

Medallion Press, Inc.

Printed in USA

For Charlie[3]

CHAPTER ONE

"HOW ABOUT YOU JUST STOP TREATING me like a titty baby?"

I thought of that one after I was already out the back door. I'm a regular genius at what I should have said.

But to hell with it. Nothing I'd said in eighteen years mattered to Dad. I couldn't swallow water to suit the man. Saturday morning, and he'd started in about a hammer he found out back by the shed. When did I use it? Why didn't I put it back? Would it kill me to ask to borrow his tools in the first place?

Like one of his hammers spending a night outside the toolbox was going to knock the earth off-balance and throw the world into darkness. I walked down the driveway, kicking rocks that belonged to him. Using up air that was his, no doubt.

"Why, hello, John!" Mary Albrecht's voice whipped my head up so fast my neck just about snapped. She was walking by with her folks. "Are you coming uptown for the spectacle?"

I said, "Why, yes, I am," and nodded. "Mornin', ma'am. Sir."

Something fun came to Wakenda about as often as the thirteen-year locusts. *Was I going?* Not *yes* but *hell, yes.* I fell in behind the three of them. Then they turned up the front walk of a house down the street before I could think of any more to say to Mary. Figured.

But the day promised to be a prize on its own. It was one of those beauties in March that can trick you into thinking spring has picked Missouri as her favorite place over all others. Houses were emptying out all along the street, and every person who stepped outside tilted his face toward the sunshine like he was receiving a blessing.

The town's two churches would be hard-pressed the day before Judgment to scare up a crowd as big as was gathering that noon. When the old Number 3 engine split the air with a mournful wail and all the hounds in town took up a chorus behind it, it was a little like a church bell and choir: *Come, all ye gawkers! Banty Wilson's about to make a jackass of himself!* Made me grin.

Banty had bought the town's first automobile a few months back and since then claimed the Maxwell could do just about everything but give birth and churn butter. Finally, he bragged it was faster than a MoPac steam engine.

But that had turned out to be one more brag than Curly Weis could stand. So Curly talked his boss into

taking Number 3 out of service that Saturday morning for the solitary purpose of shutting the blowhard's
mouth. My guess was, the big shots at the railroad
were fed up hearing about automobiles putting trains
out of business someday. Nobody with a lick of sense
thought Banty had a chance at winning the race, but
it wasn't going to bother anybody to watch his ass
handed to him either.

By the time I got to Main Street, I was walking
through a cloud of steam. Faces appeared like specters
and then got swallowed up again in the mist.

Then one figure appeared out of the fog, looking still as a statue at the sidewalk railing. When I
got closer, I saw it was Paul Bricken. Of course. Too
many people trying to get somewhere they weren't,
stepping on feet and poking elbows in their neighbors'
ribs, but around Paul there might have been a shield
keeping everybody a foot away. Like blindness might
be catching.

In the year Paul had been home after finishing high
school in St. Louis, I'd watched how folks ignored
him almost like they were the ones who couldn't see.
I did have the advantage of being used to him. But
you'd think somebody else could at least make an effort
once in a while.

I went up and bumped his elbow, and the face
that turned could have been carved out of wood.
"Hey, Paul," I said. "John Hartmann. How you doin'
today?"

His shoulders relaxed some. "Fine, John, thanks. You?"

"Aw, been better. Been better." I bent toward his ear. "Let's just say when Thanksgiving rolls around, I'll be thankful I've got only two parents."

He laughed louder than the joke was worth, and heads turned like somebody had rattled off a fart in church. I bet most of them had never heard Paul laugh.

Then he said, "Can I ask you a small favor?"

"Sure. Name it."

"Would you stand here and tell me what goes on?"

I was hoping to park myself next to Mary Albrecht, but Paul's face had gone all the way red just for asking, and I couldn't ignore that if I'd wanted to. I heard myself say, "Sure, I will. Just let me finish my rounds, and I'll come back before the race starts."

That seemed to lift his chin a fraction higher.

I came across Katie McCombs running through a forest of legs as I walked on, and I scooped her up and threw her in the air a few times to hear her squeal. My little sister had just about outgrown that. But then Ellen McCombs came steaming my way like a battleship and set in squawking like women do—putting on they're upset when really they just want everybody in the county to hear what devoted mothers they are—so I set Katie down and went on.

I wandered through the whole crowd without finding Mary, and my enthusiasm was severely tempered by the time I went back and started explaining to Paul how little he was missing. "Banty's pullin' the Maxwell up next to the tracks and makin' a show out of linin' up exactly even with the cowcatcher on Number 3. Curly's got about a week's worth of steam goin', but you can probably tell that."

I didn't much care anymore, but Paul's face looked like Christmas morning. So I filled in some. "Ruby Watts is tryin' so hard to get Billy Sweeney's attention she's just about to stand on her head. Yep, there she goes . . . Dang it! She remembered to put on drawers this morning . . . Whoa! Roy Auptman's gut is gettin' so big it's gonna need its own address before long."

Paul paid me in chuckles.

And then "There they go" was the end of it for us. Terms of the race were ten miles side by side—Wakenda to Miami Station—so we saw the start, a few others would see the finish, and in between was nothing but hot air.

That was pretty much the story of Wakenda, if you asked me. High hopes when something—anything—was about to happen, then a letdown when the same old people showed up and nothing much went on.

The town was a lot like the Missouri River four miles south. It might be different water running past the bank every day, every month, every year, but it all looked the same. High school sweethearts got married after graduation and started producing the next generation of high school sweethearts. Boys, for the most part, followed their fathers into the fields or onto the river. At any gathering, you could see the past, present, and future in one sweep.

But no matter how little happened, there was always plenty for the men to hash out over beers later on. Thank God. Even if the talk at Charlie's didn't rise above the topics of crops and the weather, it beat going home. I asked Paul if he wanted to come along, but before he could answer, his dad showed up.

"Have you had enough foolishness?"

I winced, but Paul just said, "Yes, Father," and then, "Thank you, John," with his face a blank mask. I couldn't imagine what was in his mind as they walked away.

Mr. Bricken spent his days at the bank in Carrollton saying yea or nay on crop loans to all the farmers in the area, and even my dad jumped when Mr. Bricken said the word. But you'd think he could have a kind word for his son. His only kid.

Enough foolishness? Even I had a longer leash than that.

I went on to Charlie's alone and was toward the end of my first beer when a couple of men came in scratching their heads. They'd gone to Miami Station that morning to watch Curly win the race and couldn't explain what they'd seen instead. Banty Wilson— acting nervous, they decided—had driven up in the

Maxwell while there was still no train in sight, and he'd said he better just keep on going because he had things to do at home. Everybody agreed that last part alone was cause for suspicion.

These two men had waited another half an hour, then driven their teams back to Wakenda to see if anyone there had news. Nobody did.

But pretty soon, Joe Clipner came in about to bust. He said he'd been coming home on Well's Road alongside the railroad tracks and had come upon Curly climbing the fence at the back of his own farm, with Number 3 sitting dead on the tracks nearby.

"And I got out and said, 'Curly, what the hell you doin'?'" Joe told us. "And he said he was so disgusted he couldn't even work up an anger yet. Said he was only a mile or so out of town when he pulled up even to Banty's tin can and passed the little bastard. But about then, he saw somethin' up ahead on the tracks, and before he could even reach for his field glasses, he knew. That little shit had taken one of Curly's own heifers, just about ripe, and staked her out so she was astraddle the tracks. Curly said he about busted an aorta before he got Number 3 stopped no more than ten feet from that poor little Hereford. He got her back in the pasture and had just come from cleanin' up in the house when I caught up to him."

Joe sat back then and took a long pull on his beer like he'd accomplished a great feat. When gossip is the local pastime, knowing something before everybody else does can start to feel a lot like success.

The crowd at Charlie's was too thick for me to know who was talking half the time, but some voices carried. Somebody yelled, "How did he think he'd get away with it? Banty's an idiot, but he's not stupid." The rest of the men grumbled in agreement.

Another man shouted, "Oh, he didn't think he'd get away with it. He's such a prideful lowlife he'd rather be known as a jackass cheat than be ragged about losing the bet!"

From the way they acted, you'd have thought Banty had cheated these men instead of Curly and the railroad. But I guess in a way he had. They'd been looking forward to watching a good man put a loud-mouth in his place, and Banty had taken that away from them. They started getting worked up about it, and the place got loud. Women came as far as the door, got a load of the crowd inside, and decided maybe they didn't need flour until the next day after all.

After a few beers, James McCombs, the minister from First Presbyterian, stood up on his chair and began to call for a tar and feathering. At least that's what we thought he was saying. By then, his vowels were a lot stronger than his hard-edged letters.

Somebody pointed out that tar and feathers wouldn't exactly constitute an eye for an eye, and Reverend McCombs raked the crowd with a scowl and informed us that down through the ages, "a whole raft of righteous smiting" had come to folks who hadn't necessarily smote first.

Everybody drank to that. Then the man of God halfway climbed and partly fell off his chair and wandered out the back door to take a leak.

The laughing that came after that seemed to lighten the grudge in the room. The only yelling then was from men trying to be heard over Claude Hutchison's snoring after he curled up by the stove in the corner. Finally, Charlie's old coon dog, Belle, came up and made three circles before dumping herself into the curve of Claude's body, and that quieted him down some. They slept there and snorted and twitched together while neighbors visited and drank like on any other Saturday. Nobody else around my age had come, so it was kind of like a picture show. I nodded hello a few times, but mainly I stood against the wall and watched.

The grousing started up again after somebody came trotting in to report that the Maxwell was parked in Banty's shed and not a single lamp was lit in his house. I hadn't seen Henry Brotherton come in, but he was hard to miss now. "Yellow belly!" he hollered. "Banty-ass chicken! Lily-livered coward!" I knew Henry—he'd been a year behind me in school until he dropped out—and I could see the shit-eating grin he was holding back. I knew the only thing he cared about right then was getting everybody's blood boiling. And it was working. Things started to get ugly.

Then Charlie broke out the whiskey and shot

glasses, which seemed like a bad idea on the brink of spectacular to me. I'd been all for Banty's nose being rubbed in his own stupidity, but I didn't want to see anybody get hurt. Even him. Maybe boring wasn't the worst way the day could turn out, after all.

I'd never seen a lynch mob, but I'd heard stories and had a fair imagination, and I could feel the mood starting to turn in the room. The balance was tipping over from righteous anger into something raw and mean. Men yelled. Henry yelled louder.

I started to feel sick, watching and listening. Sick and stuck—like I didn't want to stay but I wasn't able to leave. Like I needed to say something but my voice wouldn't work. It was clear that somebody needed to do something, and fast. If nobody put the brakes on, there were going to be things done that could never be undone.

Nobody was even arguing anymore. They were all just yelling about what Banty had coming to him. And I couldn't think of one word that might make them stop or even slow down. Most of them were twice my age and three times as ignorant. Even if I could find the words, it didn't mean they would listen to me. My heart was hammering hard against my ribs.

Then Henry Brotherton jumped up on the counter and held a lit match over his head. I couldn't tell his words from anybody else's at that point, but the sight of even such a small flame made my blood run cold. Chairs started scraping back as men stood up. This was it: the place was about to boil over.

"Aw, hell. He has to live with hisself. Isn't that punishment enough?" It was my father, filling the doorframe. Nobody had heard him coming, but that deep rumble of his drowned out everybody else. "Come on, John." My own face looked back at me, twice as serious and broadened by time. "Time to come on home." He turned and disappeared.

And in the few seconds he was there, he'd done what I couldn't. When talk started up again, the noise was cut by half and whatever steam had built up was gone. Vanished. Nobody was heading over to Banty's house that night.

I don't know why that didn't make me feel a lot better than it did.

I was almost to the door when Henry Brotherton's voice rang out above the others. "Hey, John. My sister Ellen wants to know when you're gonna get married and have your own kids to torment."

"Oh yeah?" I said, just to be decent.

"Yeah. I told her first you'd have to find a girl-friend that wasn't a sheep."

The room exploded, and my face got hot fast. I wanted nothing more than to go over and bust Henry one, but the smirk on his face told me that was exactly what he wanted me to do. I guess my dad had ruined his good time and he was looking for another.

I'd always heard that once, as a kid, Henry shoved a firecracker up a cat's ass and lit it. Just then I could believe it.

I walked out, shaking my head. The door banged

11

behind me. Down the street in the gaslight, I could see my father, already a block away.

Spring flirted with us for nearly a month, giving up a glimpse of her petticoats now and then before she finally gave in and showed us her bloomers. The days grew longer and warmer, and the temperature in my house rose right alongside the mercury in the thermometer.

Dad had always ridden me hard, but now I couldn't do the smallest thing right. If I left my muddy boots on the back step, I was an idiot for not knowing it was going to rain. If I brought them in, it was the wrong day for that. When he was sorting and doctoring cows, I was always running the wrong one through the chute. Never mind they were Black Angus with no markings of any kind. I should know them apart. On and on.

And Mom—good old Mom, so beaten down and tired since Catherine had come along—she was right there to tell him about every wet towel left on the floor that he might otherwise have missed. Both of them circled around, barking at Catherine and me like cattle dogs rounding up a herd.

I imagine it's just as annoying for cattle.

I think Dad's real problem was that I was graduating high school and hadn't announced I wanted to farm with him until one of us dropped dead. When I was little, he always talked like that was a given. "Old

Man Hodgkins knows I've got my eye on that forty that joins mine down in the bottom," he'd say. "We'll talk to him when the time comes to stake you." Or he talked about my buying cattle. "Pay attention to how they act in the sale ring. It's a sign of what you'll be in for at home."

But about the time my voice changed, I'd stopped answering him. Or nodding. By then, it didn't seem like he was trying to teach me so much as to whittle me down to a smaller version of him. Signing on for life sounded like a life sentence.

Why he'd even want a partner who couldn't hammer a nail to suit him beats me. I guess he thought I'd really foul things up if he wasn't there to oversee my every minute. But that's pure speculation. What I knew for sure was, the sentences that started with *someday* never got finished anymore, but they always thickened the air between us.

I didn't know what I wanted to do past May or a year or ten down the road, but I sure as hell knew it didn't involve suppertimes spent listening to a litany of each and every thing I'd done wrong that day.

I felt sorry for Catherine. Sometimes she got caught so squarely in the heat of the words thrown across the table, she got the hiccups and went upstairs without finishing her food. I even saw her sucking her thumb a few times, and she had given that up at age four.

I started going up almost every night after dinner and playing checkers with her. Reading to her. And even when we started out on opposite sides of a checkerboard, she'd end up somehow snuggling up to me with an arm around my neck. Our folks never were much for hugging us—or each other, that I knew of—but I think the need must be built into little girls the way corn needs sunshine to grow. Catherine loved me spending time with her so much, it almost felt like I wasn't doing it just to get away from Mom and Dad.

Maybe that wasn't the only reason I did it. But it was a fact that whenever I came down those stairs, the grandfather clock ticking in the front hallway sounded like a time bomb to me.

One Friday night in the middle of April, I managed to sneak outside without being noticed and hunker down in an old metal chair. Then I tried to will the weather warmer because I hadn't taken the time to grab a jacket, and I intended to stay put until the rest of them were in bed. I couldn't even remember what I'd eaten at the meal just finished—I'd been working too hard to avoid eye contact.

The screech of the screen door made my butt pucker.

"John?" Dad's thunder. "Company. The Bricken boy's at the front door."

That wasn't the last thing I was expecting to hear, but it was probably close. I stood up so fast my chair clanged over backward.

Dad seemed to think it was curious too. He'd parked himself near the entryway and was thumbing through an old copy of *LIFE*. Standing up. Like that's what he always did Friday night after supper.

The door stood open, and Paul's silhouette was outlined by the street lamps behind him. Dad had left him standing on the porch.

"Hi, Paul!" I said, louder than I intended. "Take a step back—the screen opens out—and come on in. Two steps forward, then one step up."

Over his shoulder, I could see a team out front. Mr. Bricken sat in the carriage box, staring straight ahead.

I glanced toward Dad, and his face ducked back down to his magazine. I said to Paul, "Come on in and sit down."

"No, thank you." His face told me nothing. "I just have a minute. Father wants to get home. But I need to ask you another favor, I'm afraid."

I couldn't think what I'd done for him before. It took a while to connect with that day a month earlier when I'd stood with him and described The Race That Wasn't. "Oh. Well, sure. Name it."

My dad moved a couple inches closer.

Paul took a long breath. "I'm buying an automobile. A Ford Model T from Stuart Kassen, and I'm supposed to pick it up in Carrollton tomorrow. If Sam and I come get you in the morning, could you come along and drive it home for me? I'll pay you for your trouble."

Dad gave up the pretense and stood there, slack jawed and blinking.

I started slow and tried to gather words as I went.

"Well, golly, Paul, I'd like to help you out. But, you know, I've only driven an auto once. And then not very well. I gotta ask—"

"I'm sure you have questions. But if you don't mind, I'd rather answer them tomorrow. As for driving, surely we can figure that out together. Will you help me? Like I said, I'll pay you."

"Sure, I'll come. But you don't need to pay me. Just come by in the morning. I'll be ready."

I guess he heard the grin in my voice, because he smiled back.

"Your dad's waitin', so go on, if you need to. Step to your left, and I'll let you out." I watched him make his way down the walk at the same pace I would've taken. He must have memorized the distance on the way up.

What the hell? A Model T Ford? What the holy, holy hell?

I shut the door and turned to face Dad. He has a habit of combing his hair back with his fingers when he's nervous, and just then it was sticking out every which way. He looked like he'd just met up with the family ghost and it had asked him for money.

"What the hell was that all about?"

"You know as much about it as I do."

He threw a guilty look toward his shoes.

Mom came out of the kitchen, wringing her hands around a dish towel. "What was that all about?"

"Paul Bricken needs me to do him a favor. He and their colored man are gonna pick me up in the morning." I took a step toward the stairs like we were done. Like that was it. Like that was possible.

"Oh, and has he forgotten he has a job now, piddlin' that it is? Jonas? Did you ask about that?" Before Dad could answer, she went on at me through him. "Didn't Jim ask him to work tomorrow at the elevator? Did he forget that?"

"No, of course I haven't forgotten," I lied. "I just reckon Little Jim can cover for me. He owes me a day."

I hoped with everything I had that Little Jim would be home that evening for me to ask. I'd get no sleep at all if I had to wait until morning to find out how deep I was standing in it.

Mom flicked the dish towel onto her shoulder and crossed her arms. "And is the Bricken boy paying him to miss work? Or is he supposed to work for them for free the rest of his life? Or maybe he's just made out of money now?"

"Well, no, he's not paying me—"

"And why not? Why didn't he ask him to?" Still going through Dad. "God knows his people could afford it!"

"Well, actually, he offered to pay me." I knew Dad would tell her if I didn't. "But I—"

"But you turned him down. I heard it myself." Dad had taken back the reins. "Well, maybe once you have to earn a living instead of freeloading off us, you'll learn the value of a dollar!"

"You're the one who sent me out there to . . . babysit him, summers I was thirteen and fourteen, and there was no talk of paying me then. Was that okay just because *you* got to decide?"

I hadn't noticed Catherine sitting on the bottom step, but she must have been there all along. She started bumping her butt up the stairs one at a time, thumb in her mouth.

I tried, "I just wish you wouldn't get so worked up. I don't understand—"

"No, you don't!" Dad again. "You don't seem to understand much of anything!"

I couldn't win.

I stalked to the door and was on the other side of the sill before Mom said, "And just where do you think you're going while we're still talking to you?"

I belched onions. That's what we'd had for supper— something with onions. "I'm going over to ask Little Jim to work for me tomorrow. Paul Bricken is buying a Model T Ford, and I'm driving it home for him." I slammed the door so hard the porch shook.

Goddamn it. I'd left without grabbing a jacket again. If I caught pneumonia, I'd never hear the end of it.

The next morning, I was out in the yard kicking at nothing, wearing a coat, hat, and gloves, and still wishing it were warmer. Goddamned April anyway. Paul hadn't told me what time he planned to come by, but I wasn't going back in that house even if I froze to death.

My nose was barely numb, though, when Sam turned the corner driving the Bricken team. I took the front hedge like a hurdle and bounced into the backseat of the carriage next to Paul. I said, "Good morning!" and he clipped off an answer.

Sam clucked to the horses, and we rode to the edge of town with no sound but hooves clopping. I studied Paul's profile and could see he was wound up tighter than an eight-day clock. I was starting to wonder if I would ever take a breath again without swallowing somebody's troubles.

I gave Paul an elbow and tried to sound cheerful. "Well, man, are you ready for a big adventure?"

"Not too big, I hope." His lips barely moved. He took a pamphlet from his breast pocket and shoved it at me. "Here. Read this, and when you find the part we need to know today, read out loud to me." His voice was as cold as my red, nipped nose, and it knocked me back a bit.

I turned the book over in my hands. *Ford Model T Instruction Book* was stamped front and back, the word *Ford* strung out across a pyramid with wings.

"Well, now, Paul, I turned down your offer of money 'cause I planned to do this as a friend. But if you're gonna talk to me like a hired hand, I might reconsider." I heard Sam clear his throat and didn't know if it was to comment or for necessity. I cleared mine back at him, just in case.

All at once, the air came out of Paul and he looked about twelve years old and scared to death. "It's just . . . I'm nervous, John. Heck. Afraid is what

I am." He rubbed his left thumb and index finger together—back and forth, back and forth. It looked like habit. "Everyone thinks I'm crazy. At least those who know what I'm doing. The rest will think so when word gets out, which should take all of"—he snapped his fingers—"that."

His voice was pinched. "I just don't want to make an ass of myself. I want today to go off without a hitch, and I want to get the dang thing home and figure out what comes next." The finger rubbing went double time.

A clucking sound came from Sam that I doubted was aimed at the horses.

"Okay," I told Paul. I looked at both sides of the instruction book again. "Just calm down. Nothin' to worry about. If anybody looks like an ass today, it's gonna be me."

He busted out in a choppy laugh.

"Ain't neither one of you got the sense God gave a head a cabbage," came from the carriage bench, and we both broke up. A lot of people would have been steamed at a colored man for throwing an insult at them, but I'd spent enough time around Sam that he was just like a regular person to me. We joshed each other all the time.

Besides, he was right. Probably neither one of us did have the sense God gave cabbage.

I was finally able to drink in that clear air I'd been looking for earlier. But curiosity can pester worse than a mosquito, and it wasn't more than a minute till I nudged Paul and said, "You know I gotta ask. Why you doin' it?"

His eyebrows moved toward each other.

"You don't have to tell me. But you know I'm not the only one gonna ask."

"You're right." He sat with his head down. "And I will tell you. But nobody else needs to know all of it."

I wondered why Sam didn't count, but still I knew what he meant. There were times I wished for somebody to lay it all out to, without it getting around.

"Okay," I said. "Maybe we can figure out together what to tell everybody else."

When Paul smiled, he looked like a different person altogether. He was a good-looking fellow, if you didn't look too close at his eyes. I wondered if being handsome meant anything to him at all.

"Okay," he said. "But I'm making this up as I go. I haven't said it out loud before."

I nodded, like that counted for something, and he went on. "I'm nineteen years old. I know I'm always—well, probably always—going to depend on other folks to take me where I want to go. And I'm tired of depending on Father, explaining everything even before I do it."

"I can see that," I said, then caught myself. "Aw, I don't mean *see*, but—"

He held up a hand to shut me up. Then a cough came from up front, and Paul nodded toward it. "Or there's Sam. Which is almost the same thing, really, since he works for Father."

His head fell back, and he faced the blank sky. "I guess I figure a new automobile might provide an incentive for other folks to take me places, if I ask. Give me a little more independence." He brightened up. "Heck, maybe some people will even volunteer to drive me after a while."

All of a sudden, I felt ten pounds lighter. Something had been gnawing at me, and now I knew what it was. Part of me had worried just how much Paul was planning to depend on me.

I told him it made good sense.

"I'm glad." He chuckled. "I guess . . . I . . . don't know." He shrugged.

"Uh-huh." I listened to birdsong until the next question spilled out. "Okay, but I gotta ask too. Where'd you get that much money?"

I was halfway expecting *None of your business*, but Paul looked glad I had asked. He said, "Well, I got a little when Grandfather died."

Sam bowed his head for a few seconds.

"But you see, my parents always give me money for Christmas and birthdays, and I've spent hardly any of it through the years. That's mainly the money I'm using now. Even though Father clearly doesn't approve of my owning an automobile."

I weighed those words. "That wouldn't be part of the reason you're buying it, would it?"

He was quiet long enough for me to wonder if I'd stepped in something. Then he fairly exploded laughing.

I joined in, and pretty soon even Sam got going.

A doe in the field north of the road startled and ran.

We studied the manual the rest of the way to Carrollton. I read, and Paul interrupted to have me repeat some sections. He asked a lot of questions, and explaining the answers made it all come clearer to me. I could tell he was the smarter of us, but at least I was smart enough to recognize that.

Inside Kassen's dealership, everything went okay, but there was one moment only I could enjoy. Stuart Kassen put a pen in Paul's hand and then looked like he'd been kicked in the gut. It was plain he didn't know if Paul could sign his name. Funny, he hadn't hesitated to sell the car to a blind boy in the first place.

I took Paul's wrist and positioned his hand. "Here," I told him, like it was something we did every day.

Now that the auto belonged to him, Paul became more confident with every question. It became down-right comical, watching him grill Stuart. Had Stuart filled the radiator with soft water? Had the gasoline been strained through a chamois skin before it was put in the tank? Who had adjusted the carburetor? Was Stuart positive it was Ford's head tester himself?

I leaned against the wall and shrugged each time Stuart looked to me for help.

By the time we headed out to the driveway, I do believe the man was glad to see us go. He gave a wave and handed us off to a small herd of men who had found themselves not too busy that day. They circled the Model T and made appreciative comments, but nobody asked anything. They looked at Paul like they didn't know where to start.

There was absolute quiet when I guided Paul to the driver's seat and put one of his hands on the spark lever and the other on the throttle. But when he started making adjustments, somebody gasped.

I walked around front and turned the crank. Once, twice, then hallelujah! A small cheer rose from the onlookers as I sprinted around to the left side of the car. Just like we'd planned, Paul slid over on the bench in the same movement as me jumping into the driver's seat. I took over the pedals and steering wheel and lever, and we were off—a little faster than we wanted, maybe, but I kept it reined in okay until I could get used to the controls and slow down.

At least two Wakenda men slept happy that night.

CHAPTER TWO

FIVE WEEKS PASSED BEFORE I SAW Paul again. In the meantime, the tail end of April dragged by and the better part of May dogged after it. I went to school and hung my legs out in the aisle because they were a foot too long to fit under my desk. I went to the lunchroom and heard other guys talking about either getting married that summer or the jobs they had waiting for them. Or both. I said hello to Mary Albrecht every time I passed her in the hallway and got tongue-tied if she so much as asked how I was.

I'd be in the classroom stewing about what I was going to do with my grown-up life, and then I'd be called up front to clap the erasers clean. I didn't know how old to feel.

And then I graduated, and it was with more pomp and circumstance than the Second Coming would warrant.

Mothers cried, babies cried. It was damn loud in that gymnasium on top of being hotter than Hades. There were speeches, there was music, and the knot in my stomach twisted a little tighter every time mention was made of our future. Most parents appeared proud afterward. Mine looked grim.

The Monday after was May 16, and I went to work full-time at the elevator. Jim wasn't all that happy about it. I'm not sure he had enough work or money to have Little Jim and me both around, but I'd practically begged. I might have worked for free. Hell, I almost did. Getting out of helping Dad was worth it. It wasn't a fix, but at least it was a safety pin.

Unless the doomsayers are right and the world really does come to an end this week, I thought. If that happened, I wouldn't have to worry about a job or anything else. Ever again.

At home, my folks had banished all speculation about Halley's Comet from the supper table. Anywhere else, though, the nonsense going around was impossible to avoid. Everybody knew the earth was on course to pass through the comet's tail, probably Wednesday night, but even the experts didn't know exactly what kind of hell was going to break loose then in the eastern sky and all around us. The men at the elevator had been especially generous with their prognostications of everything from the Black Death to scurvy.

Wednesday afternoon, the Brickens' colored

man, Sam, stopped by the elevator and told me "Mr. Paul" wanted to know if I could drive him to Carrollton on Saturday.

I said, "Sure, if we're all still alive."

Sam fixed me with a dead-level stare that he held steady until it was funnier than ten jokes from a laughing man. I busted up and saw the corner of his mouth almost twitch into a smile before he clucked at the horses and went on.

It wasn't really a surprise to look out the window Thursday morning and see nothing had changed, but it was still something of a relief. I was fairly sure it would be better for life to go on.

Saturday morning, I spent a lot of the walk to the Bricken farm wondering why they still lived there. Mr. Bricken's work was in Carrollton, and they for sure could afford a big house in town. It was Mrs. Bricken's old family home place, but she traveled too much to make her seem very sentimental about home. I decided it must have to do with money, and God knows I didn't know the first thing about making money.

I drove Paul to town in his Model T and then stood around Dickson's for two hours or so while Paul bought a summer suit complete with hat, suspenders, and wing tips. Out of the whole getup, I might have been able to afford the suspenders.

I didn't begrudge Paul any of it, but it was hard

not to compare the upward swing in his life with the direction mine was taking. I stood back while he chatted up the folks who stopped to ask questions about the Model T sitting outside. Nobody said much more than hello to me, but I didn't have any more to say back, so it didn't really matter.

Then Mary Albrecht walked past the store, and the front window was like a big picture frame around her and Bill Wheaton. There was her hand tucked into his elbow with his fat paw holding it there. She tilted her head back, laughing, not quite laying her cheek on his arm, her eyes telling him he was Sir Lancelot, Hiawatha, and Santa Claus all rolled into one. Some little hope I hadn't quite admitted to myself died, and it felt like a fire going out.

On the way back to Wakenda, Paul said, "What say we stop at Charlie's for a few?"

What say. I wondered if the way Paul talked didn't put people off about as much as his blindness did. But that was probably my mood doing the thinking.

Before I could answer, he said, "I'm buying, of course."

Of course. "Sure, Paul, whatever you say." I wasn't feeling very social, but it was going on suppertime and that was reason enough to avoid home.

I parked the Ford without scaring the horses at the hitching post too much. We waited for Charlie to finish measuring off some calico for Georgia Kelly, and then we bought beers at the counter. Three men were arguing politics at one of the round tables, but otherwise it was just Charlie and Claude Hutchison. No need for a fire today, but Claude was curled up asleep next to the stove in the corner anyway. Habit, I guess.

Paul made his way toward the debate, pulled up a chair, and started right in with his opinions of Taft and the men in Congress. I sat down and finished a beer without coughing up a word. Then they all started arguing about some prizefight coming up, and I was even less interested. Paul finally asked if I was okay, and I said I needed some air.

I sat at the edge of the ravine behind Charlie's store and threw rocks into the shallow water below. I was full of some kind of hurt I couldn't put a name to and anger pointed at nobody in particular, and each rock I hurled made me feel a little lighter. It was already too dark to see them hit, but every plop was some small satisfaction.

After half an hour, there were footfalls behind me.

"John? Are you out here?"

"Yeah, over here." *Find me yourself, Paul.*

"John?" The uneasiness in his voice made me ashamed.

"Here I am." I turned around and squinted. "Three yards in front of you. Sittin' on the ground."

He shuffled forward and folded his skinny legs next to me. He was cradling two bottles and wrestled the top off one before handing it to me. "That Troutman . . . It's worth starting a disagreement just to get him going." He chuckled, then took a long swallow. "Say, this reminds me of when we used to go fishing."

Except it's dark. Then I realized it always had been dark for him. I almost said it out loud anyway, just because.

When we used to go fishing. I shook my head. Not that I'd taken him. Not that I'd taught him. Not that I'd been assigned to be his companion those summer days and wouldn't have been there otherwise.

A minute later, his nose pointed up like he'd caught a whiff of something. "What's wrong? Did I do something?"

I didn't answer.

"Please. Say something."

I threw a rock across the ravine hard as I could. "Aw, Paul, look. It's not got to do with you." Then I thought better and said, "I don't mean *look*. That's just an expression—"

"Well, is there anything I can do to help?"

I laughed, then felt sorry for doing it. My day to be sorry, seemed like. "Thanks, but I don't know what it'd be." Quick as I could draw breath, I changed the subject. "So tell me. How's it goin' with the Ford? Who's been drivin' you around?"

Whip-poor-will? came a call from a distance.

"It's going all right." His tone made me doubt it. "I've been out only three times before today. Once with Stamp Grady, once with Herman Schneider, and once with Father. He decided that if I were going to own an automobile, he should know how to drive it."

I grinned into the night. "How'd that go?"

"Not well."

"Well, I heard about what happened with Stamp." No need to make him say it. What happened was that Stamp thought he had the Ford in reverse and broke through the railing and onto the sidewalk in front of Falke's store in town. He nearly flattened the little Lybarger girl and put the fear of God and Henry Ford into her mother. It took three men to lift the Model T down to the street while Paul stood by red-faced.

His answer was sober as it gets. "Yes, I'm sure you heard."

"Well, what about Herman? I didn't hear anything about that."

"He . . ." Paul's voice dropped so low I had to lean toward him. "I asked him to take me to Carrollton for a Sunday afternoon discussion group. He wasn't interested in it, of course, so I told him to just come back in two hours or so. He . . . went off and left me." Paul took a pull on his beer. "He felt awful about it, or so he said. He'd gone to Bogard and gotten carried away taking his girlfriend and her family for rides. By the time he came back, somebody else had taken me home."

I sent my empty bottle sailing into the slough. Paul's followed a few seconds later.

I said, "How about I go in and bring us a couple more? I got nowhere to be." Paul reached for his pocket, and I said, "On me this time."

Who? Who-whooo? came from across the ravine.

I came back with an armload and explained that Charlie was getting ready to close. We drank for a while, listening to the crickets.

Paul said, "What about you?"

My laugh sounded sloppy. "What about me?"

"Well, you don't have to say. But are you sure I didn't do something?"

"Naw, it ain't you. It's just everything else."

He sat there waiting for more.

Damn it. "It's just . . . I gotta decide what I'm gonna do with myself, I guess. That about sums it up."

"Well, I'm a pretty good listener, if that does you any good."

"Aw, hell. I don't know what to say." I launched another bottle into the slough.

"Well, what do you want for yourself?"

Didn't he know how to let something go? "I don't know. I mean, what me and Little Jim do at the elevator, that's a boy's job. Difference is, someday he's gonna own the whole shebang." I uncapped a new bottle. "I'd rather pull my own head off than work with Dad, and I got no designs on workin' on the river, but anything else would probably take goin' off to college. Not much else around here."

"So go."

"Right." I snorted. "It'd take a miracle on the order of Moses on the mountaintop to pay for it. And anyway, they'd want to know what I aimed to study, and all I know is what I don't want to do. I'd be pissin' into the wind and payin' to do it."

I wiped my face with my free hand, and it felt a little rubbery. "How about you? You already doin' . . . what you planned?" I had no idea what he did with his days. I'd never given it a thought.

"Hardly." He got to his feet, took a dozen steps away, and took a piss.

Back and with a fresh beer, he blurted out, "This isn't my home, you know," like he was in the middle of some story in his head. "Not really. I'd only spent a few summers here up until a year ago. And I do not want to spend the rest of my life depending on my father for everything. Not that I do, but he thinks I does. Do. You know what I mean." He took a swig. "He just assumes I have to live here, but I don't."

I started peeling the label off the bottle in my hand. "But where else would you go? Back to St. Louis?"

"I don't know where I'd go." Paul started peeling his label too. I wondered if he could hear what I was doing or if it's just instinct when you mix beer and philosophy. "I could go back—they offered me a teaching position at the School for the Blind—but that's no more than choosing the only other place I know my way around. And I don't know how many more Septembers I could stand."

I tried to see the sense in that but finally had to ask.

He told me how the first day of school every year, little kids coming in were paired up with older students to help them find their way around and learn the routines—and how some years he'd been paired up with a six-year-old who had mostly been locked in his room like a caged animal since he was born.

"All the little kids cry for their mothers at first. By Christmas, they cry at having to leave and visit their families."

"Why would that be?"

"Well, in some ways, the school is a haven. Blindness is normal there, and you get used to that. But then Parents' Weekend comes along and you can practically smell the fear and shame in the air. And then you feel like you're at the school just so you can be hidden away. It's a relief when the families go home. By the time Christmas comes, nobody wants to leave school. And it all starts over, every September."

I knew anything I said would sound ignorant.

"I don't want to close myself off from the outside world. But I sure as heck don't feel normal here, living with Mother and Father and the rest of the townsfolk." He pointed his bottle at me. "Present company excluded, of course. I don't know. I think what I need to do is to see America."

I weighed those words for a minute and asked what he meant.

"Get a fresh view," he answered, and it still didn't

sound like he was kidding. "See if there's somewhere I fit in, something I can do besides teach blind kids or tune pianos."

"You can tune pianos?"

He withered me with a sigh. "Yes. And make brooms. All the things blind people are particularly suited for."

"Oh."

"Yes."

I tried to get back on track. "How would you do it, though? Buy a train ticket and just get off in every town?"

"No." Paul sounded tired. "I don't know. It's just something I think about sometimes—that's all."

I was due to take a leak and wandered off into the dark.

When I got back, I started in the middle of a thought. "You ever think about our folks? They just got on with it, right after school. Your dad at the bank, my dad farmin'—that was that. Seems so easy."

"How do you know it was easy?"

Some late-season ducks squawked their way north overhead.

"Maybe they hated it. Maybe they just couldn't get up the . . . gumption to go anywhere or do anything else."

"Well, hell's bells." I ripped a handful of grass out by the roots and launched that into the wind. "I can't just sit here till I feel stuck."

"I know. But what, then? We're just talking in

circles." He hatched a slow smile. "Well, at least I knocked a huge hole in Father's assumptions when I bought the auto, for whatever that's worth."

We both chuckled.

A minute later, the idea hit both of us like a singular lightning bolt.

"The car—"

"Oh my God!"

We started talking at the same time, and neither of us in sentences, but it was clear what we meant. My head was buzzing, and I felt like I was on fire from the inside out. Like I'd grabbed onto a loose electrical wire and not let go.

Paul's grin lit up the dark. "Why not? Why in the holy name of God not?"

We laughed like it was the best joke we'd ever heard.

When we calmed down enough, we straightaway started talking about where we should go. It wasn't until later I realized neither one of us suggested setting out without a plan. Limited thinking or limited courage, I don't know.

Paul suggested New York, then threw that idea away even before I could. He said on second thought, crowded and dirty would be okay to come across, but they didn't make for much of a destination.

I agreed like I was worldly as all get-out, but really the notion of New York City was more than I could wrap my mind all the way around.

Paul said, "Could we make California by the Fourth of July? We could go see the championship fight."

It seems impossible now, but I didn't even ask what he was talking about. I guessed it was the prizefight they'd been arguing about inside. But all I could really think when I heard *California* was gold-rush hooligans and earthquakes. I said that last one out loud.

We knew what had happened to San Francisco in 1906—the ground had opened up and done its best to swallow the whole city. Four years later, it wasn't even close to rebuilt.

We fell damn silent for two fellows who'd been whooping it up just the minute before.

Then Paul spoke up, quiet as a prayer. "Yellowstone National Park."

I thought about it. Prairies and deserts and mountains. Cities and small towns and open space in between all of them. And at the end of it, land so beautiful President Roosevelt had set it aside for the sole purpose of being looked at. "Yes," I said.

I don't know how long we sat watching the pictures in our heads before Paul spoke again. "Should we ask someone else to come with us?"

"Why?"

"Won't you want somebody else to handle part of the driving?"

I hadn't thought about the fact I'd be the only pair of eyes. "Yes, yes, I would, I guess. But who?"

After that night, we never did agree whose idea Henry Brotherton was. The answer was probably lost somewhere in the nest of empty beer bottles around us.

I was still plenty sore at Henry for embarrassing me that day at Charlie's, and I know I pointed out to Paul that Henry could be a mean little shit. That he enjoyed being one.

Paul said something like, "But if there's trouble, wouldn't you want to have someone like him on your side?"

"There is absolutely no guarantee he would be." Of this, I was sure.

But it didn't take long to run all the way through the list of other fellows we knew. They were all tied to jobs or getting married. They'd already settled. Henry Brotherton, though—well, he'd lived like a stray dog most of his life. There was nothing tying him down.

Mainly, we were caught up in the idea and not too worried about the details. Henry was better than nobody, and that's as much as it mattered to us then.

We were fairly swimming in courage when we lit out in the Model T for George Reimer's farm. That's where Henry worked, and Paul had said he was sleeping in George's barn.

"How in the hell do you know that?" I asked him.

He shrugged. "People talk in front of a blind man like he can't hear either."

I parked the car out on the road. George Reimer

is a friendly man, but it's hardly ever a good idea to surprise a man on his own property after bedtime.

Just inside the barn door, the moon lit up a pile of loose hay. No telling what was in it. We stood in the doorway calling out, "Hen-reee," like a pair of cowardly ghosts.

Pretty soon, there was a commotion up in the loft.

I said, "I bet he's got a girl up there and he's tryin' to hide her."

Paul whispered, "I bet he's got a gun up there and he's trying to find it."

My head started to ache. I was sobering up fast.

About then, a wiggling bedroll shot down like a bomb from the loft into the hay pile in front of us. Paul and I both jumped a foot in the air.

Henry roundhoused out of the blankets like a cat fighting its way out of a gunnysack. His eyes looked as wild as his tangled red hair. But then they started to focus.

He'd still been asleep when he fell—that was all. He was just waking up, after the fact.

Like that was any better.

"What the hell are you two doing here?" He struck a pose, dukes up. He was a head shorter but probably had fifteen pounds on me, all muscle.

Paul looked like he'd been hit upside the head with a skillet.

I said, "Uh . . . we came to ask you something."

"Well, *what*?" Henry still stood at the ready.

I said, "We're goin' to take Paul's Ford and drive to Yellowstone National Park, and we want you to go along." There in the barn, with the beer wearing off, it sounded downright silly.

"Tonight?" Henry took a couple steps away.

"Naw, not tonight. We don't know when. We just got the idea . . ." I was becoming a bigger fool every second.

Henry advanced on me, studying my face. "You two drunk?"

"A little." Paul was back. "But we're sober enough to mean it."

"Well, then, what the hell are you talking about?" Henry's fists finally relaxed.

"Just what we said."

Paul nodded.

"We wanna get away. Go somewhere. See stuff. We need another driver, and you're our first choice. But we can ask someone else."

"Yes." Paul was still nodding. "We can."

"Oh, now, just hold it. What—hey, you got any left of what you been drinkin'?"

There were three beers in the Model T, put back just for this.

"Wait right here," I said.

The two of them were sitting cross-legged in the hay when I got back. I handed beers around.

Paul asked Henry, "Why are you living here?" He sounded as polite as Sunday school.

"None of your goddamned business."

I said, "Never mind. Let's stick to the subject. You wanna go with us or not?"

"Jes' hold it a minute!" His bark belonged on the end of a chain. "What the hell is this about? What do you mean, you wanna *go* somewhere? And get away from what?"

"Wakenda."

"Our parents."

Henry hacked up a guffaw. "Ain't you two a little old to be runnin' away from home? First time I did that I was six. You comin' to ask me how?"

Paul said, "No, we are not running away from home." This voice could have cut glass. "But we've been talking—"

"You ask me, the beer's been doin' the talkin'."

"Forget it." I stood up and brushed hay off my ass. "We can come back tomorrow, cold sober. Or better yet, we can go ask our second choice. Come on, Paul."

Paul moved slow enough to wait out the bluff.

"Aw, now wait. Can't you fellas take a joke?" Henry waggled his empty beer bottle at me.

I shook my head that there wasn't any more.

He reached over, took Paul's, and threw back a swig. "You guys bust in here in the middle of the night talkin' crazy—you could at least explain yourself."

"There's not much to explain." I sat back down. "You wanna die here, Henry? That what you want?"

"What the hell's that supposed to mean?"

Apparently I'd gotten ahead of myself.

Paul took over. "What John means is that he and I have been discussing the limited options available to us here."

Henry frowned at him like he was talking in Chinese.

"We're not satisfied," Paul went on, "but we see no better course available than to get away for a while, see a little bit of the country from a different perspective. We look at it as an opportunity."

"A opportunity." Henry looked back and forth between us. He finished Paul's beer and lobbed the bottle at me. "So why you offerin' me this opportunity?"

What could we say? *Because we know you're too stupid to be afraid of anything? Because there's nobody else to ask?* "Well, we thought . . ."

Paul picked up the thread. "We could think of no one better. You have no ties to speak of—"

"And we like you." My heart was thumping over what Paul might repeat from earlier, like my opinion that Henry's own family—such as he had—wasn't likely to miss him. That he might as well go. He had nothing here.

"Well." Henry laid back and contemplated the pitched roof of the barn. Finally he raised up on his elbows. "Okay, then. I guess I wouldn't mind gettin' away from this shit hole for a while."

It was as good as a handshake.

By the time I drove Paul home, it was going on midnight. We said our good nights, and I walked down their long tree-lined lane and turned toward Wakenda.

And there it was, taking up nearly a quarter of the sky between horizons. A big fist of light with a long tail that seemed to be made up of thousands upon thousands of stars. It looked like it had streaked across the sky at great speed and then frozen in place just for me.

The earth had passed through the tail of the comet and come out on the other side. Halley's Comet was now to the west of us.

It was some time before I realized I was on my knees.

CHAPTER THREE

TIME ITSELF RACED BY AND THEN slowed to a crawl again and again over the next eleven days. Every night that Paul and I were at the county library, we were astonished when Wid Albrecht told us it was closing time—it always seemed like we'd just got there.

Every meal with my parents, on the other hand, lasted fourteen years. They came out full bore against the trip—no surprise there. They imagined everything that could go wrong, from rattlesnake bites to getting lost in the desert with no water.

They weren't exactly excited about me going with a blind boy and a known troublemaker either. Mom treated me to every detail she knew about Henry's family, from his mother's death to his dad's becoming "a worse drunkard than Claude Hutchison," from his sister Ellen's kicking him out of her house to the legendary cat's-ass-Fourth-of-July. And apparently, I was the only person in the world who didn't know Henry was living in George Reimer's barn because none of his other brothers or sisters would have him. Mom was thorough.

Like I wouldn't have already been questioning the wisdom of including Henry, starting soon as I was sober. Once I'd latched on to the idea of getting away, though, nothing my folks said could change my mind about anything.

That's not to say they couldn't plant doubt. I had never been the superstitious type, but now I saw signs everywhere. If I found a penny on the ground, we were going to have a safe trip. If a blackbird flew across my path, I worried the rest of the day.

And every night, I sat on the porch and stared into the sky at the biggest good luck charm of them all. Even though nothing about it changed from moment to moment, to me it was as mesmerizing as a picture show.

Then we had clouds for an evening or two, and when the sky cleared, the comet looked half the size it had been. A few nights later, it was just one star a little bigger than the rest.

Then it was gone, and the sky looked almost empty without it. This once-in-a-lifetime spectacle was over, and the very thought of that made me mournful.

I moped around like somebody had died until I latched onto a notion that the comet was still there, just not where I could see it. I started to think of it as a big altar in the sky that would never really be gone. Hope and belief may not be the same thing, but I think sometimes they're at least first cousins.

Whenever I was around the house that last week, Catherine stuck to me like a cocklebur. She didn't ask about my going away or even mention it, but she looked up at me with huge eyes that made me feel like I was deserting her. Without a word, she—more than anyone else—reminded me I'd never been farther than eighty miles from home, and then I'd been with Dad. Anything beyond that was just something I'd read in a book.

And reading books to her became a nightly reminder that you can travel anywhere you want without ever leaving home. You can explore the world over, sitting in your safe home in your safe chair by a lamp with a good wick.

More than one night, I dreamed about stepping off into a canyon.

I tried to hide any whiff of fear from Paul, though. He had his own troubles. His mother was back east visiting relatives, and his father wasn't speaking to him.

"Surely he said somethin' right when you first told him," I'd said.

"He laughed. Then he walked out of the room."

"And he's said *nothin'* since? Not even 'Pass the salt'?"

Paul shook his head. "I guess it's supposed to

be some sort of punishment. To tell you the truth, I wouldn't much care . . ."

"Except what?"

"He laughed."

What a mean bastard. I got Paul out of that house every minute I could.

When we made it to the library, Paul and I sat over maps and newspapers and magazines. Like when we studied the Ford's manual, I read out loud and Paul asked questions. Those were powerful hours for me, and I wondered if Paul's head was filling with as many pictures as mine. If we both saw the same way when we weren't using our eyes.

We read about the Glidden Tours that had been going on since 1902 and about the two cars that drove the Oregon Trail in 1905. We read absolutely everything we could find about the transcontinental race that was run as part of the 1909 World's Fair. It had passed through the countryside not far from us and carried on west all the way to Seattle. I decided we should follow that route for the most part.

Paul's the one who suggested we leave June 1 because it was the first anniversary of the start to that race. I guess he wasn't above looking for good luck charms either.

I made notes on everything we read and took them home to memorize. I made new lists every day of what we'd need to take and what we'd need to find along the way. I was determined to be sure we were ready for anything.

We didn't get Henry in on the planning, but I was only halfway sure he'd end up going when it came down to it. I ran into him one day buying a sandwich at Charlie's and told him the date we'd decided on, and all he said was "Fine."

I asked Paul one night what he wanted to do if Henry backed out, and he said, "I know it wouldn't be easy on you as the only driver, but would you be willing to give up now?"

I believe my answer made some reference to the weather in hell. Already, I could barely stand to wake up in my own bed every morning.

Paul thought we ought to drive out to Reimers' and give Henry a pep talk, but I said no. Henry would think we were begging, and you just don't lay down and show your belly to the other dog like that. I said, "We'll drive out the morning of the first, and he'll either go or he won't."

If he did go, I knew I'd have to establish myself at the top of the pecking order right at the get-go, and that was a prospect none too attractive. Henry wasn't exactly one to debate a topic—I'd seen him in plenty of schoolyard fights. But I figured what had to be done had to be done. Only one person could be in charge, and I was the only one who could be trusted.

As bad as I itched to get going, my determination took a big hit the night before we planned to leave. Mary Albrecht showed up at my folks' door with a basket of food for the road, and it just about surprised the legs out from under me.

I wanted to grab her and kiss her. I wanted to ask her to wait for me. I wanted to tell her that Bill Wheaton was a kitten strangler and quite possibly a leper.

Instead, I said, "Why, thank you, Mary. That's right nice of you," and she giggled and ran back to the wagon waiting out front.

Then I went to my room and wondered why in the holy hell I was leaving the only place I knew.

Early morning on the first, I walked out to the Bricken farm under angry skies, but when I turned up the lane, the sun popped out and spotlighted that Model T like it was smiling at me. Definitely a good sign.

Paul was on the front porch with his bags, like he was waiting for a train running late. I helped tote his things to the car, and he got in. I looked from him to the house and figured there was no use asking if he had any good-byes to take care of.

The next act took place in front of my folks' house when we went back to pick up my stuff. For a Wednesday, there were a whole lot of neighbors out tending their puny yards.

I was tightening the straps around my bedroll a third or fourth time when Catherine came running out of the house and cried, "John!" She put a dirty little wad in my hand, and it took me a minute to recognize it as the last remnants of her special blanket.

"Aren't you gonna need that?"

She shook her head.

I picked her up and squeezed her, and she bolted into the house while a knot crowded my throat. *What if that's the last time I see her?* I thought. Then, *Stop that. Just stop.*

I stared at the front door and reckoned there was no use in going inside. I'd fought all the necessary fights. That morning, Mom had made me breakfast, but I ate it in the silence of a prisoner's last meal. She moved around the kitchen with a wordless droop about her, and Dad stared at a spot in the middle of the table while he drank a pot of coffee one cup at a time.

Neither of them even looked at me when I stood up and said, "I'm going now."

I got the Model T started again, climbed in, and did not look over my shoulder as we drove off.

On the way out to the Reimer farm, I could not shut my yap for two seconds to save my soul. Nerves, I guess. I was rattling a mile a minute. "God, what a beautiful day! Just look at that sky!"

Paul's voice came dry as toast. "Yes, I see a cloud shaped like a bunny."

"Aw, Paul . . . I'm sorry."

"I know you didn't mean anything, all right? But if I hadn't said something, you'd have caught yourself a few seconds later and started kicking yourself. I know about figures of speech. And I know you mean well when you apologize, but it's insulting."

"It's *insulting*?"

He sighed. "When people are so careful and tiptoe around, being nicer to me than they'd be to anybody else . . . well, it's almost as bad as when people ignore me."

Oh. I wondered how long he'd been waiting to say something. "Okay," I said. And then I did shut up. We were both probably glad about that.

This time, I drove up the Reimers' lane and parked in front of the barn. Margaret was walking across the yard swinging a basket of eggs.

When I yelled, "Hey, Miz Reimer," Paul nearly jumped out of his seat. I stepped onto the running board and asked low, "You wanna wait here?"

He nodded. Then he said, "No," and started feeling his way out of the car. There were plenty of nerves to go around, I guess.

I scuffed my shoes in the gravel so he could hear. Surely he couldn't be insulted by help like that.

I walked inside the barn and squinted in the dark. "Henry?" I called.

"Up here."

Nothing more came, so I climbed the ladder to the loft.

Henry was dressed but barely awake. He'd slept in his clothes, would be my bet.

"We're ready to go. You with us, or you stayin'?"

He squinted at me. "What's a matter with you? I told you I was goin', didn't I?" He stood and rolled a feather pillow with no case into the grimy quilt that covered his pallet. Then he pulled a metal box out of the hay nearby and checked inside. I caught a glint of gunmetal, and a jolt went through me.

I had thought about bringing a gun. I liked the idea of having one handy as much as I hated the thought of using it. But Dad had settled that question earlier in the week when he'd seen me eyeing the gun case and reminded me that none of the fire-arms in his house belonged to me.

I climbed down the ladder and went outside.

Henry followed me out with the metal box and a bedroll I hoped did not contain lice. He dumped both in the rear seat and jumped behind the wheel, pushing at levers and pedals. "How do ya start this thing?"

I yanked him by the shirt. "Cut it out! It ain't a toy!"

He was out of the Ford and in my face in the time it takes to blink. "You want me to bust you one?"

Here it was. Right now. We stood chest to chest, staring each other down. I tried to look braver than I felt.

Paul stepped in and pushed us apart. "Now, come on. We can find someone for you to fight along the way, if your hearts are set on it, but surely you don't need to be fighting each other."

Henry turned his back, and I was glad he didn't see Paul's hands shaking.

"Well, I believe I'll drive *since I'm the only one who knows how.*"

"At this time," Paul said and then felt his way into

the front seat.

"Oh, and I gotta ride in back?" Henry threw out. "How'm I supposed to learn how to drive from back there?"

"It's Paul's car."

Henry blew. "Oh, and we're jes' the help, is that it? He rides like a king, and we do all the work. Is that it?"

Paul stepped out, fished in his front trouser pocket, and came out with a quarter. "Fine, Henry. Heads, I sit up front. Tails, you do." He flipped the coin into the air, caught it, and slapped it against his right wrist. "Heads," he pronounced and climbed back into the car.

I fought not to laugh and walked around front. "Ready?" I cranked the car to life, then folded myself behind the wheel and tossed the crank over my shoulder. "We're leavin'. You goin'?"

It was hard work being so nonchalant. Paul looked like he'd shatter if anyone blew a breath on him.

Henry threw a look toward the house.

"We'll wait if you need to go say somethin'."

He shrugged. "Oh, they'll figure it out one of these days." He vaulted into the backseat.

I twisted around. "You haven't told 'em?"

Henry looked past the cornfield across the road. "They won't care."

I took that in before I turned forward and released the brake.

For the next forty-five minutes, Henry leaned over the back of my seat and fired off one question after another.

Several times, I said, "Paul?" since he knew more about the Ford than I did.

But Henry would jump in and ask something else, like Paul wasn't there. I wondered if it was punishment for putting him in the backseat or if Henry intended to ignore the blind boy all the way to Yellowstone and back.

Then Henry felt like he had enough information to start hounding me for a turn at the wheel.

First I told him I wasn't tired yet, then later that we should try to make some distance before we stopped.

Finally, Paul offered some help. "You two are supposed to describe the countryside to me. How can you do that if all you talk about is the car?"

Henry said, "Fine, then. I guess I'll take the first turn at that."

Enough time went by to make me wonder what he was up to.

Then he shouted, "Tree! Tree! Tree!"

My butt muscles lifted me in the seat.

Paul grabbed the brim of his hat.

Henry was leaned over between us. "Dirt, rock, dirt, tree, *fart*!"

I sped up to leave the foul cloud behind.

Next thing that was said, we all went, "Humph!"

I tried to hold a good thought, but it was hard to ignore a bad limp the Ford had developed. I stopped it and walked back to see that a rock pretending to be a hunk of dirt had punctured the left rear tire and tube.

We had made it all of eight miles.

When the three of us were standing in the road, I said, "Well, I guess I'll jack her up and put the spare on, then."

Henry snorted. "Oh, like you know how. Mr. Au-to-mo-bile. What if you get it on wrong and we turn over and git kilt? What if we have another flat before we can get this'n fixed?"

I saw a cloud of dust moving our way and pretended to watch it while I thought what to do.

Finally, the cloud revealed a team and wagon. A man who looked to be a farmer reined in his horses once he got within hollering distance. "You boys need a ride somewhere?" He took off his hat and sopped at his brow with a red bandanna.

Paul stared off toward the horizon. I fixed Henry in my sights and answered, "Naw, thanks. We got it."

I won. Henry looked away.

The farmer lifted his right pointer finger in a wave, then steered his team around the crippled Ford.

Paul spoke, first time since we'd stopped. "What happened?"

Henry leaned into his face and screamed, "Rock!"

Paul nearly stumbled backward.

Henry debated every step it took to get the wheel off and change the tire and tube. "Are you sure you know what you're doin'? That don't look like it's supposed to fit that way. Did you read the instruction book on how to do this, or you jes' makin' it up as you go along?"

I was ready to use the crowbar on him too.

Paul stopped pacing after a while and came over where we squatted. He bent down. "What can I do to help?"

"Describe the damn countryside, why don't ya?" Henry bellowed.

Paul retreated to his pacing grounds.

When the work was finished, I went to get him. "Come on. We're good to go." I hoped I meant it.

Paul climbed into the backseat without a word. Henry shrugged and jumped in up front. The two miles to Waverly passed with nobody talking.

I had been to the blacksmith shop there once with my dad, and Lewis Staton remembered me. He dropped what he was working on and ambled over. "Hey, John, when'd ya get this?"

"I didn't. It's his." I jerked my head in Paul's direction.

A gaggle of kids down the street made a beeline for us.

"Well, mighty fine-lookin' machine ya got." Lewis draped his ham-sized forearms across the frame next to my elbow. "What y'all doin' today?"

"Had a flat tire and wondered could you fix it. I mean, the inner tube and casing. You know."

Paul spoke up. "The outer casing has to be sent back to the manufacturer for repair."

I had a vague notion of having read that to him from the instruction manual and kicked myself for forgetting.

A couple kids had climbed onto the toolbox, and I waved them away like flies.

Lewis undraped himself from the car. "Oh, now, then, I can at least take a look at patchin' that tube, and you can send the other off later. This'll be enough to get you all home."

"Ain't goin' home. Not for a long, *long* time," Henry chimed in. "We'll be needin' that spare, sir." I wouldn't have suspected there was a *sir* in him.

I shooed two other children off the front fender.

Lewis said, "Well, bring the tube on in anyway, and if you really need a spare, I think Hardin's got some up the street." He motioned us to follow him into the shop.

"I'll stay here," Paul said, sounding woeful.

I grabbed the spent tube off the backseat and told Henry, "I'll take this in. You ride herd." I nodded at the children.

I wasn't quite to the shop door when I heard, "Scram! Beat it!" and the dull sound of bare feet pounding dirt.

Three minutes later, I was back. "Okay, here's the situation. Ol' man Wilcox just showed up wonderin' why his harness rig ain't done, so Lewis has got to finish that first. We should go find a spot on the river bluff and eat some dinner, then come back."

"Eat what dinner?" Henry asked.

"Well, uh, dried beef and biscuits I got. I mean, that Mary Albrecht brought by last night—"

"Oh, she brought you a package too?" Henry's smile looked as sweet as pokeberries and just as poison. "I ate mine last night."

I studied his face for a sign he was lying.

"Give me gas, though."

And then I was reeling away, gagging.

Paul stepped out of the car and several feet away. "I'll go with you, John."

Henry caught up to us half a block away. "Can't you guys take a joke?" His elbow in my ribs just about got his nose broken.

We climbed a dirt path on the edge of town and found a spot I believe would have made Adam and Eve jealous. Flat white rock overhanging the riverbed a hundred feet below, trees leafed out all around us and covering the bottomland bank on the other side. It was the kind of sight that could turn a nonbeliever around.

I dealt out half a dozen biscuits and a dozen strips of jerky. It was barely enough to keep us going but as tasty as a feast in the open air. Not ungodly hot and too early for mosquitoes—the best time of year, no doubt about it.

Between bites, I tried to do justice to the view for Paul. I told him how bright and clean the new leaves look in spring and that squirrels were building nests right above our heads, skittering up the tree trunks with mouths full of last year's leaves. I told him the river looked swollen after the spring rains. I reported on a steamboat chugging by, pushing an empty barge. A hawk circled over something on the other bank, and I did my best to describe how they sweep the sky and catch the wind to soar without moving their wings.

Henry just grunted every once in a while. I pretended I didn't hear.

I ran out of food and something to say, both at the same time. I unfolded my legs to stand up and stretch, then took one more long look around and felt like I'd been fed more than the little I'd eaten. "Gentlemen? Time to head out."

On our way back to the smith's shop, Henry and I walked on the sidewalk two abreast with Paul behind us, and we met a colored man and woman coming our direction. There was plenty of room for them to pass, but Henry deliberately angled over and walked straight toward them. They both stepped off the curb into the dirt street and looked away.

I turned to ask Henry what the hell he was doing, but his face shone with the bright smile of an accomplishment and stopped me at an unspoken *What the hell?*

I thought about somebody doing that to Sam and his wife, and it shamed me all the way red not to speak up. But it didn't feel like a good time to start up something new, either. I shook my head.

We picked up the patched inner tube, and Paul handed Lewis the five cents he asked for.

Lewis nodded up the street. "Hardin's is right up there. Post office is in the same storefront. I'm sure he's got something he'll sell you to put the casing in."

I told Henry to stay and mind the Model T.

Paul and I walked on, him following my footfalls on the wooden sidewalk. When we got away a piece, I said, "Look, Paul, I'm sorry about Henry. He's a jackass, but he'll back off once he figures out we won't take his bait."

"I find him interesting, actually. Don't you?"

Interesting was way down my list of words to describe Henry. "Huh?"

"Everything about him is so . . . exposed. He doesn't hold anything back, does he?"

"No. I guess that's one way of lookin' at it." I studied Paul's face, as unreadable as usual.

We came back to find Henry behind the wheel of the Model T, holding court with some locals. "So I says to the ol' man, I says, you never bought me nothin' before and—" He slapped the front panel of the car before he looked up and saw us coming. The lie froze halfway out of his mouth.

I walked to the front of the Ford. "You wanna set the spark and throttle?"

After three turns of the crank, the motor caught.

Paul headed for the backseat.

I grabbed his arm. "Naw, you sit up front this turn. I'll sit in back."

We waited. Henry released the parking brake, floundered with the pedals, and killed the engine. The car lurched forward and nearly hit one of the men on the sidewalk.

I climbed out with the crank and asked, "Brake back on?" before I stepped in front.

Henry looked sheepish and set it.

Once the motor was running again, I got back in and waited. It didn't take long.

"Okay, what do I do?" Henry asked in a loud whisper.

"What say?" I called.

My payment was seeing the two men smirk at each other and start away.

At first it was fits and starts, but before long we were out on the open road, on our way for sure now, just us and the dirt and the newly planted cornfields. I felt like singing. "Casey Jones" seemed to fit the moment. I sang it top to bottom, the quality of my voice making up for an occasional innocence of the words—I'm sure of it.

Paul said, "How about 'Meet Me in St. Louis'?"

I obliged. "Meet me in St. Louie, Louie. Meet

me at the fair."

He joined in halfway through. We finished out the chorus as loud as it gets and got a standing ovation from a cow in the barnyard we were passing.

Henry took his eyes off the road for half a second. "Oh, yeah, you were there when they had the fair, weren't ya? Too bad you can't tell us about it."

"What do you want to know?" Paul asked. "I went. Several days."

"I wanna know what it looked like."

"It was beautiful."

"Oh, bullshit," Henry shot back. "Like you know the difference between beautiful and cow flop."

Paul acted like he hadn't heard. "There was Festival Hall, and the Cascades in front of it—all these different tiers of gigantic fountains—and the whole thing was strung with electrified lights, so at night it was like a fairyland. They set up exhibits of different civilizations from around the world, and you could talk to the natives and see how they lived, and there was a scandal with the Igorot people from the Philippines stealing dogs from nearby neighborhoods for food—"

"Sounds beautiful, all right." Henry snorted.

I leaned forward to hear better.

"And they had the Olympic Games there. Foot-races and jumps and javelin throws, and there was this huge contraption they called the Ferris wheel you could ride on. Maybe you heard about the one they had in Chicago a few years back. You sat in something made like a big basket and went up and around and could look out over the entire city, and—"

"How do you know?" Henry interrupted.

"How do I know? You mean about the fair?"

Henry didn't answer.

"Or how do I know about anything?" Paul thought for a minute. "Trust, I suppose. When it comes down to it, I have to trust what people tell me. What about you? Don't you know about things you haven't seen?"

Henry humphed. I love it when a person with no answer pretends it's the question that's stupid.

We were quiet the rest of the way to Dover.

As we came into town, I said, "How about some real food?"

They jumped on that like ducks on a June bug.

We meandered through the streets until I spotted a storefront cafe and told Henry to pull over.

A bell above the door tinkled when we walked in.

A motherly type stuck her head out of the kitchen and called out, "What y'all want?" in a tone as un-motherly as all get-out. She didn't like our looks, would be my guess.

"Well, food! Whaddaya think?" Henry snorted.

I jumped in. "Dinner, I mean supper—whatever you want to call it, ma'am." The clock above the kitchen door read four thirty.

"Well . . ." She was still taking our measure.

"We're all out of dinner specials, and I just got supper on, so—"

"We're travelers, ma'am." I offered up my best smile. "And we'll be happy to eat whatever you can dish up."

Henry flopped into a chair and hoisted his boots onto one opposite.

The woman said, "If you'll take what I can scrounge up, fine, but take your feet off the furniture and mind yourselves. This ain't a saloon."

I yanked the chair from under Henry's feet. "Paul, you sit here, and I'll sit to your left." I called toward the back, "Ma'am? You got someplace we can wash our hands?"

She shouted without coming out. "Shoulda thought of that before. This ain't a hotel."

Henry's smile was pure evil. "Well, she's real clear on all the things this place ain't. We oughta eat and then tell her we won't pay 'cause this ain't much of a restaurant either."

Paul and I ignored him.

The woman came out carrying three plates and dealt them out. "Milk or water?" Once we'd answered, she disappeared.

Paul was groping the table with both hands.

Before I could offer help, Henry said, "What the hell you doin'?" through a mouthful of food.

Paul asked, "Where's my silverware?"

Henry guffawed and lost a wad of what he was

chewing. "You eat a sandwich with a knife and fork? Boy, them St. Louis manners is somethin'!"

"He didn't know, okay?" I hissed.

Paul felt for his food and started eating.

The woman came with our drinks.

Henry told her, "Mighty tasty ham, ma'am."

She snorted and went back to work.

"Mine's roast beef," Paul said.

"So's his," I said.

Paul was the last to finish.

The woman appeared like magic as he chewed his last bite. "Seventy-five cents," she told us.

A quarter seemed like a lot for just a sandwich, but there wasn't much to do about it since we'd already eaten them. Paul and I started fishing in our pockets.

"Rich boy's payin'." Henry nodded toward Paul.

"No, he isn't," I told him. "Fork over two bits."

Henry went all wide-eyed. "Well, now, that wasn't part a the deal."

"Sure it was. You didn't ask, that's all." Two quarters on the table and three of us waiting.

"Aw, hell." Henry took a twenty-five-cent piece from his shirt pocket.

The woman wiped the three coins off the table into her hand and took her leave.

"But I ain't goin' dutch on no fancy hotels and such."

I stood and pushed my chair in. "We'll shove you off that bridge when we come to it."

As we were on our way out, the woman stuck her head out the kitchen door to see what Paul was laughing about.

Henry drove the next stint too. I called out an oak tree with four separate trunks that made it look like it was being pulled in all directions at once. I called out wheat fields and cornfields and crows and doves and a cloud shaped like a buffalo. Henry kept his mouth blessedly shut.

The town of Lexington came into view, and I told Paul the two things I knew about it: there was a Confederate cannonball still lodged in one wall of the courthouse on the town square, and my dad had stayed at a boarding house nearby one time on a trip to Kansas City.

We were barely into town when Henry hollered, "Tavern!" He veered over to a stop so hard it threw Paul and me forward.

I rubbed my elbow while deciding I liked the looks of the place none too much. "I don't think this is the best—"

"Who said you deserved the best? Hell's bells!" Henry laughed. He jumped out of the car and bounded onto the sidewalk. "You two be as big a sissies as you want. But you ain't goin' nowhere else." He waved the Ford's crank high over his head and went inside, cackling.

I twisted sideways in the seat. "Paul—"

"I know." He opened the back door. "If you can't beat 'em . . ."

When my eyes adjusted to the dark inside, Henry was already at a table with a shot and a beer.

Paul pressed something into my hand. Under his breath he said, "A beer. And whatever you want." He folded my hand into a fist around the money.

I was almost to the bar when I realized I'd left him standing alone.

Henry's voice rang out, "Oh, Master Bricken! Come join me for tea, won't you?"

I was starting to hate that laugh of his.

There were only two other customers in the place, I was happy to see.

Paul threaded his way through the chairs and tables with Henry offering what might pass for encouragement. "A little to the left!" Crash. "Now, that there was a chair. I'd step over it if I was you." And so on.

The barkeep nodded in their direction. "He blind?"

"Which one?" I said and was sorry before I got to the question mark.

"Now, look here." He was a bear of a man and growled like one. "You ain't from around here, are you?"

I shook my head.

"Well, let me tell you—we don't need no smart boys." He nodded toward Henry. "No troublemakers neither."

"Yessir. I'm sorry." I laid Paul's dollar on the bar.

"Hang on to this, please. I'm sure we'll have more." I picked up the bottles. "And, yessir, he's blind. The other one's just stupid."

The big man's face cracked into a grin.

Henry and Paul were talking baseball when I joined them. How they'd gotten started on that, I couldn't feature. But it was one subject Henry knew something about, and there was no end to Paul's questions.

"Naw, naw, naw," Henry told him. "If a outfielder catches the ball on the fly, it don't matter if it's fair or foul. It's a out just the same."

I sat back and listened with a seed of hope.

We were on our third round when Paul said, "Uh, guys? I . . . um . . . need to go."

Henry said, "Why, go where?" with a fake innocence that told me it was way too early to pronounce him tamed.

"Okay, Paul. I gotta go myself." I stood and caught the barkeep's eye. "Out back?" I asked, and he nodded.

The outhouse was twenty yards from the back door. After I peeked inside, I told Paul, "It's a two holer. We can both go in."

We did our business and buttoned up. When I opened the door, I came face-to-face with two men and some kind of hammer falling from the sky.

Next thing I knew, I was sitting on the ground rubbing a knot on the side of my head, and it had somehow gotten dark outside.

I heard moaning sounds close by and crawled over to find Henry staring at a sticky mess in his hands. He'd wiped at the wreck that had once been his nose, and his hands were covered in blood.

"What happened?" I asked.

"We were robbed." This from Paul.

"Goddamn!" Henry went for his pockets same as I did.

Mine were hanging outside my trousers. "But what . . . happened?" I felt a little thick.

"I never saw what hit me," Henry said.

Paul let out a long breath. "Well, I was behind you when you opened the door," he said, nodding toward me, "and heard a thud. You went, 'Unghh,' and hit the ground. Then something that felt like a gun barrel was poking me in the chest, and I was told to sit on the ground. Not hard to do, since I tripped over you."

"Shit!" The faces I'd seen in that one second came back. "It was the other two guys from the tavern!"

"It was?" Paul and Henry asked.

"Yeah. Then what happened, Paul?" Felt mighty strange, me asking him.

"Then they rifled my pockets and yours and put us over by that tree." He motioned with his head. "And they told me to keep quiet and wait for our friend to come see about us."

"I was set up!" Henry hollered. "You guys was

gone so long I'd'a thought you left me if I didn't have the crank."

I startled a little.

"It's inside," he said. "I hope. Well, come on!"

He headed in with us behind him and announced, "We been robbed!" as we came through the door.

The barman didn't seem surprised or interested. "On the way to the outhouse? Somebody scare the piss outta ya? That ain't hardly robbery."

"It was the two that were in here before," I explained.

Henry jumped in. "Yeah, you know who they are? We gotta go to the sheriff—"

"Now just hold it." The grizzly reached down and came out with the biggest revolver I'd ever seen. He laid it on the bar that separated us. "You boys cook this up to try and get outta payin' what you owe?"

"We done nothin'!" Henry yelped like a kicked pup.

"Mister, we paid you before we started, remember?" I offered.

"You give me a dollar when you came in," the man said, "and Butthole here"—he nodded at Henry—"put you fifteen cents over while you two was outside. And you ain't leavin' here without payin'."

"But we were just robbed!" I reminded him.

"You think I smashed up my own face over fifteen cents?" Henry sounded ready to fight.

The man studied us. "Mebbe."

"I've got money." We all whipped our heads toward Paul, who was feeling around for a chair.

The revolver came up off the bar. "Oh. So you was all robbed but him. Is that it?"

"Paul," I said, "maybe you don't know it yet, but even your watch is gone."

"Yes, I'm well aware." He sat down. "Is there anybody else in here besides the four of us?"

Henry and I cased the room.

"No," I told him.

"Why?" Henry said.

"Yeah, why?" The barman's voice bounced off the rafters.

Paul's answer was to untie his left shoe. He took it off, then peeled his sock just past the heel and came out with a dollar. He held it out to me, and I laid the soggy thing on the bar. The barkeep made change and slammed it down so hard coins bounced in all directions.

"What the—?"

I motioned Henry quiet. "So now that you're paid, sir, would you tell us who it was?"

The big man snorted. "I still ain't convinced you was robbed."

Henry took a step forward, and I stepped in front of him.

"But one of the fellers here was Virgil Jones. I dunno who he had with him."

"Well, that's very helpful," I said, "and would you tell us how to get to the sheriff's office?"

"Find it yerself." The man already had his back to us.

I grabbed Paul's arm and headed for the front.

Henry bolted over to where we'd sat. The crank. I'd forgot. He held it up like a trophy, and I took a breath again.

At the door we all stopped. It was clear none of us wanted to be the first to step outside.

"Come on," I said through my teeth and pulled Paul along.

Outside, we all started gulping night air.

I said, "I'll drive."

Nobody argued.

Once I found the town square, it didn't take long to locate the jail. I knocked.

Henry said, "Go on in. We ain't exactly company."

My hand was on the knob when the door flew open.

A man, half a head taller than me, stood there with a chicken leg in one hand and a napkin tucked into the open neck of his gray work shirt. "Whaddaya want?" was his way of saying hello.

"We been robbed!" Henry shouldered Paul and me apart and took a step forward. "It was Virgil Jones and—"

"There was two of them," I said.

"But we don't know who the other one was," Paul offered.

The man showed us his disgusted look. "That's who I thought you was." When he pulled the napkin away from his throat to wipe his mouth, I saw the tin star pinned above his left pocket.

"What do you—?"

He cut me off by stepping outside. "Now you listen to me." The man shook the drumstick in our faces. "I heard about you all. Virgil was by here not fifteen minutes ago and interrupted my supper the first time tonight to tell me there was three troublemakers over at Red Schmidt's place. He said he didn't know what you was up to, but you was drinkin' up a storm and didn't look like you had no money."

Henry and I blinked at each other, openmouthed.

"But he's one of 'em who did it!" I said. "And we had money before we was robbed."

Paul nodded fiercely.

"How'd ya think I got this?" Henry pointed to his nose, twice its normal size and showing purple under the gaslights on the stoop.

"Well, now, I don't know," the man said. He threw the chicken bone into the bushes, and his eyes got pig narrow. "But you look to be the one Virgil said in particular was a loudmouth gettin' fallin'-down drunk. I got no sympathy for you."

"But, sir," Paul tried, "what they say is true. We were just—"

"My cousin's no thief," the sheriff said. "An' I don't appreciate you sayin' he is. Now I suggest you take your butts back where you come from and think twice before you set foot in Lexington again." He stepped up through the doorway and reached to shut us out.

Paul tried again, "But—"

"Sir, before you go"—I gulped—"we know there's a boarding house near town and—"

The man cut me off with a murderous look. "Well, now, seems to me if you was robbed you wouldn't have money for a boarding house. You boys better get your story straight." He slammed the door, and we heard the dead bolt turn.

Henry reached to knock.

I grabbed his fist midair. "What are you doin'?"

"What are *you* doin'? We can't jes'—"

"You heard him. No use talkin' to somebody who won't listen. Let's get away from this man's front door."

I thought out loud while we walked toward the car. "I know one thing. Sleeping inside tonight, someplace safe, just got real damned important to me."

Their mumbling didn't sound like argument.

Five minutes later, we were standing on the front step of a two-story house looking at a brass plate that said *Mrs. Bentley's*. Now, I don't know squat about running a boarding house, but the brass gargoyle with a ring through its nose for a knocker didn't look too friendly to me. A dog next door started yapping. I hit the striking plate three times, and we waited.

Before long, that dog was working on my last nerve. I was about to bolt when the door opened an inch and an eye appeared in the crack.

"Yes?" An old woman's shrill cackle.

"Mrs. Bentley, ma'am?" I asked.

"Mebbe." The eye narrowed. "What do you want?"

"Why, a place to stay," I told her. "My name's John Hartmann, and my father stayed here last year. Jonas Hartmann? He told me what a nice place you have, and—"

"Why didn't you write ahead and hold rooms, then?" The doorway lost half its open inch.

"Well, we didn't know we'd be here tonight, exactly, and—"

"Just where did you think you'd be?"

"We weren't sure, ma'am. You see, we're travelers and—"

"This is a respectable house, young man. We don't truck with hoodlums and hoboes." The door was going to shut any second.

"My mother has died, ma'am." Henry took a step forward.

I just about choked. How low a man could Henry be, to beg the devil for that kind of curse? Everybody knows you can attract a disaster just by mentioning its name.

Then I remembered his mother had died—when he was born or some such—and I guessed nothing he said was going to change that.

"We was in Kansas City doin' business when I got the telegram," Henry went on. "We been drivin' all afternoon—we live in Wakenda—but we're awful tired and we need some rest before we . . . can go on."

His voice cracked on the last few words, and I had to marvel at that.

"Look up at me, young man."

Henry did.

"What happened to your face?"

"Why, I . . ." Henry faltered.

Damn. We were camping out for the night.

But he stalled with a deep, ragged breath and went on. "When I got the news, I just fell down prostate with grief, ma'am."

I managed, "It's true."

"Uh-huh," Henry said. He felt around his backside. "I think maybe I even rent my garment."

"You smell like you been drinkin'," the woman said.

Paul stepped forward. "Well, we poured a little whiskey down his throat to bring him around, ma'am, but he nearly choked on it, unaccustomed as he is to strong drink."

She looked at Paul for the first time. "You blind?"

"Yes, ma'am, I am, but I always have been. That did not happen today, no, ma'am." He tried to pat Henry on the shoulder, and Henry helped by shifting a step closer.

"Well, I only got one room left tonight." She said it like she doubted her own honesty.

"That's fine," I said. "We wouldn't want poor Henry to be alone tonight anyway." I patted his other shoulder.

"Well . . ." She blinked, and I knew we were in.

"It'll be two dollars for the room and three meals in the morning, and I'll have to have it in advance." She looked sympathetic towards Henry. "No offense, son, but this is a business, and I don't know you all."

Paul held up two damp-looking bills, and Henry started to push on the door. "If you don't mind, ma'am, I still feel kinda faint—"

She threw the door open, and he nearly fell on her.

"You get in here and sit down." Two minutes after she'd tried to run us off, she was clucking like a setting hen.

When I stumbled through the door with all our gear, Paul behind me, Henry was tucked under a crocheted afghan on the divan in the parlor.

I dropped everything and went to him. "Where the hell did that story come from?" I hissed.

"Got us in, din't it?" His dimples made a wicked frame for the wreck of his nose. His face and hands had been washed clean of blood.

"Yeah, but—"

"You're forgettin' I lived with Ellen and the reverend most a my life," he said. "You wanna learn how to lie like the devil, live with a preacher awhile."

I nudged him with my boot. "Well, what are you doin' layin' there?"

"Oh, I'm sure my weakness will pass once all our stuff has been carried upstairs." He grinned.

Mrs. Bentley appeared with a cup of something steaming hot. She gave Henry orders to rest, then lit into us. "And did you take him to let a doctor have a look at that nose?"

"Uh, no, ma'am," I told her.

"We wanted to, ma'am," Paul said, "but he wouldn't let us. He just wanted to get on the road soon as possible, and . . . and . . . it was all we could do to convince him to stop here. He wanted to keep on driving." The admiration in Paul's voice was so deep I hoped I wouldn't step in it.

"Oh. Well, then." Mrs. Bentley blinked. "I got a doctor stayin' here, travelin' through. Seems nice enough. I'm sure he won't mind comin' down for a minute."

"Oh, don't go to any trouble on my account. I ain't worth it."

I saw the glint in Henry's eye.

She didn't. "You poor dear," she clucked, and I wondered how much time had passed since she had a chick in the nest. She turned to me. "You two come on up with me. Bring Henry's gear too, you hear me? I'll show you what's what and get the doctor."

Last one out of the room, I glanced back at Henry and saw his eyes cross and his tongue come dangling out the side of his mouth.

Mrs. Bentley showed us our room and hurried off. I flopped onto the bed and stared at the electric light fixture in the ceiling. Paul found his way to an oak rocking chair in the corner.

I said, "Well, at least somethin's goin' right."

"We've got to turn back," Paul blurted out.

I shot upright. "What are you talkin' about? Where the hell did that come from?"

"What choice do we have?" Something in Paul's throat was interfering with his words. "Here it is our first day, and look what's happened. We've already had automobile trouble—"

"We had a flat tire! That's all! It's no big deal."

Paul started rocking.

"Did you think we were gonna drive all the way to Yellowstone—and back—and have nothin' go wrong with the Ford?"

"Yes." He sounded miserable.

"Well, then, you weren't thinkin'. A flat tire's nothin'. We're adventurers! Travelers! We're—"

"Broke. Or very close to it. We were robbed, John. Have you forgotten?" He covered his face with his hands. "We could have been killed! Henry's hurt, we've got no money, nobody cares—"

"Paul, Paul, Paul. Slow down. If it's the money you're worried about, well, you still got some anyway, and me and Henry can always pick up work."

"You and Henry." Paul's ears turned bright red. "But I can't?"

"Well, of course you can, if you need to. I just . . . didn't know how much money you had left. We all can. We can make enough along the way to pay expenses. It won't take much, and we won't get robbed every place we go." It was all I could do not to knock on wood.

He shook his head.

"You were enjoying yourself downstairs just a minute ago. Don't tell me you weren't—joining in on Henry's cock-and-bull story like that."

"I wanted to make sure we had a place to stay tonight—that's all. I've . . . lost my nerve, John."

I kicked at his chair and rocked him backward. "Well, then, you didn't have much to begin with, did you? I don't believe that, Paul Bricken. You're tougher'n that."

"But what if—?"

I pounced. "Aw, hell, Paul. This ain't a *what if* kinda trip—you know that. It's a *so what* kinda trip. So what if we had a flat tire? We'll probably have a hundred more! So what if we were robbed? We weren't killed, and that's what matters! And Henry . . . well, if nobody else had busted his nose by now, you and me would probably be fightin' for the privilege. We figured he'd be a hell of a guy in a spot, remember? If we thought there wasn't gonna be trouble along the way, why in holy hell ask Henry to come along?"

Paul kept rocking, his face like stone.

After a minute, I said, "Indoor plumbing here, remember? Want me to show you where it is?"

No answer.

In the toilet, there was a mirror over the sink. I peed, washed my hands, and took stock. My face was chapped from the day's sun and wind, and I could see my headache staring back at me. I felt the knot on my head and winced. Then my stomach growled to remind me it had been ignored since late afternoon in Dover. *Damn it*. Maybe Paul was right. *Damn it to hell anyway*. Maybe we weren't up to this. I wasn't sure what had made me believe we were.

When I got back to the room, he was facedown on the bed. From what I remember, I must have been out before my head hit the pillow.

I didn't hear Henry come in, but his snoring woke Paul and me up in the morning. He was on top of the covers at our feet. Asleep, his busted face looked like a sign saying he wasn't as tough as he thought he was.

I nudged him in the side. "Shut up!"

He was on his feet, fists raised, before he was even awake, just like the night we'd gone to see him in the barn. I couldn't imagine what would condition a man to wake up ready to fight. "Goddamn," he said. "Wha'd ya do that for?"

I rolled out. "You snore like a damn buffalo. Nobody could sleep within a mile of that racket."

"Goddamn sissies. I'm goin' down to breakfast. Go back to your beauty rest." He slammed the door on his way out.

Paul gave out a loud yawn.

I said, "We'd better get downstairs before Henry eats all the way through Mrs. Bentley's pantry."

We found Henry sitting at a long table in the dining room behind a plate of food already half gone.

Three other men looked up and grunted before going back to their own plates. I sat down opposite Henry and started to speak, but one look at his face shut my mouth.

The dim light upstairs had told only half the tale. Now I saw his nose was swelled up like an eggplant and crisscrossed with white tape. Plenty ugly for sure, but it was his eyes that gave me the creeps—crocodile eyes swollen to slits and buried in thick purple lids. My eyes watered just looking at him.

"Pretty, ain't I?" he said.

Mrs. Bentley burst through the swinging kitchen door, and I was glad for something else to look at. She balanced platters of biscuits and sausage in one hand and carried a pitcher of milk gravy in the other.

Henry filled a second plate and lit into it like he'd always heard wondrous tales about food but this was the first he'd had. Mrs. Bentley served up some of everything on a plate she set in front of Paul. Then she fluttered around filling coffee cups.

I leaned over a little and told him, "Biscuits and gravy at twelve o'clock, sausage at six," and started in on my own.

Henry gulped a wad of bread and said, "What do you do when nobody else is around?"

Paul never hesitated eating.

"Hey! Paul!"

Paul looked up. "Yes?"

"How do you get by when nobody's around?"

"Oh." Paul tapped at his mouth with a napkin

and took a sip of coffee. "Well, Henry, have you ever heard that if a tree falls in the forest and no one's around to hear it, it doesn't make a sound?"

"I guess so . . ."

It was clear he hadn't.

"Well, if there's no one around to see me, I don't exist."

"You don't . . . Huh?"

Paul said, "Yesterday, you implied you live by the old adage 'Seeing is believing.' Isn't that what you were saying?"

"Well, you were talkin' about the fair like—"

"And you know I can't see myself. So I guess if nobody else is around, I'm not there, am I?" He started eating again.

We all sat and stared at him. I knew he was having fun at Henry's expense, but his face held no clue that he was anything other than serious. And it's hard to laugh at a fellow's joke when you're not sure what it is. The room was completely still other than Paul's fork traveling from plate to mouth.

Then Mrs. Bentley appeared with a milk pitcher, and regular conversation took up again. Sugar was passed, and the weather was reported upon and predicted. Henry wolfed a third plateful of food and headed upstairs.

Seconds later, Paul asked, "Has anyone here read the morning newspaper?"

There were grunts that sounded like *no* from around the table.

The man opposite Paul said, "Why?"

"Keeping up with news on the Johnson-Jeffries fight—that's all."

The same man grunted. "Jeffries and Johnson, you meant to say, din't ya?"

"Not gonna happen," said the man to his right.

This time the grunts sounded like *yes*.

The man continued, "John L. Sullivan hisself said it was prob'ly a frame-up, and the governor of California said the same. It's just a setup to cheat people out of money."

I had barely a clue what they were talking about.

Paul said, "Yes, I've heard that."

Mrs. Bentley reappeared and started clearing the table, and we all pushed back our chairs and went upstairs to our rooms.

The room we'd slept in looked like a tornado had hit it, and I had to stop myself from asking Henry if he was raised in a barn. Instead, I said, "Okay, then. Let's figure out what we're gonna do."

"Whaddaya mean?" Henry grunted. "What's to figger?"

I scuffed my toe in the flowers on the rug. "Oh, it's just that last night when you were downstairs and we were up here, Paul was sayin'—"

"Last night I was saying we should shoot you and put you out of your misery. It's true. But now I think we should keep you alive and torture you as long as we can." Paul put on a cheerful smile.

"What the—?"

I grinned at the woolen roses at my feet. "Let's go. Load up the car and get outta here."

Mrs. Bentley was waiting by the front door when we banged our way down the cherrywood staircase with our bags. "Seems to me you could of shaved," she told no one in particular.

Paul was still jolly. "We would have, ma'am, but Henry wants to get on the road so he can be a comfort to his father soon as possible."

"Well." Her dark little bird eyes darted over our clothes as if she just now noticed we weren't dressed like businessmen.

Paul said, "But could you tell us the nearest place to buy a newspaper, please?"

Henry snorted.

Paul ignored him. "Ma'am?"

"Well—" She was blinking telegraph code, trying to sort us out. "Just go on up to the square, and you'll see Stanford's. You can get one there."

"Thank you, ma'am. For everything." I pushed Henry out the door with the bags I carried.

I drove as we headed out.

Paul leaned over the backrest. "Don't forget to stop at Stanford's."

Henry twisted around. "You meant that? I figured you was jes' pullin' that ol' woman's leg."

No answer.

"What are you gonna do with a newspaper?" Henry said.

"I get one every day."

"But what do you do with it?"

"Have somebody read it to me."

"Oh." Henry faced forward two whole seconds. "Who?"

"You or John . . . it doesn't matter."

"Naw, I mean every day, like you said. Yer ma or yer pa take all that time out of their day?"

"No. Sam reads to me."

"Oh."

I was concentrating on pulling up to the rail in front of Stanford's, and I jumped when Henry yelled.

"There wasn't no colored schools around when Sam was comin' up! You think I'm stupid?"

I didn't hear Paul's answer before I walked into the store.

Henry was guffawing when I came back out. I maneuvered into reverse and told Paul while I was turned around facing him, "We oughta buy gasoline before we leave town."

Henry leaned over and slapped my thigh hard. "You missed a good'n."

I gritted my teeth against the sting.

"Ol' Paulie here's been tellin' me he learned their boy Sam how to read!"

"Well, then, I'm sure he did." I could feel the outline

of Henry's hand burning my leg.

"Aw, phffft! Now how would he? Jes' tell me that."

I kept my eyes forward and headed west. "Seems like you're askin' the wrong person." Over my shoulder, I said, "Paul? Gasoline, if I can find a place?"

"Sure, wherever you think."

Henry buzzed like a mosquito again. "Well, then, you jes' tell me how the hell you teach somebody else to read when you can't. That's what I wanna know."

"I can read."

"Not like normal people, you can't!"

"Oh? And what is normal? If everyone around but you were blind—"

"Don't start in on that shit again," Henry hollered. Then to me, "What are you laughin' at?" His fist came at my shoulder.

I caught it and shoved it back at him. "You. And if you hit me one more time, I'm gonna pull the car over and lay you out. I mean it." I checked his reaction with a split-second glance. "You hear me?"

"Well, tell me what's goin' on!" Henry bleated like a calf.

"Sounds to me like you're doin' your best to make Paul mad and he won't play along."

"No, I ain't! I jes'—" He threw up his hands. Like we were the ones being ornery. "I just wanna know how he could learn a man to read when he can't even see. That's all."

"Oh. Then why didn't you say so?" Paul asked.

I shot Henry a look that prevented an answer.

"Well, I do know my letters. At school we were taught the shapes with carved wood blocks."

"But—"

"And I can write. I need paper guides, but I can turn out writing as good as yours, I'd wager. I drew the letters for Sam first and taught him those. Then it was just a matter of teaching him what they sound like and how they fit together. If he got stuck, he'd describe a letter to me or draw it in my hand with his finger and we'd go on from there."

"Jiminy," I said. So simple.

But not simple enough for Henry. "But how can you write? How do you know what you've wrote when you can't see it?"

"If you wrote something in pitch darkness, it might come out messy, but you'd know what you had written, wouldn't you?" There was a smile in Paul's voice.

"Oh." Henry frowned, then said, "But what about the readin' part?"

Paul leaned forward. "I read things printed in Braille. It's a raised-letter code that's stamped into paper, and you read it by running your fingers over it. It's named after the man who invented it."

"A code? You mean it's like readin' a whole 'nother language?"

"That's right," Paul said. He was resting his head on his arms between us. "Have you heard of Helen Keller?"

"Yeah . . ."

"Well, she can read and write in four or five different languages, and she's blind *and* deaf! What do you think of that?"

Henry snorted. "I heard my pa say she weren't nothin' but a trained monkey. That's what I think of that."

Paul's words came like bullets. "I once heard your father say that you killed your mother. Do you believe that too?"

Henry made a noise like he'd been kicked.

I braked and turned around to look at Paul—I guess to make sure that comment had really come out of him, the Paul Bricken I knew.

He looked about ready to puke.

We drove until noon and into the town of Levasy without any more said, but Henry cleared his throat a lot. My stomach clenched like a fist and burned like it always does during a brouhaha with my folks.

I had the awful thought that maybe home wasn't the problem any of us thought it was. Maybe what was wrong hadn't been left behind at all.

CHAPTER FOUR

"WE'RE IN LEVASY," IS HOW I SURFACED from the gloomy silence. "You got enough to buy us gasoline and a meal, Paul, or do we need to rob a chicken house?"

"I can pay." His voice was flat as train tracks. "Stop somewhere for fuel and ask if there's someplace to eat that's not too fancy."

Now, there was a remark only a blind man would make. The town of Levasy made Wakenda look like Paris, France. The whole town looked like it could do with a bucket of soapy water and a new coat of paint.

But there was a cafe. The town blacksmith carried gasoline for sale, and he pointed us toward Maggie's after he pocketed Paul's money. Outside, it looked like the place where we'd stopped to eat in Dover.

And inside, it was about the same, except it had a lunch counter and we were in time for the meat loaf plate special. I would have put us in a line at the counter staring at anything other than each other, but the stools were all taken.

There was one woman running the place, both cook and waitress. Second time over, she brought our plates. "Sure you don't want separate tables?"

We all frowned at her.

"You ain't said boo to one another since you come in. I just wondered."

Even Paul found a spot on the table to study in answer to that.

That afternoon we passed more pastures, more corn-fields and farmsteads. I drove and was glad for not talking. My description of the countryside would have sounded like Henry's. Tree. Rock. Dirt. More dirt. But maybe that was just my mood. If we'd been getting along, I might could have turned out poetry. It's hard to find the poet inside you when your insides are on fire.

We met one automobile and three teams on the way to Independence. The first horses reared, and we had to stop and help the farmer load barrels back into his wagon. After that, I pulled over and stopped to let the dumb animals pass.

I asked if anybody needed to stop in Independence for anything, and neither one answered, so I drove on through. Once I'd found my way through the maze of streets and we were back out in the open, I pulled the car over and killed the engine.

It took about three minutes before anybody spoke up.

"Where are we?" Paul asked. "Is there another wagon passing?"

I turned sideways in the seat. "Nothin' passin' here except the god-awful gas that meat loaf gave me."

No response from either one. Not even a smile. Hell, everybody likes a fart joke.

"Naw, I was just thinkin' maybe we should turn around and go home after all."

That got their attention.

Henry popped a "Whuh—?"

Paul's nose came up like a bird dog on point.

"Yeah, I've had a lot of quiet here to do some thinking, and seems to me it won't be car trouble or robbers or broken noses that kill this trip. It's gonna be infighting. What's the point of driving all the way across the country with people you ain't speaking to?" By God, I was finally coming up with the right words when I needed them, instead of three days too late.

"He started it." Paul.

"Like hell." Henry.

Gott im Himmel, as my grandpa used to say. What were they, three years old?

"You could both do with apologizing," I told them. I nodded at Henry. "You're a damn trouble-maker." Then I turned all the way around to talk to Paul. "And that was just about the shittiest thing I've ever heard anybody say to another person." I looked back and forth between them. "You don't need to be

best friends—I don't even care if you like each other—
but if you can't be decent, I'm turnin' it around right now."

They pouted for a minute, and Henry sneered,
"Thanks, Grandma."

"Well, stop actin' like a baby and I'll stop treatin'
you like one."

They both grumbled.

Paul finally said, "That was . . . a stupid thing for
me to say. I'm sorry."

Henry's bottom lip stuck out so far I wanted to
smack it. "I didn't do nothin'," he said. "You gotta
learn not to be so goddamned thin-skinned, is all."

I was ready to head for home. "Henry," I said
through my teeth, "you've tried to stir things up every
time you opened your mouth and you know it. Are
you gonna quit it or not?"

"Seems like I can't walk anywhere without steppin'
in some kinda shit."

I waited.

He shook his head. "Oh, all right. I'll try."

I got out of the car with the crank. "Can you see
out of those bloody slits well enough to drive?"

He slid behind the wheel, and we were soon on
our way.

Half an hour down the road, we came by a barn that
listed so far to one side it looked like the wind from
a chicken walking by might take it down. I turned
around to tell Paul and found him leaning at a similar

angle against Henry's bedroll, sleeping. I faced forward and settled in for a break.

Which lasted less than a minute.

With no preamble, Henry said, "It ain't like I never heard it before."

I had to think for a minute what he meant and then said to myself, *Oh, hell.* "Well, damn, Henry. Women die birthin' babies. It's a natural fact. You can't hardly blame the babies."

Henry said, "Especially when they're four years old." An undertaker's laugh.

"I don't understand." *Oh, Lord,* I thought, *he didn't really kill her, did he?* It seemed like I'd have grown up knowing *that* story.

"Mama didn't die birthin' me. But Pa said I tore her up so bad comin' out ass first it ruined her for— well, she just never got over it. He said she started dyin' the day I was born, and it just took her four years to get done."

"Good God." I thought about Catherine for the first time since I'd left home and went back two years to remember her at four—so little, so breakable, seemed like. I couldn't imagine anybody like that without a mother.

I finally ventured, "Well, he didn't tell you it was your fault, did he?"

"Not when he was sober." That same laugh. It sent a chill down my back. "But that started comin' around less and less often. I barely remember him before he got bad. I don't really remember her at all."

I sneaked a look. He was blinking fast.

"Where are we?" Paul was awake, and I was glad.

"About ten miles from Kansas City would be my guess," I said. "Ought to be there in a half an hour."

"You got a plan?" Henry threw over his shoulder.

"Well, not really," I answered for Paul. "Just that Paul and I talked last night about picking up some work along the way to pay expenses. We didn't go into it, though."

I made note of the fact Henry didn't crack wise about Paul working. He just frowned. "Well, for you and me, I gotta say the stockyards is gonna be our best bet for work. We wanna look for someplace close around there to stay?"

The stockyards. Of course. Work tailor-made for the two of us. I was surprised Henry had thought of it before I could.

"Well, I was thinking," Paul said, "I can take the trolley downtown from wherever we are. I'm sure there's a music store there. So you two may as well take the Ford while we're here. I mean, we don't need to stay right next door to the livestock."

Henry wrestled with this.

I offered, "Paul knows how to tune pianos."

But Henry was on a different path. "You use the trolley in St. Louis?"

"All the time," Paul said.

"Huh."

For the two of them, it was downright civilized.

Once in the city, Henry's Halloween face scared two people away and convinced us I was the better man for asking directions. We all changed places to put him in the shadows of the backseat. About thirty dead-end streets and wrong turns finally got us to the stockyards, locked up tight for the night. Every one of my nerves was jangled by then from the noise and traffic and more people than I'd ever seen in one place. I wanted nothing more than to pull over and sleep in the car.

Instead, I drove us all around there to get our bearings. Then I drove in a bigger circle each time around, looking for a place to put up. The Ben Bolt Hotel declared a vacancy, and the looks of it promised it couldn't be too expensive.

Once we got to our room and inspected what little was there, I commented, "It smells like feet."

"It smells like dirty socks stuffed with onions," Paul volunteered.

"It smells like George Reimer's barn," Henry said. "Hey, wait. Maybe it's just me you smell."

Paul froze, and I stared.

Henry busted out laughing. "Hell, I can't even make a joke about *me*? Gawd, you guys are the worst schoolmarms I've ever seen!"

Paul and I laughed, but it sounded like raw nerves.

I flopped into the one chair and got butt-stuck by

a spring. "Food" was all I could manage to say.

Paul was the only one with money. Henry and I waited.

"Should we walk somewhere?" Paul said. "Drive? Does either of you know someplace to go?"

My eyes were already half shut. "I'm starved to death and still don't want to move. Just find some food and stuff it in my mouth, okay?"

They were likely as beat as me, but I didn't have enough energy to feel bad about it.

Henry finally said, "Gimme a dollar, Paul. I'll find somethin' and bring it back here." Paul hesitated just long enough for Henry to add, "Okay, you go. I don't care," before he flopped onto the bed.

"No, I just—" Paul was doing that finger rubbing I'd seen before.

"You just don't trust me." Henry let out a ragged breath. "Well, I won't take the Model T. The crank's right here." He threw it near my feet.

I was too tired even to jump.

"And I ain't gonna take your dollar and go whoopin' it up. And I'm too tired to argue." That trip up the hotel stairs seemed to have taken the last energy any of us had. "I hope I don't get any farther than the old biddy behind the desk downstairs. Surely she's got some bread and meat back in the kitchen."

I guess he left. I had dozed off when I heard, "John? John?" and realized it wasn't Mary Albrecht.

"Huh?" I rubbed my eyes.

Paul was sitting on the bed holding out the newspaper I'd bought that morning. "Would you, please?"

"Aw, hell," I said before I could stop myself.

"Oh. Well, if it's too much trouble . . ."

Yeah, yeah, Paul. I'm traveling in your car. I'm eating on your nickel, at least for now. Hand me the goddamned paper. "How 'bout headlines?" is what I said out loud. "You interested, you tell me."

"That's what I always have Sam do, every day." Even with his citified English, he'd never sounded prissy to me before, but now I wanted to smack him upside the head. Amazing what bone-tired will do to a person.

"Okay." I took the paper. "Mrs. James Carroll is home after surgery at Liberty Hospital. Harold Weames had a boar hog stolen night before last. *Farmers' Almanac* predicts a rainy July."

"No, no, no." Paul's hands erased an invisible blackboard. "News from Washington, DC. New York. California. Anything on Jim Jeffries or Jack Johnson?"

"Who? Oh, those fighters they said ain't gonna fight?"

"Never mind." Paul laid back on the bed and threw an arm across his eyes. Downright girly.

"It's the Lexington paper, Paul. Give 'em a break. We'll get a *Kansas City Star* tomorrow."

And I hope I'm not as tired after a day at the stockyards as I am after driving your two sorry asses around and playing referee.

In the morning, we told Paul the address of the Ben Bolt and put him on a trolley headed for downtown. I felt anxious, but Henry was like the parent who kicks his kid out the door first day of school.

"Be sure and write!" he yelled. Streaks of green already showed through the purple on his bruises. Like a mallard drake and just about as loud.

We walked over to the stockyards and wandered around looking for the office. A bald fat man wearing a visor looked up from his desk and eyed us over his glasses. "What?"

"We're looking for work," I told him.

He landed on Henry. "What happened to you?"

"I ran into a door."

"Uh-huh." He sized us up some more. "Go to the first building south of here and find Jim Miller. He runs the works. We lost so many men last payday you may be in luck." He went back to his paperwork.

When we got to him, Jim Miller was curious about Henry too. "What happened to you?"

"I ran into a fist."

"Uh-huh." He dropped his chin and eyed him until Henry looked away. He turned to me. "You ever worked cattle, son?"

"All my life, sir."

Back to Henry. "You look like the sort that wouldn't mind shootin' dumb animals."

"I'd shoot my own dog if I's tired of it."

"Well, that's more'n I needed to know. But all right." Miller lifted an eyebrow and pointed out a window so dirty it was close to useless. "Yonder over there's the slaughterhouse. Go see Pete Willis." He nodded at me. "You come on with me."

And no more than fifteen minutes later, I was put to work. There were five of us to run cattle through the chutes, some straddling gates and prodding animals to cull and sort. I was down in the mud, shoulder to shoulder with the beasts. Before long, I knew which way they were going to cut before they did. It was way easier without Dad yelling at me nonstop. Jim Miller walked the grounds all morning, but twice I saw him stop and watch me awhile, nodding.

At noon, I went to the warehouse with the rest of them and sat at a picnic table in the near-empty room they used for a mess hall. There must have been fifty men tearing into their dinner pails all at once.

The fellow next to me, brown as a nut and skinny as leather stretched over bone, said, "How come you ain't eatin'? Watchin' your girlish figure?" and he elbowed me right where I'd just got kicked by an ornery steer.

I winced and mumbled something about leaving my lunch pail at home. He tore his sandwich in half and handed one part to me.

I shook my head. "Naw, I can't do that. It's okay— I'll eat plenty tonight."

He set the food on the table in front of me. "Eat

it. Your sorry ass keels over this afternoon, they'll process your carcass, and my luck you'll end up on my dinner table."

I nodded my thanks.

We worked seven to seven. When the bell clanged at quitting time, I was tired but happy. I'd been told I was a good worker for the first time in my life and half a dozen times more.

I caught up with Henry at the stockyard gate. His shoes were spattered with blood to go with his fright mask of a face, and nobody walked too close to him even in the rush to leave. He ran his mouth all the way to the Ben Bolt.

"Blam!" he said. "Twenty-two rifle shot right between the eyes! Blam! And they drop."

The knot on my head from the pistol-whipping in Lexington throbbed in the sunshine. "Is that all you did all day?"

"For the most part. Swished a little water around sometimes to keep the floor from gettin' too sticky to walk on."

I felt queasy around the edges.

"Only had to shoot one of 'em twice, and that was the fault of the damn fool holdin' her. Blam! Blam! And for this they're payin' me a dollar and a half."

"Sounds like you oughta be payin' them."

We were on our way up the stairs to our room.

"Man alive, I would, and that's a natural fact."

I opened the door.

We stopped at the sight of Paul, facedown on the bed. He offered a muffled hello into the pillow, which answered my first question: he was alive.

I sat down and studied the crust on my boots and thought, *Well, at least the room doesn't smell like feet anymore.*

Henry didn't look like he could sit down if he was paid to. "I'm goin' down to the crapper," he said, and we heard him "Blam! Blam!" his way down the hall.

"Bad day?" I took a wild guess.

His "No" surprised me. But then Paul rolled over, and his face was calling him a liar. "Not today anyway. Bad day comes tomorrow."

I took off my boots and pulled out my pocketknife to scrape mud and manure onto yesterday's newspaper. "You're gonna have to help me out there, Paul. I'm no good at seein' tomorrow."

"I made two dollars today."

My knife stopped midair. "You what? Good God, man, that's fantastic!"

He sat up on the edge of the bed. "I tuned every piano Stiller's had on the showroom floor, and they paid me forty cents apiece."

Tired was catching up to me again, and I snapped, "So what's wrong with tomorrow?"

"Tomorrow they said I could go with the deliverymen and tune pianos in people's houses. A dollar apiece."

"God a'mighty, that's great! What's wrong with

you?" I wanted to grab his shoulders and shake him.

"I met the delivery team today. Two gorillas who make Henry seem like John D. Rockefeller at a dinner party."

"Oh." That was a picture. "Aren't you maybe exaggerating?"

"You tell me." Paul snorted. "Ape Number One told me, 'Good luck finding your way back from our first stop.' And Ape Two said, 'Even if you do, you won't make your way back from the second one. Not naked, you won't.'"

Christ on a biscuit. "But, Paul, don't they know you can get them fired? *You* know that, don't you?"

"They said—Ape Number Two, that is, said, 'Just in case you got some big ideas, piano wire is just perfect for shutting up tattletales.'"

I couldn't get my mind around it. Henry offering to shoot his pet dog did sound refined by comparison. "I just can't feature. Why?"

"It's nothing I haven't heard before," Paul told me. Same as Henry talking about his dad. "There are thugs, and I met plenty in St. Louis, who think anybody . . . different should be drowned at birth like an unwanted cat. Or at least institutionalized, so that so-called normal people don't have to be insulted by looking at them."

"How does looking at you insult anybody?"

Paul let out some air. "It doesn't, really. But it scares them."

"You're about the least scary fella I've ever known. No offense."

"None taken." Paul's mouth pulled into a straight line that might have been a smile. "I guess seeing me reminds them of the hand they could have been dealt."

Henry came busting through the door and took a look at each of us. "Somebody die?"

"No, it just smells that way." I stood and lifted Paul's elbow an inch. "Come on. Everything looks better over a full stomach."

We passed a drugstore before we came to a restaurant we liked the looks of. I bummed two cents from Paul and ducked in to grab a newspaper.

Over food served on a table with a red-and-white-checkered cloth, I read headlines out loud. "The Wright Flyer exhibition team was at that new motor speedway in Indianapolis the other day."

"That was almost a week ago," Paul said.

Henry rolled his eyes.

"Well, here's something about Jack Johnson. Wasn't that one of them you were asking about?"

Paul sat up straighter. "Yes!"

"Well, he was scheduled to put on an exhibition with Kid Cotton in San Francisco today, for whatever that's worth."

"Hmm." Paul found that worth consideration. He nodded. "Showing people that he really is training, likely."

"That uppity nigger?" Henry said around a wad of potatoes. "I hope you're askin' 'cause you wanna see his ass handed to him bad as I do."

Paul flinched. "Would you not . . . Could you use the word *colored* instead? Please? I know how Sam feels about . . . that."

"Can't call a spade a spade?" Henry thought that was so funny, he whacked the table hard enough for people to turn and look.

"Please." Paul's cheeks each sported a spot of red.

"Oh, okay, Mr. Schoolteacher," Henry said. "You wanna see that uppity . . . *colored* handed his ass bad as I do?"

"One of you wanna fill me in on what you're talkin' about?" I asked.

"Where you been?" Henry said.

"Boxing." They both spoke at once.

"Yeah, I know there's a fight comin' up—or not, depending on who you talk to. But what's this . . . colored got to do with it?"

"You don't know?" Henry looked astonished. "That's Johnson. He's a pretender to the championship." He snorted. "Jim Jeffries is comin' out of retirement just to show him what's what. The Great White Hope. That colored never should've been fightin' white men anyway, let alone the real heavyweight champion."

"Why?" Paul asked.

Henry made a face at him and grinned at me. "Because the colored's inferior—that's why."

I wondered where he'd picked up a two-dollar word like that.

"If he's inferior, how did he beat any white men at all, let alone what you call the *real* champion?" Paul said.

Henry laid down his fork with a clatter. "All of 'em's jes' monkeys in clothes, is what I mean. White men shouldn't have to fight 'em."

"Hey, Henry," I said. "How'd you come to know all about it?"

He mumbled something, and I cupped a hand behind my ear.

"They was talkin' about it at the slaughterhouse today," he admitted.

Paul was quiet a good long while before he said, "So you've never heard of this fellow Jack Johnson before today?"

"Yeah. So?"

"But you're automatically against him fighting for the title? You only want to know who's the best fighter with skin the color of yours?"

Henry leaned forward and hissed, "There's more to it than color of the skin, you know."

Paul leaned toward him. "No, I didn't know. What else is there?"

Henry's scalp showed red at the part in his hair. "They're different—that's what." He picked up his fork and started shoveling it in again.

"I see. They're different from whites? But all white people are exactly the same as one another? And that goes for all colored people too?"

"There's some things you gotta see to know enough to understand."

I waited for Paul to pounce, but he just said, "Ah," and went back to his food with a little smile.

We were walking back to the hotel when I said, "Well, Paul, you can't go back to that store, and that's that. So don't lay awake tonight thinkin' about it."

"Go back where?" Henry asked.

I'd forgotten Henry missed the earlier conversation. I filled him in without too many details.

"Why, I oughta go down there and beat the shit outta those goons."

Funny how battle lines shift in a war.

Next morning was pure misery. "What will you do all day, Paul?" I had bummed a quarter for food and was hanging on the door.

"Figure out how to get to a library." He looked lower than a snake in a wagon rut, being the one left behind without a job.

"Well, be careful."

The bell rang a half hour early that evening, since it was Saturday. We all lined up to get paid. I looked around for Henry and thought he must have been first in line and already gone. I hoped he wouldn't drink up his pay before morning.

We all filed through and saw the man at the desk with the visor. He asked my name, checked his log, and said, "Jim Miller says good things about you. Hope to see you next week," before he handed me three dollars and marked something next to my name.

I flashed him a grin. "Thank you." Monday was a whole world away, for all that could happen by then.

Tired as I was, I walked back to the hotel with a light step. I could see myself maybe coming back to the stockyards to work when we got back from Yellowstone. They liked me. And Kansas City was just about the perfect distance from home.

But then I remembered the older guys. The ones who took half an hour to limber up in the morning and were shuffling along like cripples by the time they lined up to get their paychecks. I thought about getting kicked in the ribs every day for thirty years. There was a lot more to it than it seemed on the surface.

But at least it was something to think about. It seemed like a possibility.

Paul was back at the room when I got there, and I was glad to see he'd bought a newspaper. A way to ease into conversation.

We went through the whole thing, including what Jack Johnson had said the night before, promising the Fourth of July fight was on the up-and-up. Paul explained some people assumed Johnson would throw the fight so he wouldn't be obliged to whip every other white man around too. Bored out of my head with not caring, I told Paul we ought to get ready to leave on Sunday.

"Why? You two haven't made enough money to get very far."

"No, but we all three need work. Time to move on to someplace friendlier." I was about to say something more when Henry came busting in so fast Paul and I jumped a foot.

"Hey, come on!" he yelled. "Payday! Let's go get us the best supper we can find and hit the trail." He was all over the room, picking up everybody's stuff and shoving it all together. He turned his back when he picked up his metal safe box.

"What the hell are you doing?" I said.

"Let's go!" He made scooping motions toward the door, shooing us out. "Grab your stuff. Time to move on!"

"What's the big rush?" I asked.

He was already pounding down the stairs and couldn't hear.

"Paul?"

He shrugged.

I loaded his arms and took the rest.

I was pretty sure the Ford had been moved since that morning. Henry was behind the wheel and threw the crank at me when I was still four steps away and not expecting it. It hit my arm before it clattered to the sidewalk.

"What the hell is wrong with you?" I yelled.

But I didn't really want an answer. By then I'd figured whatever it was Henry knew and Paul and I didn't, we were probably better off not knowing.

Henry jumped out, shoved our gear into the luggage carrier, and picked up the crank to hand it to me. "Come on. Time to go!" He was already behind the wheel again.

I got the car started and climbed into the back.

Henry took off at a clip, and I sat down hard and muttered under my breath.

Soon I was saying prayers as Henry sped through the streets of Kansas City, scaring horses, other automobile drivers, and people out for a Saturday evening stroll. He careened so close to a mother and child I saw the woman's eyes show white all the way around.

"Slow down!" I screamed.

In ten minutes, we were out of town and headed west, and my heart was sinking faster than the sun in front of us.

I leaned over the seat back between the other two. "What did you do?"

"I had some good luck," Henry shouted.

"What kind of luck?"

"I said *good* luck!"

Paul said, "I think John's asking you at whose expense?"

Henry hooted. "Let's say I found a . . . whatchacallit. A sponsor. For our trip."

"A sponsor," Paul and I both repeated.

"Yep."

"At the slaughterhouse?" I asked.

"Nope. Somebody downtown." Henry turned and flashed me the devil's smile.

"D-downtown." Paul's voice shook.

That grin was so evil I'm sure Paul heard it. "Yep, downtown."

None of us spoke for the next five miles. Then Paul cleared his throat and asked, "How much?"

"Four hundred dollars."

I felt like I'd been punched in the gut.

A mile or so went by that might have been filled with circus elephants and tigers, for all I saw of it. Then I blurted out, "How long are we on the run?"

"Jes' till my face heals." Henry chuckled, and the wind carried it back to me. "Jes' till I don't look like this no more."

CHAPTER FIVE

HENRY DIDN'T SAY ANY MORE ABOUT his newfound wealth, and it just about killed me not to ask. But I didn't. If the law caught up to him, I wanted to be able to say that all I knew, by God, was that he said he'd found a sponsor. Let him hang alone. I wasn't about to be punished for something I had no hand in.

But profiting from somebody else's wrong did present a dilemma. I could feel saintly all I wanted and tell myself I was above all the ugly details, but at the end of the day I was eating pork chops paid for by sin, and I knew it.

Outside Kansas City, we passed through Bonner Springs, Kansas, and stopped at a store for food. Henry's money in my pocket made me feel dirty. When I handed some to the man behind the counter, I couldn't meet his gaze.

I found out, though, that half an auto seat loaded

with bread and cheese and cured meat and root beer raised my spirits considerably.

We found a copse of trees on a lonesome stretch of road outside town and pulled over to make camp.

We sat in the car and tore into the food.

"Is it safe to build a fire, do you think?" I ventured.

Henry looked all around. "Well, I don't think we're gonna burn down the countryside, if that's what you mean."

I swallowed a hunk of sandwich. "No, I mean if somebody notices it and comes by to see what's going on, are they—?"

"Are they gonna recognize me from a wanted poster or somethin' and haul us all in? Hell, no. Besides, there's nobody around for miles. I don't know what you're all hinky about."

"Well, you damn well ought—"

Paul cut me off. "Oh, calm down, John, would you? Damn it. You're worse than a long-tailed cat in a room full of rocking chairs."

Paul was taking Henry's side? And swearing? What the hell was this?

Later, when we turned in, I put my bedroll a little farther away from both of them than was absolutely necessary.

Next morning, I saved some of the food back and warned the other two that it was Sunday and we might not be able to add to what we had on hand.

They grumbled about it, and I told them to stop being babies. They might not think about little stuff like how to stay alive and keep the Ford running, but I did.

We set out across Kansas and tried to make some distance. And even if I hadn't wanted to get Henry as far away from Kansas City as possible, that turned out to be the way to go. The hardest thing about describing the Kansas countryside to Paul was explaining there was nothing to describe. Land so flat you could see for miles in every direction. Mile after mile of dirt, wherever you looked. The areas that hadn't been scoured clean by prairie wildfire were covered in long grass that was doing a poor job of holding the dirt down beneath it.

We ate a fair amount of Kansas that day. We were covered in brown silt before noon and coughing our heads off, trying not to swallow it. The windscreen might have kept the wind down some, but it was powerless against blowing dirt. It was hard to keep my eyes open, and I thought maybe those fancy driving goggles I'd seen pictures of weren't as silly as I'd judged them to be.

Paul took out a clean handkerchief and tied it over his nose and mouth like a stagecoach robber in a movie picture. It made me uneasy. I didn't need any reminders of thievery.

When the sun was directly above us, we stopped near a small creek and laid down belly-first on flat rocks to scoop cool water over our faces.

I doled out a ration of food and unfolded the map Stuart Kassen had given me a week before we left home. I calculated how far we'd come and how long it took and did some ciphering. "Gentlemen? We should try to make Mission Creek by dark so we can get our clothes off and get clean."

Paul and Henry just kept eating and didn't look at me.

I counted to twenty in my head instead of telling them *again* to stop acting like babies.

When Paul finished, he brushed his hands together and said, "What's it look like?"

"What's what look like?" I asked.

"Around here. What's it look like?"

"Like I already told you." I tried to sound patient. "Not gonna be much to see in Kansas other than Topeka, and I'm not gonna stop in a big city just now."

Henry's face was a rainbow of colors in the sunshine.

"Don't we get a vote?" Paul said.

That put me back on my heels. "Well, yeah, I guess so. I just—"

Henry interrupted. "There's a little bridge here, Paul, that we haven't crossed yet. Wood floor, looks like iron frame, old enough to be all rusted."

"What color is the sky today?" Paul asked.

I had no idea what was going on with them, but it was starting to make me mad.

"Oh, I dunno," Henry answered him. "Blue like

always. It's the color of hot, you might say. You know how when the sun's beatin' down, you see kind of shimmery lines in the air?"

"No."

Henry snorted. "Aw, hell, course not. I'm no good at this. I can't tell you about somethin' you never seen."

Paul spoke before I could. "What about the water we just washed in. Is it clear? Is anything living in it?"

"Well, we didn't let you wash in mud." Henry guffawed, but he took a look. "Yeah, there's some minnows, half a dozen tadpoles I see. Water bugs skittering around on the surface."

Paul smiled. "See? You do just fine."

Henry spat a wad of phlegm so close to Paul's shoes I flinched. "Yeah? How do you know? I could tell you gypsies were dancing naked on the other side of the creek."

"Okay, then. You're doing fine for a horse's ass."

To my surprise, Henry grinned.

Paul turned to me. "We haven't passed a single person all morning, John, is that right?"

"Yeah."

"How do you know we've not gotten off the main route?"

My eyebrows went to visit my hairline. "Well, hell, Paul, Stuart Kassen got me this map from the Automobile Club of America. You know that. We haven't passed any towns today, but this thing's marked out pretty well with forks in the road and dogleg turns at the township lines. And don't forget the one gigantic tree we passed early on today. That's right here." I pointed to the map before I realized how useless that was.

"Uh-huh." His expression was the same as if I'd said we were lost nine ways to Tuesday.

"Paul. It's Sunday. Folks go to church. They go home. It doesn't mean nothin' we've seen nobody. We've *not gotten off* anything, Mr. English Teacher." I told them to pack up so we could move on.

We got to the edge of Topeka an hour later. Mature person that I am, I did not scream, "Told you so!"

In the thick of the main business area, Henry let out a whoop and veered across oncoming traffic. He stopped in front of a shop with *Ford* painted on the front window in front of the flying pyramid I knew so well.

I was about to remind him it was Sunday when a man in a suit and a black derby came out and locked the door behind him.

Henry vaulted out. "Kind sir," he started.

I rolled my eyes.

"Could you be troubled to sell us some spare parts? A tire casing, for sure, and anything else you might recommend for a long trip?"

Paul piped up from the passenger seat, "And some gasoline too, sir, if you could."

The man looked the car over. "Well, now, boys, I wish you well in your travels, but today's Sunday and we're closed. I just came down to check on something nagging at me, and the missus is expecting me home for dinner five minutes ago." He started toward his own Model T.

"But, sir," Henry said, "we're travelers headed for Yellowstone Park, and we've already drove a hundred and fifty miles or so. We're likely gonna need somethin' for the car before we get to the next town that's got it."

The man squinted at Henry's face. "What happened to you?"

I slid lower in my seat.

"Defending her honor, sir," Henry said and bowed his head.

"Whose honor?"

Henry's voice tolled like a bell. "The Ford." He shook his head and went on. "Fellow back in Kansas City had an Eye-talian car, the Eye-tala, I believe it's called, and he called my Ford a piece of junk. I reminded him that a Model T whipped his heap of scrap iron last year and anybody with a brain knew it was the rightful winner of the Guggenheim Trophy and, well"—Henry pointed to his nose—"he did not care to be reminded."

The dealer debated for so long I knew Henry had won even before the man sighed and got out his key. "Oh, well," he said. "That woman would have found something wrong with me coming home an hour ago."

We left with a full tank of gasoline, two tire casings and a spare inner tube, a gallon of oil, and a list of the few Ford dealerships scattered between Topeka and Cheyenne, Wyoming.

I cranked the Ford to life and hopped in.

Paul piped up from the backseat, "Sir? Do you know where we can get today's newspaper?"

After the man puzzled at that, looking at Paul's cloudy eyes, he walked over to his own Model T and came back with a folded paper. He handed it to Paul, who thanked him profusely as Henry started away.

The dealer looked confused but nevertheless waved us off with, "Good luck, boys! God be with you!"

Henry yelled back, "I hope not! We ain't got room in this piece a shit!" but we were far enough away that he couldn't have been heard. Then Henry cut the wheel sharp toward the right, and I grabbed for handholds. Two colored men were standing on the sidewalk talking, and Henry came within a foot of hitting them.

They jumped back, wide-eyed, before he turned back onto the street proper.

I took a breath to yell at Henry, but the look on his face struck me silent. That same look of satisfaction he'd had in Waverly when he forced the couple off the sidewalk. That look of accomplishment. I shook my head and was glad Paul didn't ask what had happened.

When we were almost out of town, Henry pulled over and set the car to idle. He turned sideways in the seat and said, "Well, I ain't seen no food for sale yet. I'd say we head back into town and find a hotel with a fat woman in the kitchen, but I'm afraid Nervous Nelly here would piss his drawers."

It took a minute to realize he meant me.

Paul did his finger rubbing thing.

Oh, and I'm the Nervous Nelly? I thought.

"Well, tell me, Henry," Paul said, "how does your face look today?"

"Bee-yoo-ti-ful," Henry said, snickering.

"Bad enough for that fellow back there to ask about it," I said.

We all waited.

"Aw, hell," Henry said and put the car in gear. "We only camped out one night so far. And we don't want Nelly to get too soft."

It didn't feel a lot like victory.

The first house outside the city had a road stand the likes of which we hadn't seen since home. A basket of eggs, some dried beef, early peas and potatoes, and a price list next to a box for money.

Henry grabbed my duffel and started stuffing it full.

"Whoa!" I said. "What do you think you're doing?"

"The man said, 'God be with you,' and I figure this is Him providin'."

"Goddamn it, Henry!" He was piling potatoes and peas on top of the beef. "We don't even have a pan to cook that stuff in!"

"I do," Paul said. "Well, I guess I do. What is it we're talking about?"

Hell's bells. "Potatoes and peas."

"Yes, I can handle that," Paul said. I threw up my hands and Paul went on. "Although if Henry is planning not to pay, I'd remind him our sponsor can take care of it."

"Like hell," Henry said.

Paul held up the Model T's crank, the signal for *You're not going anywhere.*

"Shit." Then Henry laughed and said, "Oh, yeah. I guess I do got more money than God now." He started taking food out of the duffel and putting it back.

I guess we needed a lot less food that was paid for than what might be free.

When we were on our way again, Paul passed the newspaper up front to me. "Just the highlights? Please? While you've got light?"

I glanced at the front page and threw over my shoulder, "They're putting on a Sherlock Holmes play in London," then looked back to see Paul pull a sour face. "What?"

"Unless there's a natural disaster or a war has broken out, just tell me if there's any news about the fight."

Behind the steering wheel, Henry harrumphed.

I read to myself for a bit and then reported, "San Francisco is just about going nuts. That's the long and short of it."

"Nuts, how?"

I could feel a harrumph coming on, myself. This was getting old. "Preachers are all preaching against the fight and hoping they can stop it. All the stores got statuettes of both guys, Johnson and Jeffries—"

"Jeffries and Johnson," Henry interrupted.

"Jeffries and Johnson. Anyway, it looks like the whole city—more like the whole country, really—is pretty much split up between them that want to stop it, them that think it's a fix and won't happen, and them that can't wait."

Paul nodded. From his expression, I had no idea what he was thinking. And he still hadn't explained why he was so all-fired fascinated with the subject.

We made it to Mission Creek just before sundown and found a good spot off the road to bunk down. The ground was so hard we drove the Ford over and parked it under a tree. I got the map out again and figured we'd made a hundred miles that day. That was really something, considering the farthest I'd ever been from home before was eighty miles, with that distance spread over two days.

Home. If you couldn't wait to get away, is it right to still think of it as home?

I thought about my mom making sad pancakes and bacon the morning I left. My dad staring a hole in the table. The neighbors pretending they weren't watching. I wondered how Catherine was doing with me gone. I wondered where I'd end up after this trip was over and if, wherever it was, it would feel like home. Five days on the road and already I felt rootless.

I jumped up and got busy sorting out what we needed from the auto. Busy enough to stop thinking.

Once we got unloaded and got the kinks out, we stripped down and got Saturday-night clean. Paul had even brought soap. I washed out my dirtiest set of clothes and hung them over a branch to dry. I offered to do the same for Paul, but he stumbled around washing out his clothes in the shallows. He fell hard on the wet rocks a few times while I shook my head. Then he did ask for help hanging up the clean clothes to dry, and I wanted to kick myself for feeling flattered.

Henry washed out his one set of clothes and went about building a fire in nothing but his underdrawers.

In no time, potatoes and peas were cooking. We laid back away from the heat with the last of our root beer and some dried beef. By the time we'd finished the vegetables and some leftover cornbread, my stomach was as tight as a tick. It must have shrunk some over the meals I'd missed.

I laid there food-stupid and watched the fire for a while.

Out of nowhere, Henry said, "What's it like?" He was looking at Paul.

Time went by before Paul said, "I assume you're talking to me?"

"Yeah."

"It helps if you say my name. What's what like?"

"Being blind."

Paul blinked a few times. "Well, shut your eyes. It's like that. Except imagine you can't open them."

"No, I know that. Feelin' your way around and runnin' into stuff. What I mean is, what's it like livin' around normal people?"

Oh, hell. Here we went.

"Hmm. Well, that depends. Around most people I just feel normal as well. Around people who think I'm some kind of monster, I feel normal, but I want to bash their heads in." At least he smiled.

"Real funny." Henry grunted. "But seriously. Wasn't it easier when you was in St. Louis?"

"Ohhh." Paul nodded. "I think I know what you're getting at. Wasn't I more comfortable living around my own kind?"

"Yeah, exactly!"

"I see." Paul thought for a minute and went on. "Well, it was physically easier at the school with everything set up for blind students—that's for sure. It might have been a little easier in public, since there were so many of us people didn't seem so surprised to come across us." He picked up a twig and threw it into the fire. "But it's not a home, you know. You graduate. You move on."

"But aren't there places you could live—?"

"Institutions?" Paul sat up a little. "Well, yes, there was a time blind children were sent off to live with the mentally deficient and the insane. A few still are."

"But wouldn't you be happier—?"

"No. I would not feel happier locked away somewhere. But I get the feeling what you really mean is that you would be more comfortable if I were. Isn't that it?"

I couldn't believe how matter-of-fact he was.

"Well, yeah, and not just me." For once, I didn't get the feeling Henry was baiting Paul. He was thinking so hard I could practically hear the wheels grinding. "But for your own sake too. Instead of walkin' around with people thinkin' you're some kind of circus spectacle. Wouldn't you at least be better off just stayin' home, then, and lettin' your folks tend to you?"

Paul crossed his legs stretched out in front of him. "John, remember asking me where I got the money to buy the automobile?"

"Yeah."

"And I told you I got some when Grandfather died, but most of it came from my parents giving me money for Christmas and birthdays?"

"Yeah . . ." That day in April seemed years ago.

"Well, I threw a fit when I was ten, and they gave me a cloth doll for Christmas. Ten years old. A ten-year-old *boy*. After that, they gave me money because they couldn't imagine what I might want. Because they don't have a clue who I am, really."

"Oh—"

Paul cut me off. "No, no, no. I'm not asking for

sympathy. I'm just trying to explain. Mother sent me away to school when I was six. Father didn't care where I went, as long as he didn't have to look at me. Twelve years later, I graduated and was suddenly *around*. This millstone hung around their necks.

"Henry, you can think I'm a freak all you want. Those goons in Kansas City can threaten me because the very fact that I exist scares them. That's nothing compared to living with my parents and being completely alone."

His blank eyes seemed like a drawn curtain, hiding whatever he felt.

The fire was almost dead, and none of us reached to add more wood. It just faded into embers, into silence, into dark, into sleep.

I woke up at first light to a crack of lightning so close my hair stood on end. The three of us clambered to stuff bedrolls into wads, gather clothes off tree limbs, and pick up pans and utensils, beaten by a driving rain. Fast as we worked, the ground was already getting sloppy by the time we had loaded the car and started wrestling the canopy top up for the first time since Paul and I had done it for practice at home.

"Goddamn it, Henry, you can't just bully the thing up!" I yelled, and I don't think his elbow in my ear was an accident.

We struggled putting the top into place and then started the engine. The tires moved three inches and rolled back into the ruts they'd made just since the rain began. "Shit. Piss. Damn." I beat the steering wheel hard enough to hurt the heel of my hand.

Then I jumped out and said, "Well, get movin' and lighten the load, would ya? Sittin' there like a couple of jackasses." I blinked rain out of my eyes again.

Henry barked, "No, you stay there, Paul. Get over and steer while we push."

Paul slid over behind the wheel.

Henry positioned himself with his hands on the front axle. "Get over here and push, Nelly!" Henry threw the crank at me, and I ducked just in time. "Paul, you got it in reverse?"

Paul moved the hand lever and kicked at a foot pedal. "I do now."

"Fine," Henry spat. "Give 'er gas."

He did, and when the Ford got to the end of the three inches it had moved before, Henry gave a mighty push and kept it going. They were halfway to the road before I had my hands on the axle. We bumped up the embankment.

Henry yelled, "Whoa!" just before the car started down the other side.

Paul stood on the brake and took the car out of gear.

Henry nudged him over and jumped in, whacking his head on the canopy. He looked at me like it was my fault. "You gonna go get the crank or stand around lookin' pretty?"

I bolted back for it, if you can call it that when you're suck-stepping in mud.

It rained all morning while we took turns driving and getting out to push. The last of the cornbread was all we'd saved for breakfast, and it was ruined, watered into meal inside a pillowcase. By noon we were starving.

We saw a light up ahead for the first time in so long I might have feared I imagined it if Henry hadn't said, "What the hell you suppose that is?" It gave us something to aim for the next two times we got out to push.

Shadowy outlines that might have been woolly mammoths finally took shape as a farmstead—house and barn—and it looked like heaven driving up that lane toward dry shelter.

Henry's face was way closer to normal than it had been even the day before, but I still made a better representative for the group. He and Paul hunkered down in their seats.

I ran through the rain to the back door of the house and knocked hard. There was no gutter above the stoop, and the rain poured off the roof onto my head in a solid sheet. June or not, I was chilled to the bone.

A farmer about my dad's age and size opened the door. He looked me up and down, squinted past me at the Ford, and then settled on my face and waited.

I said, "Good morning, sir. There are three travelers—I mean three of us and we're travelers, you see. And, well, sir, we're cold and hungry and we're not making much headway in this rain. Could we trouble you? For some food and shelter, I mean. We'll work. Whatever you need done."

He squinted past me again and then looked down at my shoes.

I followed his line of sight. I was nothing but mud from midthigh down.

"Three of ya?" he asked. "The other two as dirty as you?"

"Well, one of them is, for sure."

"Why one of 'em?"

Couldn't he see I was drowning while he stood and chatted?

"Well, sir, it's kind of a long story, but our one friend is blind. It's his car, and we've had him steer while the other two of us pushed. I mean, whenever we got stuck this morning."

He sucked on his teeth and nodded. "Blind boy's got hisself an automobile."

I nodded back.

"So you let him drive while you pushed."

"Something like that."

"Well." He reached an arm over his head and scratched above the opposite ear. "You can't set foot on my wife's clean floor like that. Why'n't y'all set up in the barn, and I'll see what she can scare up?"

"Much obliged, sir. Much obliged." I threw it over my shoulder at him, already running to tell the others.

The clothes in my duffel were wet, but not like the ones

I was wearing. I changed in the barn, shivering enough to make buttons hard to manage. Paul changed too, while Henry just stripped down to his drawers like the evening before. We slung our stuff over the doors of empty stalls and said hello to a pair of draft horses stamping their feet and snorting at us.

Henry said, "Do you think we can find a dry match?"

That was the moment the farmer appeared in the open doorway wearing a full-length slicker and carrying a five-gallon bucket draped with oilcloth. "Don't even think about it." The man had his chin down like a bull ready to charge. "I'm none too fond of puttin' the three of you up and feedin' you to begin with, but my wife takes that shit in the Bible serious about angels comin' to your doorstep in disguise, and she won't turn nobody away. Me, I don't care if you're Jesus H. Christ his own self—you ain't gonna burn down my barn. You hear?"

Paul and I just about broke our necks nodding. Henry held the man's gaze.

"You're trouble on the hoof." The man nodded at Henry. "And it looks like somebody's already tried to get that through your head lately. Now, I mean it. You start a fire with all this hay around, I'll kick your butt so hard you'll have to breathe through your asshole." He stalked off, head ducked against the rain.

Cold fried chicken. Hot biscuits. A jar of pickled beets and another of last year's green beans. We tore into the food in that galvanized bucket. There were tin cups on hooks above the pump there in the barn, and that water tasted as cold as melted spring and as sweet as tea. The farmer might have begrudged us the grub, but as far as I was concerned, his wife had earned her throne in heaven.

When Henry and I had inspected the bucket two or three times and reconciled ourselves to the fact it was empty, I took a look outside and wondered if we ought to be building that sweet woman an ark. It was raining so hard I couldn't even see the Ford.

I pulled down some horse blankets and threw one to Paul. "Kind of scratchy," I told him, "but better than the hay. May as well make up for that rude awakening this morning. We're goin' nowhere today."

Some people say they can't sleep in a thunderstorm, but I am not one of them. Thunder, even a big rumble that shakes the house, sounds like a lullaby to me. Maybe because my mom always said that thunder was just God's way of saying hello.

I had no idea how long I'd slept, but there was no question what woke me up. Nothing else in the world sounds like a shell chambering in a shotgun. Cha-*chung*.

I shot upright and saw the farmer filling the doorway with a gun pointed just left of me. Henry was standing in his underdrawers, hands up in surrender. In front of him was a little pile of wood scraps, the kind you find around anybody's workbench. And in one hand, he held a match.

Damn him to hell anyway. I looked past the farmer outside. At least the rain had let up.

I nudged Paul awake.

"Huh?" He rolled himself tighter into his blanket.

I pulled it away and hung it back where I'd found it. "Come on, Paul. We're movin' on. Get your stuff."

"Why? You're the one who said we weren't going anywhere today."

"That was before Henry wore out our welcome." I pulled Henry's clothes off the stall door and slung them at him. While I was at it, I grabbed the match out of his hand and jammed it into my pocket.

The other two walked out with their gear, and I hung back. When it was just us, I turned to the farmer. "Sir, I know I have no right."

The barrels of the gun came up again.

I talked faster. "But if you could see your way clear to give us lengths of saw board—whatever you can spare, but I mean two—it might help us get farther away from here in this mud than we could without 'em."

I could see him weighing it. Finally, he pointed with the gun one-handed toward the back of the barn. "Go get yourself two pieces of board, and don't even look at nothin' else."

I ran like a rat. "Thank you, sir." I passed back

through with two lengths of pine board under my arm.

"Go" was his send-off. He did not suggest that God travel with us.

We made it out of his lane and onto the road before we had to get out and use the boards the first time.

"Goddamn it, Henry," I said.

"Oh, right. Like it's my fault it rained."

"I wouldn't be surprised. I can't imagine God likes you any more than I do right about now." I had wedged the wood in front of the back tires and taken my place at the back axle.

And so went our day. We would slither side to side no more than two hundred yards at a stretch before getting mired down in the wagon ruts. Henry and I got out, Paul slid over, and pretty soon we moved on without a word. My boots came to feel like they weighed about twenty pounds each.

By midafternoon, the clouds had burned away and the sun was so hot steam came off my damp clothes when I got out to push. We kept the canopy up on the car just for shade. There wasn't a tree in sight—nothing but flat acres of mud that looked like they might start to boil.

"Damn it," I told Henry. We were shoulder to shoulder at the back axle for what might have been the hundredth time. "I am going to personally burn those clothes first chance I get, and right now I don't much care if you're still in 'em. You smell like a damn pigpen."

He grunted as he pushed. "Well, I'm sorry to offend your sensitive nose, Nelly."

I shoved him down before I knew I was going to, and he came up as fast as a wet cat. A fresh swath of mud went up to the crown of his head. Then I was spitting mud and digging with my fingers to get that moldy-tasting gumbo out of my mouth. He had pushed me back hard enough to roll me down the embankment.

A lot of grunting and cussing went with all this, and I guess that and the car not moving told Paul what was going on. He stepped out in his goddamned spotless clothes just as I finished fighting my way back up in the boot-sucking goo. It was like climbing a hill of molasses.

Paul said, "Now, ladies—"

I punched him, God help me, without a thought. Straight on the jaw.

He was no more down than Henry spun me around by a fistful of shirt. "What the hell's wrong with you, hittin' a blind boy?"

I jerked away. "He wants to be treated like everybody else, fine. That's what a smart mouth gets." I brought up more nastiness and spat it out. "What the hell's wrong with *you*? Only time you seem to care is when somebody else is being mean to him. Why? Is that your own personal province?"

He came at me, and while we rassled, Paul tried to push us apart. But his feet got tangled with ours, and we all went down the embankment together, one rolling and grunting ball of mud.

At the bottom, it took us a while to get separated. When I could, I sat up and wiped mud out of my eyes. Henry had landed face-first in a murky puddle and came up sputtering and coughing. Paul pulled out a handkerchief and wiped his face clean. We all panted like dogs in the afternoon sun.

Nothing happened for a good long minute. Then Paul reached in another pocket and came out with a coin. "Heads, we go on. Tails, we kill each other here."

I stood up and slogged my way up the embankment before he tossed it. I was pretty sure it would come up heads.

We got stuck a hundred more times that day, but something in the air between us had cleared. Stupid as it was, what Paul said had reminded us that for the time being, each other was all we had.

Along about starving o'clock, we saw the first farm-stead we'd come to since Farmer Shotgun's. Sunlight reflected off the brass weather vane on the barn like a beacon.

I wanted to stop and have a talk with Henry, but that would mean getting stuck again, and I was just about all in. As I gave the Ford some gas and fish-tailed up the lane, I just said, "Henry—"

"I know, and don't worry. I paid for that today."

I shot him a look that was only a little hateful,

seeing as how we were getting along.

"Oh, okay. I'm *sorry*," he said. "But I wanna get dry bad as you do, okay? I won't do nothin'."

"You won't do *anything*," Paul offered.

"Oh, jes' shut up."

Paul smiled for the first time in recent memory.

We had barely come to a stop under the canopy of a huge sycamore before two men banged out the back door of the house and came at us. One of them had a little hitch in his get-along, but other than that, they looked like exact copies and moved as fast as men thirty years younger.

I looked down at myself caked in mud. Mud they owned, no doubt. Their land and us, trespassing on each other. "Oh, shit," I said. "Get ready to go on."

But we would come to know that the Heverson brothers, for that was their name, ran a better boarding house than Mrs. Bentley back in Missouri. "Hello! Hello! Welcome!" they said as they got close to the car and looked us over. "What a fine automobile!"

"Well, good heavens, look at you! You're wearin' half the countryside!"

The Heverson brothers didn't get a lot of company, would be my guess. They were unloading our gear before we could even ask to stay.

When they started for the house, I said, "Sirs? We can stay in your barn. That's plenty good."

"Nonsense," one of them yelled over his shoulder.

"You heard the man." Henry grinned, and

either his face had come close to finished healing since morning or the mud provided some good camouflage. "We're just angels in disguise."

I had to smile in spite of myself.

Once we got inside the house, one of the brothers held out his hand and said, "I'm Orville."

The other said, "I'm Amos," and he shook with us too.

We must have looked confused, because they both busted out laughing. They were on the short side and looked a little like potbellied stoves wearing overalls. Their whole middle sections shook when they laughed.

"Don't worry," Amos said. "Even we forget which one of us is which sometimes." They laughed at this too. Their shiny red faces were creased with smiles baked in by the sun.

After supper, they shooed us off to the back of the house into a room that looked like it hadn't been opened in years. On one side there was a big bed with a fancy carved headboard. A matching walnut dresser and chest of drawers sat against the wall facing it. The bed was covered with a fine-pieced quilt that looked like something my grandma might have made, but it was an ivy vine design I'd never seen. Its reflection in the mirror made it look like twins too.

On the wall there was a portrait of the brothers taken when they were babies and another from when they were about four years old. I couldn't imagine how their mother had told them apart. If she had.

Their present-day versions came back with a cot that one brother unfolded while the other shook out sheets and a pillowcase. Then they said, "Good night," and left us alone.

Henry shut the door and turned on me. "I can't keep straight which is which. Can you?"

I smiled. "Well, when they're walking, Amos is the one with the bad hip."

"And when they're not?"

"Orville's got one freckle up on his right temple that's a little bit bigger and darker than the rest." The Heverson twins had grown out of the hair they wore in the portraits on the wall and, these days, wore freckles on their heads.

Henry frowned. "What if they've got their caps on and they're not walkin' anywhere?"

"Then all bets are off." I shrugged. "But they don't seem too concerned about it."

Paul spoke up. "You can't tell them apart by their voices?"

Henry and I exchanged a blank look.

The next morning, I woke up to the smell of bacon and heard one brother and then both of them singing. I would come to learn it was a morning ritual.

After breakfast, we left Paul on his own in the house while Henry and I traipsed out to the barn after the Heversons and helped them with what little chores there were to be done while the fields were too wet to work.

By the time we got back, Paul had found their mother's old upright piano in the parlor and was almost done tuning it. He'd never said he could play, but man alive. As soon as he had all the strings where he wanted them, he sat down and played some stuff that was fancier than anything I'd ever heard. Songs that had lots of notes and no words at all.

It didn't take long before Henry was fidgeting.

I saw the Heversons exchange a look before Amos spoke up. "That's just wonderful, Paul. Just beautiful. But how about we save some for later? From the looks of things outside, you're going to be with us a while."

He was right. We would come to spend three more nights there before the roads were dry enough for us to move on.

I had never thought of a house as being happy before, but theirs was. In all our time there, I never heard a cross word spoken.

We played whist and gin rummy. We all sang songs while Paul played the piano for us. The brothers cooked, and we three visitors started tugging at the waistlines of our pants, filling out like bears before winter.

But mainly, we kept company. We told the brothers how we came to drive up their lane and everything that had happened to us up until then. "Oh!" they said. "Oh my goodness."

They weren't nearly as keen to talk about themselves

as they were to hear new stories, but we did learn they'd lived on this farm their whole lives.

"Neither of you ever married?" I asked.

They seemed genuinely surprised by the question. "Why would we?" one of them asked.

Well, okay, then.

I'd been halfway convinced, up to that point, that Henry was just plain mean from the inside out. But he minded his manners with the Heversons almost as nice as Paul and me. I think what it was, the brothers just expected everyone they met to act kindly, and not even Henry could bring himself to disappoint them.

He'd always seemed like he was built out of wires and springs, but at the Heversons', he started to move more like a lazy cat. Every time one of the twins patted him on the shoulder or draped an arm around him, he practically purred. He walked around with a smile even when no one had made a joke.

Maybe he'd never been shown that much kindheartedness. Whatever the case, he soaked it up like a sponge.

Wednesday evening during supper, Amos asked if we'd written home since we'd been gone. We admitted we hadn't, and he exclaimed, "Why, it's been"—he counted off five fingers on one hand, and his brother took up and counted off three on his—"eight days. And you haven't sent word that you're okay?"

If I'd been a dog, my tail would've been dragging.

They got up and bustled around the kitchen. "I've got some lined paper and some envelopes here somewhere."

"Do we still have any stamps?"

"No, but we need to get some next time one of us goes to town anyway."

"Where did all the pencils go?"

Once they'd found everything, they doled out the supplies, sat down across the kitchen table from us, and smiled, expectant-like.

Paul spoke up. "Do you have a ruler I could use as a paper guide?"

The Heversons went wide-eyed. "Why, yes!" Orville said. He rummaged through a drawer and came up with one.

They were so interested in watching Paul write that it took a while for either of them to notice Henry sitting there staring at the blank page in front of him. His pencil laid on the table beside it.

"Can't think of anything?" Orville asked Henry. His voice was gentle.

"Got nobody." It sounded like Henry gargled the words.

I could hear a loose shingle out on the barn clapping in the wind. It was that quiet. I tried to step in with, "But there's Ellen—"

"She quit me too." Barely a whisper.

After what seemed like a year, Orville said, "Henry, come down to the root cellar with me, would you? I need you to hold the lantern while I look for a quart of cherries. I do believe I've got a taste for pie."

Paul and I finished our letters and addressed the envelopes while they were gone. All I wrote was *Dear Mom and Dad, I just wanted to let you know I'm doing fine. Tell Catherine*— I debated. I love her? Hello? Not to take any wooden nickels? I settled for *I miss her.*

I sneaked a look at Paul's envelope while he was addressing it. He had written to Sam. I guess I shouldn't have been surprised.

When we heard boots on the steps, the envelopes were whisked away from us and put in the secretary by the kitchen door. And then everybody was in the kitchen again, and the Heversons were arguing in their good-natured way over which one of them made the best piecrust.

They were a marvel.

Thursday, we knew the roads would be dry enough for us to leave the next day if it didn't rain again. So that afternoon, we knuckled down and cleaned up the Ford and checked out all its parts. We added some oil to the crankcase and took a gallon of gasoline the brothers offered. Everything else seemed sound, once we got the mud off.

While we were visiting after supper that evening, Paul asked the Heversons how they got their news, and it startled me—theirs was such a closed-off little world, it had been some time since I'd thought about anything that laid beyond it except the folks in Wakenda. Like those were the only two spots on the globe.

Amos said, "Why, we take turns goin' into town for supplies," and they laughed like it was their favorite joke.

Paul said, "But seriously. Do you keep up with what's going on in the world?"

The brothers got as serious as I'd ever seen them, and Amos said, "No. We do not," while Orville shook his head.

Henry said, "Paul likes to read the newspaper."

That sat them up straight.

"I mean, he has somebody read it to him, but he's like a encyclopedia. Go ahead. Ask him somethin'." He might as well have been bragging about a pet that did tricks.

The brothers studied their hands a while before Orville said, "What are you interested in, Paul?"

"Oh, everything. Politics, world news, sports. I've really tried to follow the championship fight coming up. A study in human nature, to say the least."

"Fight?" The Heversons looked upset.

"Well, yeah, surely you know about that," Henry said. Like he hadn't first heard of it in Kansas City the week before. "The one with Jim Jeffries and that Jack Johnson."

Amos said, "Why are they fighting?"

Henry guffawed. "Why, to settle the championship! To prove once and for all who's the best—that the whites is over the coloreds, always have been and always will be."

Orville said, "Why?" His expression reminded me of my little sister, Catherine, untarnished by sin from within or without.

"Well, b-because—" Henry sputtered. He looked back and forth between them. "We have to . . . We can't just . . ." He gave up, his mouth still hanging open.

Every time I looked at him the rest of the evening, he seemed troubled.

Orville went on like they'd just gotten done talking about the weather. He asked about the route we were taking to Yellowstone, and I brought out our map. The brothers huddled over it and hmmmed and decided we'd gotten off course by a few miles. They told us how to get back to the road that ran parallel along the Central Pacific rail line.

"That's where you want to stay," Amos told us. "If you have trouble along there, at least you know somebody will be along sooner or later."

Of course. I should have kept an eye on the train tracks all along.

But then we would never have found the Heversons. And three days with them was worth running from ten double-barrels.

Friday morning, we ate all the breakfast we could hold, and the brothers packed a big parcel of provisions for the road. After we had tucked it in with bedrolls all around, there was nothing left to do but say good-bye.

It wasn't easy for any of us, but it about half killed Henry. I couldn't imagine what three days with the Heversons had meant to him. He pulled the brothers together in a fierce hug, and when they wrapped their short bear arms around him, I had to look away.

When Henry let loose, Orville asked to see my map again. He unfolded it and pointed to the red X he'd made. "We're right there, son. Right there. Ten days or ten years, the door's always open as long as we're alive."

And that's how we left.

CHAPTER SIX

FOR THE FIRST COUPLE HOURS BACK on the road, we might have been the lead carriage in a funeral procession. I don't know about the other two, but I had this deep-pitted feeling of dread, like we'd been swinging in a big, safe hammock at the Heversons' and now we were naked to the world for it to do with us what it would. I drove first and hightailed it to the crossroads where a turn toward the south would lead us to the railroad line. I hoped a better sense of well-being was waiting for me there.

We got to our intended road just as a train was steaming past, and that did lighten the air a little. We weren't completely alone for the buzzards to circle over.

"Gentlemen, I'm going to predict we make Junction City by noon," I said.

There was no answer except Henry sniffling and coughing to clear his throat.

I thought, *Damn, we should leave him with the*

Heversons on the way back, if he's taking it that hard.

We did make Junction City before dinnertime, but by then it was clear Henry's problems weren't sentimental. He was shaking so hard his teeth chattered, and when I put a palm to his forehead, it was on fire.

I found a hotel near the middle of town and went in. The man behind the desk told me noon was a mighty strange time to be finding a room for the night. I was beginning to think some older folks tend to distrust bucks our age. I explained to him about Henry being sick.

He went out front with his hands on his hips. Henry was laying across the backseat and breathing mighty hard for a corpse. That's how bad he looked.

The hotel owner was already backing through the door. "I don't need no typhoid in my hotel. No, sir, boys. You just move on."

I said, "Oh, but wait—"

"Typhoid!" Paul said.

I tried to take things down a notch. "But, sir, we're hundreds of miles from home and have to stay somewhere. And there's no reason to think he's got the typhoid."

"No reason to think he's not." He started to close the door.

I jammed my foot in the opening. "Is there a doctor in town?"

"Two blocks that way." He tilted his head.

I stepped out to look.

He slammed the door.

Paul and I hauled Henry into Dr. Osgood's storefront with his feet barely touching the ground.

The doctor stuck his head out of a back room. "Be right with you."

He came out in a minute, wiping his hands. "No need asking what you're here for. Bring him back."

We laid Henry on a table, and the doctor went about taking Henry's temperature and listening to his heart and feeling under his arms. "Hmm" was his first opinion. Then he asked, "Has he had any water of questionable cleanliness lately?"

My mind provided a picture of us three laying on the rocks beside Mission Creek, scooping water over our heads, then one of Henry spitting puddle water the day it had rained and I'd shoved him down. I explained to the doctor.

"No, not that recently," the doctor said.

Paul and I both let out a breath.

"Think back a week or two."

Paul said, "We left home the first of June. Before that he was living in a barn."

Dr. Osgood's eyebrows went up.

I counted back. "A week ago, he spent two days workin' at the stockyards in Kansas City." I knew that was true, but it didn't seem possible. We'd lived two lifetimes since then.

The doctor wiped all over his face with his bare

hand. "Well, it's likely just some kind of influenza, although it's not common this time of year. But this town has buried two this past month from the typhoid, and we'll have to be sure. Sheriff lets me use the jail for quarantine. Your friend needs to give me some blood to look at and then spend some time as a guest of Sheriff Larkin. You two boys'll just have to get a room somewhere and wait."

"We won't leave him." Paul spoke like it'd been put to a vote.

I was thinking a little distance from Henry might actually be in our best interest.

The doctor chuckled. "Well, then, you'll have to share a cell."

"We're all the family he's got," Paul announced.

I'm not sure how I would've voted on that one either. But there was no use in arguing just then.

We could've done worse. The sheriff's wife brought a big supper over and put it on the front desk to come get after she left. Good thing too—someone had stolen our parcel from the Heversons out of the Model T while we were at the doctor's office. Apparently they didn't need ratty bedrolls or spare tire casings.

The jail was like a hotel all to ourselves. A hot, concrete hotel with bars on what few windows there were, and all the hard floor we wanted for sleeping. But it beat sleeping outside with the rest of God's creatures and would give my bug bites time to heal.

A big bowl of brown broth came along with our suppers.

"Aw, let's eat first," I told Paul. "It's not like Henry's hungry, the state he's in."

He laid on the bunk and shivered and moaned. I couldn't even tell if he was awake.

"It won't help him any to get weaker," Paul said. "Fever burns up a lot of fuel." He picked up a spoon.

I grabbed it away. A poke in the eye with hot broth wasn't going to help Henry either. I sat as far away as I could reach to feed him.

The next morning, we had a breakfast of eggs and sausage and cornbread, along with yellow broth for Henry. I felt stir-crazy afterward.

I told Paul, "I can't sit around here all day. I'm gonna go for a walk around town. You wanna go with me?"

He shook his head.

"All right, then. I'll be back for dinner. Shouldn't be any hotter than a boiler in here by then."

Junction City looked to be about the size of Lexington, but it was a lot more western in flavor. Men dressed like cowboys more often than not. Spitting tobacco juice seemed to be a popular hobby, and the horses hitched up along Main Street were sharing it with only one car, a Maxwell. I strolled the streets and saw what was there, then ducked into the general store to pick up a Topeka newspaper for Paul.

When the sun was high enough to make sweat

trickle down the back of my neck, I went back to the jail and walked in just in time to see Paul take a bowl off a tray and poke Henry in the shoulder with the spoon.

"Come on, Henry. Time to get stronger."

Henry groaned.

I hurried over to take the spoon from Paul.

He jerked back like I was trying to steal from him. "Paul . . ."

He ignored me and ladled a couple sips into Henry, without any hesitation I could see. "Now," he said, "that's better."

I looked around to see if there was food for us. There didn't seem to be.

"Doctor says he's 99 percent sure it's not typhoid," Paul said.

"When was he here? Why didn't you send somebody for me?"

Paul went on like he hadn't heard. "He's still standing by it being some kind of influenza, though he can't say why we haven't taken it too. He said we may still."

Influenza sounded a lot more serious all of a sudden.

Paul said, "We can't stay here on the county's penny anymore, so I asked if there was someplace other than the Typhoid Arms to stay. I don't particularly want to give that man my business."

Neither did I, but I would have liked some say in the matter. Paul went on before I could tell him so.

"There's a Mr. Williamson who has a livery stable

and smith shop nearby, and he's got a room in the loft he rents out. It's none too fancy, but neither are we, right?"

I nodded.

"Right?"

Oh yeah. "Right."

Henry had soaked through his clothes, a sheet, and a thin cotton blanket by then. His eyes were closed, but his mouth opened and shut like a baby bird's while Paul kept the spoon going back and forth.

"So?" Paul said.

"So what?"

Paul scraped the bottom of the bowl. "Why don't you go check things out with Mr. Williamson before we move Henry?"

"Right. I was just going to do that."

"Um-hmm." His mouth was set in a white line. I didn't know what was eating him.

Jack Williamson looked so familiar I might have known him all my life. He was a barrel-chested, smiling man with arms the size of tree trunks and thick black hair that curled over his forehead.

After we were introduced, I told him our situation.

He stopped working to listen and draped himself over his anvil, like it was hard work to hold up all that weight on his own. He was nodding halfway through my first sentence. "Go on up and look," he said. "If it'll do, it's empty right now. Dollar a night and all the hay you can eat."

From somewhere, a horse snorted at the joke.

"Oh, I'm sure it's fine. We just wanted to make sure we could have it before we moved our friend."

"That sick, is he?"

Oh, shit. I hoped I hadn't scared us out of our shelter for the night. "He's pretty sick, sir."

"Jack. Call me Jack or I'll have to arm wrestle you." He was pounding out a shoe on the anvil, and his muscles bulged even bigger. My eyes must have bulged too, the way he laughed. "I was just getting ready to unhitch that team back there"—he tossed his head—"but why don't you take the wagon over and bring him back on that? If you think it'd be easier than puttin' him in the auto."

I stood a little taller just for being trusted. "Thank you, sir. Jack."

He grinned and went back to work.

I spread out Henry's bedroll on the wagon before Paul and I hoisted him between us and dragged him outside. We were as sweaty as he was when we got back to the livery.

Jack Williamson ambled over and took stock. He squinted at Paul. "You, I haven't met. Call me Jack." He held out his right hand.

I was about to explain Paul couldn't see when Paul took the man's hand and shook it. My mouth stayed open.

"Paul Bricken, Jack. Pleased to make your acquaintance."

Jack went over to the wagon and, in one motion, picked Henry up and slung him over his shoulder.

Henry promptly threw up all down his back.

"All right, buddy," Jack said. "Better here than in your quarters, right?" He made some adjustments to Henry's position. "We'll fill you back up after we quit jostling you around." And with that, he started up the ladder to the loft like he was carrying no more than a cat.

The ceiling of the room sloped down on both sides from a gabled roof, but it was plenty tall for standing in the middle. There were two cots tucked into the short sides. Jack laid Henry down on one of them like he was handling a newborn.

He stood and stripped off his shirt, bundling it around the mess in back. "I'll get you another cot and have my wife bring up some soup."

This man was larger than life its own self.

"Oh, no, sir—Jack—we don't expect—"

"Eh." He waved me off. "Woman can't have children and tries to mother everything that gets within a mile of her. Do her good to leave off on me for a while." His face was a picture of what good-natured means.

Mrs. Williamson—Anna, she insisted—was a vision. She had curly brown hair, dimples, eyes as green as shamrocks, and a waist that Jack could likely span with his hands twice over. I broke a commandment or two just looking at her.

She cooed over Henry while she sat on the edge

of his cot and fed him clear soup. Then she told me, "If you'll change him into dry clothes, I'll wash the ones he's soaked. Just that much should help him feel a little better."

"Those are the only clothes he has, ma'am. At least all he brought along."

She fixed me with a green glare. "One dollar at the dry goods store and he could be clean and dry. I'll loan it to you myself, if you don't have it to spare."

"Oh, he can pay," I said. "I guess . . . well, I don't know, ma'am—I mean Anna. I reckon Henry just never put much of a premium on havin' clean clothes to change into." I stopped short of telling her he was pretty much a jackass and a lout, to boot.

She nodded, watching me. "Well?" she finally said.

"Oh." I had gotten stuck, looking at her. "Right. Right away." I skedaddled.

By the time I got back, Paul was in love with her. The way he looked when she spoke to him made me feel flat-out jealous. Of course that was crazy. When the courting only takes place in your head, there's plenty of any one woman to go around.

The following morning, when Paul and I came down to find the outhouse, Jack was already in the stable filling water troughs. "Sleep okay?" he asked.

We assured him we had.

"How's your friend?"

About the same, we told him.

"How long you boys fixin' to stay?"

I hadn't thought about it. Big breath. "I really don't know, Jack. Do you . . . need to put us out soon?"

"Oh, no, nothin' like that." He grinned. "But that boy likely doesn't need both of you all day long, and I can always use help around here. Switch off, if you want to. Dollar a day between you and all the hay you can eat." He did like that joke.

"Well, I don't know." I looked at Paul.

"You go ahead," he told me. "I'll take care of Henry."

I was starting to think Paul was getting sick himself, between the ears.

But Jack gave him a warm look and said, "You do what you need to do, son."

So I went to work for Jack and found it a pleasant way to spend the day as well as earn an easy dollar. I mucked stalls, changed out hay, cleaned and polished tack, brushed and fed and watered horses—did everything but work the forge. Jack stayed busy with that and thanked me for everything I did. That would have been payment enough.

The work at the stockyards and now this. I was very nearly rid of the voice inside my head that second-guessed everything I did.

It occurred to me that maybe I'd be a smith when all this was over. Maybe I could learn that trade. But then a little more time watching Jack—seeing how strong he was and how hard he worked all day, every day, without seeming to get tired—got me thinking some things can't be learned. Some places you just can't get to from where you are. And from my puny arms to Jack's looked to be one of those distances.

Paul wouldn't leave Henry longer than it took to visit the outhouse, and so Anna insisted on bringing all three of us Missouri boys our meals. It didn't seem right, what with Jack already paying me same as we owed for the room, but one wink from him told me Anna was enjoying herself.

When we quit for the day on Monday the thirteenth, I climbed the ladder and found Anna reading the newspaper to Paul. He looked like hell, and I asked if he felt sick too. He shook his head but didn't offer any assurance beyond that.

I sat down and listened too. I didn't much care what was going on in the world, but I did like the sound of her voice. Suffrage meetings, speeches by Theodore Roosevelt and President Taft—even stories about Jim Jeffries and Jack Johnson—they all sounded like music when she read about them.

Middle of the night, I woke up and knew something was wrong. I lit the lantern and it showed Paul's bed empty. I got up to check and found Henry's cot groaning with the weight of the two of them. "What're you doing?" I hissed.

"Keeping him warm," Paul whispered back.

"But what the—?"

"Didn't you hear him crying out? I can't believe you slept through it." Paul hadn't put in ten hours of manual labor that day. "He was shaking with the chills so hard the whole bed rattled."

"Well, there's blankets in the chest." I started across the room.

"He was calling for his mother, John."

I stopped.

"I just—he needs more than blankets. And the way he was thrashing around, they wouldn't stay on anyway."

"But, Paul—"

"Look. If he's delirious enough to call for his mama . . . Well, look at him. He's so slick with sweat he was freezing. At least he's quieted down."

I shifted foot to foot. "You think I oughta go try to find the doctor?"

Paul shook his head. "He already said there's nothing he can do for influenza. Either he'll get better or he won't."

I went back to bed unsettled and didn't get close to sleeping through any more of Henry's outbursts. Sometimes he called for his mother, sometimes for Ellen. It was a pitiful and eerie sound. Each time I got up, I found Paul wrapped around him, whispering, "Shhh. It's okay. You're gonna be just fine."

I hadn't had a thought about Henry not getting well. But he'd been nigh on inhuman going on four days at that point, and this was something still beyond that. One time I got up when he cried out, and I asked Paul if this was it . . . if he was dying.

"Either that or getting well." Paul looked even worse than earlier.

I felt my own forehead. It seemed fine.

When a rooster crowed at daylight, it took me a minute to realize what it meant—it wasn't Henry that had woke me up this time. I sat up and saw Paul in the gray light, sitting on the edge of the cot across from me. He had his head in his hands, crying. I stood up so fast I cracked my head on a low rafter.

"What?" I whispered. "What happened, Paul? Is he—?"

Paul managed a snotty laugh and shook his head. "His fever broke about half an hour ago. Just went, all at once, the way it came. Come see."

I knee-walked over, holding my head. Henry's breaths were deep and calm. I touched his cheek. Clammy, cool.

"Thank God." I was ready for more sleep if it was available.

Paul broke down all the way, heaving and all-out sobbing.

"Hey now." I felt as awkward as a one-legged dog. "You're wore out—that's all. You need to get some sleep your own self now."

He finally nodded and felt his way back to his own cot.

I dropped off to the sound of him snuffling.

Both of them slept all day. I went up the ladder a few times to check and then waved Anna away when she came with food. I figured they needed the rest more.

I was still trying to figure out Paul in all this. I told Jack about it, how it was almost like Paul had taken it as something personal, Henry getting sick.

Jack didn't seem surprised at all. "He knows what it's like to need comforting, don't you think?" He had a point. "I think sometimes the best things we do for others are really just the things we wish someone would do for us." He finished hammering a horseshoe and flipped it into a trough of water to sizzle.

"Don't get any ideas that the reason I make your meals is because I really want you to cook for me."

We spun around to find Anna with yet another tray.

Her green eyes danced. "I have eaten your cooking, Jack Williamson."

They both laughed.

I sneaked up the ladder and reported back that Paul and Henry showed signs of waking up.

Anna sent me up with the tray and said she'd be back.

All five of us ate supper in the loft that night, and it felt like a party. Henry was still so weak Anna fed him with a spoon, but his broth had some noodles in it, and she gave him sips of cold milk between bites.

When Henry found out it was Paul who had

nursed him around the clock, he looked stunned. "Thank you." His first real words in over four days. He closed his eyes and laid his head back with the effort.

He had no memory of any time in Junction City—everything we asked, he shook his head. And since the Williamsons had never met him in any way that counted, we spent a lot of that first conversation catching everybody up.

We stayed two more days while Henry got his feet under him. Anna still insisted on feeding us, although we wiped our boots and ate at her table once Henry could make it that far. After supper, she read aloud from the newspaper and we all daydreamed to the sound of her voice. Well, I know I did.

Thursday evening, Anna asked Paul, "Are you still interested in that fight in San Francisco?"

He sat up straight. "Yes, ma'am. Is there news?"

"Hmm." She frowned while she scanned the story. "It seems Governor Gillett has banned the whole spectacle from his state."

"What?" Paul said. "Why? Does it say?"

Anna read on and chuckled. "Well, he seems to have decided this is to be a prizefight, which is illegal in the state of California."

Jack joined in. "What did he think it was before, a tea party?"

"Before, it was a boxing *exhibition*," Anna said.

"Ohhh," we all chorused.

"What's going to happen now? Does it say?" Paul was tapping his foot.

Anna read to herself. "Well, it says this Mr. Rickard has three weeks to find another place to hold it, or the contracts they signed are null and void."

"Oh." Paul took this in.

"I still don't understand," Henry said. He had lost half his swagger and all his edge, and it was strange to hear him talk in such a quiet voice. "Why are you so all-fired interested, Paul? I mean, I can see why the white people are. And why the coloreds are, for that matter—"

We all busted out laughing, and it took him a minute to catch on. "You know what I mean."

"Well, I think you've just answered for yourself why I'm interested. All this building it up to be bigger than it is—the Great White Hope, the Black Man's Colossus. All the fear that goes along with that. It's ghoulish, but it's fascinating to follow."

"What do you mean by the fear that goes with it?" Anna asked.

"Something I've known— Well, here's an example. As recently as Kansas City, a pair of goons threatened to beat me up or even kill me. I hadn't done anything, and a skinny fellow like me is hardly intimidating, right? The fact that I wasn't like them scared them into wanting to hurt me."

The room was so quiet I heard the clock chitchatting. Henry blurted out, "I robbed them."

That got everybody's attention.

"That's what I figured." Paul nodded.

"Those thugs that threatened Paul," Henry explained to the room. "I was so mad, I cut out of work early and followed them on their last delivery of the day. I guessed that they collected cash for the store, and I was right. That's where our . . . sponsor money came from."

"You did it because of me," Paul said in a quiet voice.

"Well, hell, yeah—excuse me, ma'am. They had no business jumpin' on you. They didn't even know you, just that you're different. That's not fair."

"But saying one man can't be champion of the world because of what he looks like—that's fair?"

Henry looked like all the air went out of him. The rest of us shifted in our seats, and there was a fair amount of throat clearing.

"Who wants to play gin rummy?" Jack asked the room.

We all thought it a fine idea.

CHAPTER SEVEN

FRIDAY MORNING, THE SEVENTEENTH, we said good-bye to the Williamsons. Jack shook hands, and Anna gave us hugs a lot more innocent than the thoughts they inspired. She sent us off with a parcel to rival the Heversons' and told us to be sure and stop back by on our way home later in the summer. We had no problem promising we would.

We'd been stopped so long it felt like we were starting our trip all over again—but with a different group. Henry didn't spend any time at all trying to get a rise out of me, his laugh didn't raise the hair on my neck, and—best of all—he'd started talking to Paul like he might have been anybody.

I didn't know if it would last. In his quiet moments, it was pretty clear Henry was wrestling with something. He couldn't think too hard about anything without the effort showing up on his face. But as long as he was being civil, I was determined to enjoy it and not ask. Like my mom always says, when you see a can of worms, remember it's for the birds.

The company was more pleasant, but the drive itself was starting to feel like work. West of Junction City, past the farmed ground, there still wasn't a lot to Kansas other than flat miles of blowing dust. Trees here and there, but none close to the road and not enough of them to anchor the dirt anyway. Then more grain fields as we got closer to the next cow town that looked just like the one before it. Carry Nation and her temperance union had shut down every saloon in the state long before we got there, so there wasn't even that distraction at the end of the day.

We did find a rhythm. We'd drive into a town—Abilene, Salina, Ellsworth—find the biggest store, and go in for provisions. We could tell by the way we were told hello and the way people acted toward Paul whether we wanted to find a room in town or push on and camp out. Mostly we camped out.

We'd build a fire, and after we finished cooking supper, it was like a hearth with the whole prairie our parlor and the sky a ceiling shot through with stars. More than once, I thought of the great comet that I knew was just out of sight. If it was still there to see, the night sky would've been even more spectacular, but I always hurried that thought away as quick as I could. I didn't want to be regretful about any part of it whatsoever. A good luck charm is a good luck charm.

We'd listen to the coyotes sing, and the wood

would crackle and send sparks spiraling into the black sky, and we'd talk. Henry and I saved up things to describe to Paul at night—since swallowing road dust was not a favorite pastime for either of us.

Often as not, we'd sit around the fire and argue over what we'd seen. One night, I described a scene of three men on horses driving a hundred head of cattle off to the north of us, and Henry remembered it as more like two hundred. The same night, I said we'd seen a rotting horse carcass being pulled apart by buzzards five miles west of Salina, and Henry said it was a dead cow east of town. Before long, we were all three laughing so hard we couldn't talk. But the truly funny thing was, Henry and I both meant what we said—we just remembered some things different from one another, even a very few hours later. That was as much a revelation to me as the fact that folks could disagree without getting mad.

We took turns telling our own stories too. Paul told us a lot about the twelve years he'd lived at the Missouri School for the Blind. The time he and another fellow rode the trolley all the way downtown on a steamy August day to buy the biggest catfish Soulard Market had on hand so they could bring it back to lay overnight in the desk drawer of a teacher they hated. How another teacher lied to Paul's parents about a summer job two years in a row and let Paul live with her and her husband so that he wouldn't have to go home. How most of the teachers were caring but some were downright mean, like they were set on punishing the students for their affliction. How some of the blind teachers were the worst about it.

And through all of it, Paul's face told us nothing. When he was learning Braille, he said, he had a teacher who burned his hand on a flatiron when he made a mistake—and Paul told this as though it held no more weight than a comment on the weather.

He described being beaten up on the streets of St. Louis half a dozen times and joked, "Not once did I see it coming."

Neither Henry nor I could manage a laugh.

Henry, for his part, told about how he could almost, but not quite, remember his mother and how some nights he woke up thinking she had just been there in the room like a wisp of smoke barely gone. He talked about how his father got serious about his drinking after his wife died and how he'd said, "You think I care?" when Ellen asked to take Henry into her own household. How his other two sisters and two brothers seemed like distant cousins because he only lived in the same house with them a few days whenever Ellen was having one of her babies. How his older brothers beat the living daylights out of him every day for sport until he was allowed back at Ellen's. How they especially liked to jump him when he was asleep.

That explained how he could come out of a deep sleep into a fighter's stance. He said he'd never had a pleasant dream in his life that he could remember.

I gambled to tell him he'd cried out for his mother and Ellen during the worst of his sickness, and it didn't faze him at all.

He said, "I'll tell you the honest truth. I even thought one of them was there with me for a while, keeping me warm and telling me I was going to be okay. I know it was the fever talking, but at least that made it seem worthwhile to fight my way back. I was pretty close to givin' up there for a while."

Neither Paul nor I said a word.

The other two asked me to tell my own story, but I found I hadn't lived much of an interesting life. Only child until age twelve, doted on by my mother and father until sometime after Catherine came along and Mom was busy and tired all the time and I couldn't do anything to suit Dad. I told them Mom said two men under the same roof were like two bulls in the same pasture, but Paul's life and Henry's had been so different from mine they couldn't say they knew what I meant.

As we traveled on, one thing was becoming clear: even though we were way different from one another, each of us had something we were better at than the other two. We were rock, paper, scissors.

Paul was the smartest and the best educated. He knew more about the rest of the country away from home and how things worked than I ever would.

Henry—even the new Henry—was the toughest. If

there was anything he was afraid of, we hadn't come across it yet. He was also as strong as a bull when the Ford had to be pushed. And, boy, could he invent a convincing lie on the spot when one was needed to pave our passage.

As for me, I held everything together. I kept track of the map and how much gasoline we had in the car. I made sure we bought food before we needed it. I changed the flat tires we had every other day and replaced the spare in the next town we came to. I was the organized one, the practical one.

At least that's what I thought.

Monday, June 20, was our fourth day of driving since we'd left the Williamsons', and we hadn't changed clothes or spent the night in a bed since. Around noon, I studied the map and decided we could make Goodland by nightfall. I told the other two we ought to find a room there and stay overnight.

They didn't want to. Henry said he wanted to "get the hell out from under Carry Nation's hatchet," and Paul said he didn't want to spend the money when it wasn't necessary. I had to bargain with them the way I might bribe my little sister to leave me alone. And even after they agreed to go along, they pouted.

There had been another shift since Henry's sickness that I didn't understand even a little. When we'd first set out on the road, Henry thought Paul didn't know anything. Now if Henry wanted to know how often the Model T's spark plugs should be cleaned, or anything at all, he asked Paul and wouldn't let me get a word in edgewise. Paul could've told him brown cows give chocolate milk and Henry would have believed him.

And Paul was so damn polite to Henry. Like when Henry said we should smear our faces with motor oil to keep from sunburning any more than we already had. I practically laughed out loud while I waited for Paul to shrivel him up like a slug under the saltshaker.

But Paul said, "Hmm. Interesting," and I nearly pissed myself. "Well, the sun does dry out your skin, for sure, but it seems to me that dark clothes feel hotter on a summer day than light colors, so I wonder if the dark oil might just make things worse."

"Not to mention the next wagon we pass might mistake us for traveling minstrels and make us sing and dance for 'em," I added.

Neither of them even smiled.

"I guess that makes sense, Paul," Henry said. "Now that I think about it, I've been burned with frying pan oil and just plain fire, both, and the oil was worse."

"I think you're right," Paul said.

I wanted to puke. Or suggest they run off and get married to one another.

When we pulled into Goodland, with me driving, I meandered through town until I found a place called the Hotel Louise. It had wooden window boxes with pansies out front, and I figured a woman's touch meant home cooking. The other two just shrugged, so I went in and got us a room.

They were still in the car when I came out. "Well, come on and help carry stuff," I yelled.

They slouched out with all the cheer and cooperation of a couple of tomcats.

They were like that all night. We ate in the hotel dining room, and there was as much conversation at our table as you'd encounter in a graveyard.

"What's wrong with you two?" I finally asked.

After a minute Paul said, "You tell us."

Henry seconded. "Yeah."

I figured I'd give them a talking-to if they didn't come around by morning.

But everybody felt better after a bath and a night's sleep in real bunks. While Paul was packing up, he started singing something with words I didn't understand.

"What is that?" I said.

"Opera."

I didn't ask what that was. Just then, I'd rather have him believe I knew.

Henry started the day driving, and Paul rode shotgun, singing French or Mexican or whatever it was. At least they were both pitching in.

About twenty miles outside of Goodland, we saw three white clouds billowing toward us way too low in the sky. There wasn't anything else to see but dirt behind us clear to the horizon and more dirt trying to turn to desert in front of us, so the clouds were an eerie sight. They kept growing bigger until they were close enough we could make out covered wagons and the people driving them.

Even from a distance, it felt like three big clouds of despair coming toward us. The air was thick with it.

Henry stopped and killed the engine when they were still a hundred yards away. That right there was a sign of how much had changed. Before he got sick, he would have sped up just to scare their horses into bolting.

When they got closer, we saw that each wagon held a family. By the looks of them, they were all related. Their long, thin faces looked like they were pulled that way by the weight of the world.

Two boys, about eleven and thirteen, walked along behind the wagons, barefoot and as sullen as Henry and Paul had been the night before. Little heads popped out the front of the prairie schooner canopies, and eyes grew to saucers at the sight of the Model T.

The first wagon came up even and stopped.

"Mornin'," Henry said.

The man nodded.

His wife looked ahead like it was her job to hold the horizon in place.

"Where you all headed?" Henry asked.

"Back to Indiana."

The wagons had stopped, but the two boys kept walking. They circled the Model T without a word, their faces empty even of curiosity.

"We're travelin' out here from Missouri, goin' to Yellowstone Park," I offered. "You been out west long?"

"Too long," the man said. Then he touched the brim of his hat and clucked, and the wagon train was moving past. Second wagon, eyes forward. Third wagon, the same. The two boys fell in behind as before.

We sat there until their canopies looked like wisps of smoke. Then I jumped out to crank the car, and we went on.

Half an hour down the road, Henry said, "Look." He stopped and cut the engine.

"What is it?" Paul asked.

"A wood cross."

"There's a little pile of rocks in front of it," I added. I looked all around. "They were here some time. Look over there, Henry, where they had their fire." There was enough ash and char to account for three or four days.

A circle of ground fifty feet across was packed down by shoe leather, and off a ways from that was evidence of where the six horses had been tied up.

"They stopped for the child to get well," Paul said.

I said, "And they just left this morning, a little before we came across them. No wonder they looked like the end of the world."

"Mighta been you buryin' me, just as easy," Henry said.

A shiver went down my back like a goose had just walked across my grave.

"Seems like we oughta do something," I said.

Henry and I stared at the cross and the pile of rocks not much bigger than a family Bible.

A gust of wind blew a swirl of sandy dirt at us, and we all spat and rubbed our eyes red.

Paul said something so low I missed the first few words before I caught on. "Now I lay me down to sleep" was what it was. "Pray the Lord my soul to keep."

Henry joined in. "If I should die before I wake, I pray the Lord my soul to take."

That gave me the willies same as it had when I was little.

After a couple seconds, Henry said, "Amen."

Paul and I repeated it.

Henry finally spoke again. "Men?"

I said, "Let's go," and got out to crank the Model T. When I got back, Henry put it in gear, and we drove off.

My guess is we got lost in our thoughts about the family we'd just passed and what they'd left behind, because none of us said another word till I yelled, "Henry!"

Paul let out a yip.

Henry hadn't noticed the dirty ditch we were coming up on, and I was damned near too late.

He got us stopped before we hit water and before the back wheels left land, but our front tires sank past the axle in wet quicksand as we quit moving forward.

Before the motor could take in more muck, I yelled, "Turn it off! Get out! Climb over the seat back here and take the weight off the front of the car. Come on. Move before we sink any deeper." I seemed to be the only one able to think. "Come on! Grab the back axle and pull!"

One try proved the folly of that undertaking.

Paul said, "Now what?" calm as could be. He couldn't see how close the Model T had come to turning into a submarine.

"Henry drove off in the goddamned creek, is *now what*," I yelled. "What the hell were you thinkin', Henry? You weren't. That's what! Didn't I tell you to keep an eye on the railroad tracks?"

I couldn't stop. I was scared and mad and shaking all over. "How long we been off the road? Do you know? Of course you don't—you weren't paying attention!"

He didn't even look embarrassed. "Oh, shut up, Nelly."

A field of red swam in front of me, and I charged like a bull. My chin ran right square into Henry's fist, and my ass hit the ground so hard my teeth hurt.

"I think you should shut up too," Paul said. "Are you going to take a run at me next?"

I rubbed my jaw and looked back and forth

between them. They looked more mad than worried. "You wanna tell me what the hell's going on with you two?"

"You tell us. You're the expert," Henry answered, and they both started laughing.

"I have no idea what you're talking about." I was still on the ground.

"Really?" Paul's turn. "Usually it's us who don't know what we're talking about." That was hilarious to both of them too.

Not much makes you feel as small as being laughed at. I climbed to my feet so at least I could stop looking up at them. "All right, start with *Nelly*. What the hell's that about?"

Henry spoke in a fake high voice like a girl's. "Stop actin' like a baby, and I'll stop treatin' you like one. What were you thinkin'? You weren't thinkin'. That's what!"

"I never said that."

"You said it to me not three minutes ago!" Henry crowed.

"Well, yeah, but—"

"And you said it to me back in Lexington," Paul chimed in. "Did I think we were going to drive all the way to Yellowstone and back without having any car trouble? Well, then, I wasn't thinking!"

"Well, I was just tryin' to help."

Goddamn if that didn't set them off again. Stuck in the middle of nowhere with a bona fide dilemma is what we were, and they saw fit to laugh.

I was about ready to blow a gasket. "What? Why are you doing this?"

Henry spat to the side. "Ever since we left home, you've done everything but tell us how to pick our teeth after a meal. You even told me to go use the shitter this morning before we left Goodland."

I had told Henry that, but only because he'd become famous for making us stop right after we got underway while he looked for a place to squat.

"But—"

"You've decided when we stop and when we go, John," Paul said in a quiet voice.

Henry dropped his voice to match. "And what we'll eat and when we'll eat it."

"And when to buy gasoline. And God knows nobody but you could possibly change a tire—"

"Okay, okay! I get the point! It's just . . . somebody needs to be in charge and—"

They jumped on that.

"Why?"

"Says who?"

"Okay, fine. Nobody's in charge." *Let's see how fast you come begging for help* is what I was thinking.

I nodded toward the Model T. It looked like a horse bending to take a drink from the stream. "What do you wanna do about the car?" I realized I had my hands on my hips like a fishwife and dropped them to the sides.

"Help me out here, Henry," Paul said. "How bad is it?"

Henry scratched his head. "Pretty bad."

"No chance of using our two boards behind the front wheels?"

Henry looked again. "I'd say that's a no chance in hell there."

Especially since we burned them for firewood two nights ago. I was too mad to say it.

Paul said, "We haven't crossed any railroad tracks since we left Goodland this morning, have we?"

Henry said, "No."

"Well, then, we know the tracks are still south of us. If we walk in that direction, we'll come to a bridge or the line itself, and either one will lead to help."

Damn it, he made sense.

"No need in all of us going," Henry weighed in. "Won't take three to bring back help. Somebody prob'ly oughta stay near the auto anyway."

"I'll go." I wanted as far away from them as possible. I found Paul's hat, jammed it on my head, and stalked away in a line with the creek.

Henry yelled at my back. "Because you just want to help!"

Goddamn them to hell, they were laughing again.

The heat I felt rising had little to do with the sun climbing higher in the sky. My thoughts ran along the line of the horrible ways they should both die and how right now wouldn't be too soon. After I had them good and dead, I started picturing how I'd keep walking and never come back and their poor rotten carcasses would spend eternity feeling sorry for what they'd said to me.

How could they? Hell, they wouldn't remember anything if I didn't remind them. They were practically helpless if I didn't tell them what needed to be done, useless until I decided what to do next. I wasn't being bossy. I was just . . . just . . .

I stopped in my tracks, stunned.

I was just like my dad. Holy mother of God.

How many times had my mom explained him to me by saying he was just trying to help? How many times had I chafed because he predicted my mistakes and named my shortcomings before I did anything wrong?

Thinking about it like that, I guessed I could understand Paul and Henry. But what I'd done was only to take care of them. Only because I worried about them. Because I was afraid . . .

Jesus Horatio Christ. My dad was *afraid*?

"Evvabody's sunzabitches 'cept me and Jimmenently, and I ain't sure about Jim." I was singing and swinging my arms by the time I got to the railroad tracks. The sun was hot, and I was hungry enough to feel lightheaded, but this was more than that. I had taken on a weight of responsibility at the beginning of the trip, and now my friends had cut me loose.

It felt good just to be alone. We'd been gone three weeks, and I'd been by myself no longer than it took to use the outhouse. No wonder we were at one another's throats. Why, maybe the other two didn't really mean what they'd said.

I interrupted myself with another original tune before that thought could take root: "Gonna climb right up in the tallest tree and show my butt to the world—"

Sure, they meant it. Did I resent my dad trying to control every little detail of my life? Damn straight.

Woooo-wooooo!

I was so deep inside my head I hadn't even heard the train coming. The engineer waved as he passed, and I crossed my arms in the air, waving back too late. I was still signaling like crazy when the caboose came by, and that trainman waved too—like it was a normal thing, seeing a man out here in the middle of nothing, jumping up and down, saying howdy to the Central Pacific. Oh, well. At least I'd found the tracks.

Not fifty yards west, I found more: a handcar sitting idle on a side switching rail. I pumped it onto the main track and looked behind and ahead. Plenty of view and nothing in sight. That would sure beat walking. I didn't know what I'd do about the handcar if a train came along, but I knew I'd have enough warning to save my own behind. And I was no longer responsible for anything beyond that.

"Come, all you rounders that want to hear . . . the

story of a brave engineer . . ."

I sailed along and made my own breeze. Up down, up down. It felt like I was flapping my wings and flying.

Once I got a little winded, it was hard to keep singing. "Casey Jones—goin' to reach Frisco. We're gonna reach Frisco, but we'll all be dead." Two verses was all I could manage.

An hour later, I'd estimate, I had to stop and rest. The sun was nearly overhead, and I was wishing I'd taken more from the Ford than Paul's hat. Like lunch. I took the map out of my pocket and studied it. The little creek we'd run into was nothing but a line. It wasn't even named. But at least I determined it was almost halfway between Goodland, Kansas, and Burlington, Colorado. I wondered if I'd have been better off going back to a town we knew.

So what? That's what I'd told Paul way back that first night, that this was a *so what* kind of trip. No use looking back. I started westward again.

I made it to the Burlington train station and celebrated that fact until I saw the stationmaster steaming out the door toward me. He was just a little over five foot nothing, round as a barrel, with a face like an apple just starting to shrivel. "What are you doing with that, you hooligan? Where do you think you're taking it?"

"Well, good afternoon, sir. I'm part of a group of travelers, you see—"

"You're part of a group of jailbirds if you don't get

down from there this instant."

I accepted his invitation to join him on the platform. Both arms had seized up into solid knots of deadweight. "I came for help, you see—"

"And you're going to need it when I get through with you."

I clasped my hands behind my head and twisted left and right, working the kinks out of my back. Looking down on the flat top of the stationmaster's hat gave me the notion he might not get to bully anybody very often. I did him a favor and kept my mouth shut.

"You stay right here while I go get the sheriff!" He started away and changed his mind. "No, you come with me. I don't trust a horse thief like you to be here when I get back! March, mister!" He was on tippy-toe, trying to get up in my face. He'd had sauerkraut for lunch, and my stomach growled back at him. I turned and marched, hands still behind my head.

When we walked into his office, the sheriff was sitting with his long legs crossed at the boots on his desk. His hands were folded where a belly would be if he ever grew one, and he looked like the kind of man who's never seen a hurry worth getting into.

"Well, hell, Ed, what'd you expect him to do? Sit there and hope for a miracle?" That was his view of the situation after Stationmaster Ed tattled on me.

"I was gonna offer to take it back when I got help," I said.

Ed practically jumped up and down. "You'll do

nothing of the kind! You are never going to touch railroad property again. Do you hear me?"

"Speaking of railroads, Ed, don't you have one you're supposed to be running?" The sheriff's mouth curved up the least little bit.

Ed took his big watch out of his pocket and looked at it. He yipped like a puppy with its tail in the door and was gone.

"Thank you, sir," I said.

"Welcome, son. Ed doesn't mean any harm. The little dogs always bark loudest when the parade goes by, you know?"

"I do know."

We grinned at each other.

He undraped himself from the desk and stood, and then I was the short man in the room. No wonder he was so easygoing. He could scare the devil out of people just by standing up.

"George Windom. Or you can call me Sheriff." He held out his hand and I had to reach up to shake it.

"John Hartmann, sir."

He walked me over to the sidewalk in front of the drugstore where some benches seemed to serve as town hall. On the way there, I told him how the three of us had left Missouri first of June in our blind friend's auto to see America. How we were headed for Yellowstone Park.

He just nodded, but he was listening to me. You can always tell. Some grown-ups, you can practically hear another conversation going on in their heads while you talk to them. Not him.

When we reached the benches lined with old men, the sheriff took off his cowboy hat and scratched his head and laid out my plight—including the getting up of Ed's dander, which proved to be a high source of amusement.

One old man provided the name of a farmer who had a steam engine tractor, and another asked how far I'd had to walk to the tracks. I told him, and Old Man Number Two reminded the first how far the nearest bridge was and how one might come in handy what with us stuck on the opposite side of the creek. A third old man suggested they load the tractor onto a train and ride it out there and back. Nobody even answered that, like they were used to hearing harebrained ideas come out of him.

A fourth old man said, "What kind of automobile did you say it was?"

I hadn't, but I told him.

He nodded. "They're real light, aren't they? Made out of some newfangled steel Henry Ford conjured up?"

I told him yes, but that no car was light enough to be lifted up out of quicksand and then pushed out by men mired in the muck themselves.

"Hog feeder lid," Number Four pronounced.

All the others nodded.

I looked from one to the other, waiting for somebody to explain.

They let Number Four go on since it was his idea. "You ever seen a hog feeder, son?"

"Sure." I thought back. Reimers' farm: steel tub in the corral that looked like a tin can squashed by a giant. Big, round piece of steel for a lid. It might work. "Um, do you gentlemen have any idea where I might find one?"

They laughed enough for me to think there must be a ready supply in the region.

"Or how I can get it out there?" I added.

This sobered them up and called for a round of "Hmm."

"You can take the handcar back out," Sheriff Windom said. "Leave it where you found it."

"Oh, no, Sheriff, I don't think Ed—"

"Aw, hell." He spat into the street and made a patch of mud the size of a quarter. "I'll handle Ed. Tell you what—I'll *commandeer* that handcar for official business."

All the old men haw-hawed at that. Ed was obviously more entertainment than friend.

"You got any money?" the sheriff asked.

I looked in my pocket and came out with two dollars. "Why?"

He squinted off to the west. "It'd be dark before you could get back out to the creek and do any good today. Buy yourself something to eat come supper-time and walk over to the jail after. You can sleep there for free." He swept the bench with a smile made of mischief. "All these fine gentlemen have done so at one time or another."

There was another round of haw-haw-haw, paying the sheriff for the joke.

I went into the store where the old men sat guard, and I bought a newspaper. Habit, I guess. Then I came back out and asked the information committee where I might be able to buy supper.

Old Man Number One pointed with a finger that shook a little. "Well, you can drink your supper over there."

I looked across at the first saloon I'd seen since Missouri.

Haw-haw-haw, they chorused.

Number Three said, "Why'n't the sheriff just take him home for supper?"

The others gave him a look that might have withered a smarter man.

Another spoke up. "Miz Henderson sets a fine table, from what I hear, over at the hotel there. Got colored help and everything."

I looked where he pointed, thanked them for their help, and tipped Paul's hat before walking away.

I walked past the saloon and on to the hotel. The lobby looked like it had been nice when it was new but had seen too many years of cowboys and dust storms to keep living up to its past. I stood, hat in hands, and finally coughed a few times to draw notice.

A colored girl stuck her head around a velvet curtain like a wren peeking out of a birdhouse. No more than she laid eyes on me, she ducked back in.

Before long, I heard footsteps, and a woman my mother's age shouldered her way through the curtain, drying her hands on a tea towel. "Yes?" Her face was friendly but meant business too.

"Miz Henderson?"

"Yes?"

"The fellows"—I pointed—"holding down those benches over there told me I might buy supper here. Said you set a fine table, in fact."

She walked over and squinted out the window. "Nice of them, seeing how not a one of them would part with a quarter to eat here."

I didn't know how to answer that, so I didn't.

She looked me up and down. "Thirty-five cents tonight. I'm cooking pork roast. But it won't be ready for"—she turned to look at the clock—"another hour or so. If you don't spend all your money between now and then, you'll eat like a king." And she was gone before I could say boo.

I sat down with my newspaper in one of the lumpy chairs in the lobby but couldn't get comfortable no matter how I folded my legs. After fidgeting like a two-year-old in church, I folded the paper and walked outside.

The benches in front of the drugstore were empty now, and that made it easier to walk back to the saloon and go in. I'd had enough haw-haws thrown my way for one day.

It took a minute for my eyes to adjust to the dark. Then I saw four men talking together at the bar, each with a boot on the rail, and some other men playing cards at two tables. A few looked my way and then went back to their game like they hadn't seen anything interesting. I paid a dime for a beer, then looked around for the table with the most light.

I had been squinting at the paper for only a minute when the barkeep came over with a kerosene lamp and set it in front of me.

"Thanks," I told him.

"Ruin your eyes" was how he said I was welcome.

I scanned the front page. Theodore Roosevelt was back from hunting in Africa and was raising hell over what President Taft had done while he was gone—such as filing an antitrust suit against U.S. Steel, one of Roosevelt's pets. "Shoulda stayed home, then," I could hear my dad say. Yet one more person wrote about how great Mark Twain was and how he was still dead, two months running. And Arizona had got the go-ahead to think about becoming a state.

I turned to sports. The Cardinals had lost to Pittsburgh the day before, but the Browns had won over Detroit, so that was a wash as far as I was concerned. I never could pick one St. Louis baseball team over the other. There was a short piece saying George Rickard was looking at two towns in Nevada for the Jeffries-Johnson fight—Goldfield and Reno. Paul would be interested to hear that.

Paul. Henry. I wondered what they were thinking, stuck out there with prairie on one side and desert on the other and a car no good to them.

Damn them. They'd be starving if it weren't for me, and they were probably having a party because I was gone. The ant and two grasshoppers—that's what we were. I ought to have let them run out of provisions, just to see what it was like. I drained my glass, and the barkeep caught my eye. I shook my head, stuck the paper under my arm, and saluted the man on my way out.

When I came into the hotel lobby, the velvet curtain had been tied back and the smell of heaven came from the dining room behind it. I ducked under the swag and saw two married-looking couples and one table of three men already eating. The colored girl I'd seen before was scurrying back and forth with plates and pitchers, and I caught her eye for just a second. She cut her face away like a head-shy horse and nodded to a small table in the corner without looking at me again. I sat myself down.

I guess Miz Henderson cooked two choices in the evening—take it or leave it—because the girl served me without a word of asking what I wanted.

I was glad for still having the newspaper, as it gave me someplace to look. I had never eaten by myself in public. Miz Henderson was a fine cook, but her food would have gone down even easier with conversation.

Damn them. I didn't want it to matter.

I already knew the cost of the meal, so when I finished, I left the coins on the table and left. I felt like a cipher that had blown through without anybody seeing me. I remembered Paul's talk about a tree falling in the woods with no one around.

I started for the jail, but it was still early, and I figured one more beer would be a sleeping tonic, good for me. Yes, sir, it would be.

Off to the west, long pink and orange spikes poked the sky, and I wondered what waited for the three of us in that direction. I looked to the east, and the sky over Paul and Henry looked gray and doubtful. I let out a long breath.

The saloon was much more popular now. The piano in the corner was playing all by itself, and I couldn't help staring at that. But then a girl in a shiny green dress with a pretend hat, no more than a feather and a little veil, headed my way with a determined look in her eye, and I bolted for the bar fast as I could. I'd read about working girls in dime novels, sure, but I'd never had relations with any woman—during my waking hours, anyway—and wasn't near ready to think about paying for the privilege.

My old Missouri work boot fit on the rail just as well as the cowboy boots all down its length, and the barkeep gave me something to watch. I could feel my heartbeat when I reached into my shirt pocket for change. My hand even shook a little when I first picked up my glass, and I was glad Henry wasn't there to give me the razz. Damn him.

I managed to finish my beer and get out the door without looking at the girl again. Outside, I took a big swig of clean evening air and looked toward the east again. I stood there long enough I had to remind myself to move.

The door to the quarters next to the jail opened. A beautiful woman with features sharp enough to cut glass greeted me with "What?" Her eyes were dark blue, and there was a fire in them that reminded me of somebody else I couldn't place right away.

I took Paul's hat off. "Evenin', ma'am. Sorry to bother you, but Sheriff Windom said—"

The door opened wider, and the tall man appeared behind her, taking a hat off a nail and squaring it on his head.

"I said he could sleep at the jail, Alma," he said as he brushed past her. "I'll be right back."

"Well, you'd better! Cook all day and you leave, you ungrateful—"

The door closed behind him.

We walked next door, and the sheriff put a key in the lock.

"Sorry to upset the missus," I told him.

"Oh, you didn't, unless you're the one who

slapped her when she was born." I understood why he hadn't invited me to dinner and why that came as no surprise to anyone but the village fool.

He showed me to a cell and said he was going to lock the front door because all the guns inside were too much temptation for some elements. That's what he called them: *elements*.

"I'll be back early, though, so get some sleep. I aim to ride that handcar out with you."

I thanked him, but he just waved it away on his way out. His key turned in the lock, and then I heard his wife carrying on when the next door over opened.

It was still early for bedtime, and I'd read more of the paper than I cared for, so there was little choice but to lay on the bunk and think. Those poor broken people and the sad little grave they left behind came to me. Thoughts of that turned into a vision of Catherine, back home, looking like she was all eyes and hope when she gave me her blanket. I wished I had it. It was stuffed into a rip in the seam of my pillow ticking, back at the auto.

I wondered what she thought about her big brother being gone. Three weeks is a long time to a girl that little. I wondered once again where I'd end up after the summer and how long she'd go without seeing me then. I decided I should send her a postcard the next day; that's what I should do.

I wondered if they talked about me—about us—

around the supper table. Wondered where we were, how we were. Three weeks with one short letter. My father was probably worried half to death, but not so as anyone could see. Mom too. A postcard to Catherine would help them too.

I thought about Paul's parents. Did they miss their boy and suppose the adventures he might be having? Was it any different to them from having him off in St. Louis?

And what about Ellen McCombs? Had she possibly had a change of heart about Henry since he'd been gone so long?

Or were the three of us trees in the forest? Once gone, did others close in where we'd been and leave no clearing?

My throat tightened up and made me glad I'd had no more beer. Enough of this. Time to sleep.

The next morning I was roused with "Rise and shine! Get up, you lazy sinner! We need the sheets for table-cloths. It's almost time for dinner!"

I sat up so fast I banged my head on the brick wall behind my bunk. Sheriff Windom was standing there with a big grin, holding a tin cup of steaming coffee and a saucer with two biscuits.

"What the—?" was all I managed.

"Aw, something my ma used to say. Don't have any kids to use it on, and don't think I'd risk it on Alma." He chuckled and handed over the plate.

I downed the first biscuit in one bite and stuffed the second one in behind it. Eating a good meal the night before had made me that much hungrier come morning. "Whadfimindat?" I asked him.

He just looked amused and waited.

I swallowed. "What time is it?"

"Why, you gotta be somewhere?" The sheriff took the saucer and traded me the cup of coffee.

"No, I just— Never mind." Always thinking about the schedule. *How many miles can we make today? What towns and when? Where's the next food? Fuel?* Piss on it. That was going to be my new attitude. Just piss on it all.

The sheriff nodded like he'd heard me. "Get yourself situated, and empty that chamber pot in the outhouse when you go. Then let me know when you're ready. I got plenty at my desk."

We headed for the rail station half an hour later, and when we got there, I sneaked a look at the big clock inside. It read half past five. We were almost ahead of the sun.

We hadn't gotten ahead of Ed, though. The little stationmaster rolled toward us like he was on wheels as soon as we were through the door. "Aha! I see you've come to your senses and arrested this hoodlum!"

"Oh, calm down, Ed," the sheriff said. "You see nothing of the sort. We came to get the handcar to go back out there."

For a second, it looked like Ed's head would explode. Then he sputtered, "Y-you will not! W-why, the very idea of you coming in here—"

"Give it a rest, Ed." Sheriff Windom pulled his shirt away from his chest and nodded at the badge pinned there. "Official police duty. You got no sway over that."

The little man's neck had to hurt, craned back like that to look the sheriff in the eye. Maybe that's why he gave up so fast. He flapped his arms once and let them slap to his sides before he walked away.

"Ed, wait!"

The sheriff turned him around. His cheeks were drooping like a basset hound's, and he didn't even muster the question.

"Any trains going past the creek out east the next couple hours?"

Ed looked out the front window so long I thought his mind had wandered. Then an engine came chugging into view, and he pointed to it. "Last one before noon." He slumped away and disappeared behind a door marked *Office*.

I almost wanted to go after him and invite him to yell at me just to lift his spirits.

On a side rail out front, there were three handcars, which made me feel a little better about taking one. Ed could look out while we were gone and see he was still a wealthy man, handcarwise.

Sheriff Windom had been carrying a covered

peck basket, and now he set it down on the platform. We climbed on.

A mile or so outside of town, we stopped to borrow a hog feeder lid from a farmer the sheriff called Pete. He helped us wrestle it onto the handcar. The only way it would ride was if Sheriff Windom stood on one edge while most of the rest stuck straight out behind like a turkey gobbler tail.

Pete waved us away with a chuckle. "Just bring it back. Ain't gonna rain today anyway."

Once we got going, we sailed along twice as fast with half the effort I'd put in alone. At least that's how it felt. We got to the little side spur where I'd found the handcar in what seemed like no time.

I told the sheriff, "The creek's just up ahead."

He grinned and said, "Really? Same place it's been since Hector was a pup?"

I guess that was pretty stupid.

We unloaded the hog feeder lid by the creek, and I told the sheriff to sit and rest while I took the handcar back where I found it.

He laid down with his gun belt and the peck basket beside him, pulled his hat over his face, and said, "Call me George. Least till we get back to town."

George was asleep when I came back, and I didn't know what to do. He'd already done so much it didn't feel right to wake him up to do more. But being so close was making me edgy, wondering how the boys had made out overnight, if they were okay. I deliberated turning the feeder lid on edge and rolling it along by myself. The sheriff—George—would figure out from the tracks where I'd gone. Either that or he'd think somebody else came along and took a snake for a walk.

But he snorted and sighed and sat up before I decided anything. He looked all around and smiled. "Kinda nice to wake up without all the screaming." He sure seemed to take it well, being married to a crazy person.

A jolt went through me. Selma Clark—hers were the eyes the sheriff's wife's reminded me of. Crazy old woman, crazy all her life. You'd walk past her family's house in Wakenda and she'd be at a window, staring out and screaming something you couldn't hear. Little kids dared one another to go closer.

I had to wonder. Selma Clark never got anywhere close to married—the very thought was funny and cuckoo both—so how did this handsome, smiling man get hitched up to Alma, the Wild-Eyed Yeller?

And some think the nighttime sky is mysterious.

We moved along, carrying the metal disk between us like we were trying to signal somebody in those heavens with the sun's reflection. It was awkward going, walking crooked with the lid tilted my way because of the difference in our heights. Sheriff George hummed a song. Maybe the going was easier for him.

When the Model T first came into sight, looking like a big bug crawling backward out of the creek, it was all I could do not to take off running. George must have sensed it, because he picked up the pace.

There had been nothing around to make a fire, so there was no campsite to speak of. We came upon Paul and Henry in their bedrolls, sleeping like babies without a care in the world. Damn them.

Clang! Clang! Clang! We had set the feeder lid on edge, and George banged it like a gong with the butt of his revolver. "Get up, you lazy sinners! We need the sheets for tablecloths. It's almost time for dinner!"

Henry shot to his feet and into his fighter's stance. I'd have been disappointed if he hadn't.

But Paul just opened his eyes and froze.

"Hey, Paul."

His jaw relaxed.

Henry's eyes focused and he stared at George, then the feeder lid, then me. "Where the hell you been? We was worried sick—well, Paul was, anyway—and we didn't know if a bobcat got you or—"

"Are you okay, John?" Paul sat up and spoke in a quiet voice. "I'm sorry. We're both sorry we—"

I cleared my throat. "Paul. Henry. This is Sheriff Windom from Burlington. He was good enough to put me up for the night and come out here this morning to help."

Henry stepped forward and shook hands, as serious

as a judge in his none-too-clean drawers.

Paul stood up with his blanket wrapped around his waist.

George stepped toward him. "I'm guessing you're Paul."

Paul's head knocked back like he was shocked at the height the voice came from.

Henry scrambled into his britches while the sheriff holstered his gun and went to survey the car's situation. His face was fierce when he whispered, "Why'd you bring the *law?*"

I laughed out loud, and George turned to see. I waved that it was nothing. We had a whole state between us and Kansas City, and Henry looked nothing like he had when we'd lit out from there anyway. He didn't even remember sleeping in the Junction City jail while he was sick. But *now* he was worried. I laughed again.

Paul was dressed and putting his bedroll together. "John, what happened when you left here?"

"Well, there was this band of wild Indians," I started, "and we got to talkin', them and me, and they said it sounded like I knew it all, just everything, and they begged me to come back to their village and tell them what to do and how to do it. They offered to make me their chief, but I told them . . ."

But I couldn't rub it in any more than that. I had my payment, knowing they'd worried about me. "Oh, well. When I got to the railroad tracks, I found a handcar just a little down the line," I told them.

"Took it into Burlington, met the stationmaster, and he introduced me to the sheriff here."

George turned around with a sly smile.

"It was too late to head back, so we got up a plan and, well, here we are."

"What's the hog feeder lid for?" Henry asked.

"Same idea as the boards," I said. "Except more surface area, keep it from sinking. We hope."

George walked over to us. "I hope you boys don't mind getting dirty. I've studied twelve ways to Sunday, and the only way this is going to work is you three get in there and lift the front axle while I stand on the bank and slide the feeder lid under the front tires."

I was about to unassign Paul the job, but I gave myself a *piss on it* reminder instead.

Then Henry said it for me. "Why'n't we put Paul on the bank instead?"

"Why?" the sheriff asked. He looked like an oak outlined by the sun. "He feeble?"

"No, sir. He's blind," Henry explained.

"He deaf and dumb too?"

Henry said, "Well, no, sir. He's—"

"Then why's he using your mouth to talk?" George grinned at me. "And what's being blind got to do with it, unless you're explaining how the auto got there in the first place?"

Henry's ears got red, and I turned away to smile.

Paul looked confused. "We're going in? Into the quicksand?"

"Either that or donate your Ford to the state as

some kind of statue," George told him. "It is your car, isn't it? I'd strip down, if I was you. Clothes aren't going to help."

None of us was what you might call modest. But it felt mighty strange—naked as jaybirds wading in hand in hand, Paul in the middle like he was going to be baptized. Baptized, bare as a hairless baby possum, in sand that got deeper every step. George was good enough not to laugh, but his grin muscles were working overtime.

We got to the front of the car and put Paul's hands on the axle. He and I were buried up to our waists. On Henry, the wet sand was halfway up his chest. I hoped pushing up on the car wouldn't tamp him down all the way under. Not worrying isn't as easy as it sounds.

We were out of breath from dragging through the muck, so we rested before we tried anything else.

George yelled, "Ready?"

We nodded.

He got into a crouch with the feeder lid as close to the front wheels as possible. "On three. One. Two. Three!"

The axle lifted about an inch at first, but the quicksand sucked at it as if to claim it for good. We grunted and heaved in a tug-of-war. The bed we stood on was none too solid either, and we tilted and banged into one another's shoulders as we pushed.

After about ten seconds that felt like an hour,

George said, "Want to rest and try it again?"

We all yelled, "No!" We weren't about to give up that inch we'd gained so far.

My teeth clenched so hard they ached. And just when I was afraid we would have to take a second shot at it—*slurrrph*—the tires broke free of the muck. George shoved one edge of the feeder lid under. The big piece of metal started to tilt toward us, toward sinking.

George yelled, "Lift again!"

This time was easier, with no enemy pulling against us.

George shoved the lid forward until it thunked all three of us in the chest hard enough to take our wind away. "Sorry! Step back now!"

It was like Mother May I in sorghum molasses. My thighs ached with the effort of taking even a couple steps. Henry had one of Paul's elbows, and I grabbed the other. But then we stopped and beheld Model T on a platter.

It had worked. The feeder lid had too much surface area to sink. To sink very fast, anyway.

George wore a mighty grimace and gripped the back rim of the feeder lid. "Get out!" he yelped. "You're not done!"

Of course. The weight of the car was trying to push the feeder lid forward, away from the bank, and it was working against George in a new tug-of-war. My legs burned, straining through the muck as I pulled Paul along behind. We were winded again when we finally rolled up on the bank.

But George hollered, "Get over here. Now!" I heard pain in his voice.

We all scrambled. Henry got there first and grabbed the feeder lid.

George gargled out, "No! Grab the axle. We gotta pull the car, not the lid out from under it!"

Henry's face registered confusion.

Once all three of us were in place, George let go of the metal disk, grabbed hold of the axle, and grunted, "One, two, *three*," and we pulled and strained with all we had.

And then the Ford's front tires sat on solid ground for the first time in twenty-four hours, and we were laying on a creek bank huffing like we'd run ten miles.

George climbed to his feet and towered over us. "Grab that feeder lid, Henry, before you have to go back in to get it."

Henry was still gasping for air, but he crawled over and spun the disk onto the bank before he broke down and laid on his side, panting again.

George stood over us and started laughing.

"What?" Henry knew it had to do with him and didn't like it. That was all there in one word.

George waved his hands in front of him and said, "Oh, no, Tar Baby. Don't say nothin'." He broke up.

I looked at the other two and down at myself. Our faces and arms were burned Indian brown by the sun. Our nether halves were covered in a thick coat of muck drying fast. We looked like we'd been dipped in chocolate and pulled on pink undershirts afterward. I started laughing too.

Paul could picture the silliness of it and joined in.

"*What?*" Henry said.

That set us off harder.

I had to wipe my eyes when I could finally tell him, "Look in the mirror, buddy."

"What the hell? You know there's—"

I pointed to myself and then Paul.

Henry frowned, looking back and forth. About the time the other three of us calmed down, he exploded laughing.

We laid around resting and drying our husks for half an hour or so while we decided what to do next. Then George remembered the peck basket he'd been toting all morning and came out with boiled eggs, cornbread, biscuits, and honey. Paul and Henry dove in headfirst.

George watched and chuckled. "Thought you might feel a little peckish. Sleeping out in the open air will do that to you."

They ate like they were wolves and it was raining sheep.

Even Paul forgot his manners for a while. Then he said, "John? Did you get some?"

"You all go ahead. George fed me at the jail this morning."

Henry took the last corn muffin and tossed it to me. "Have one anyway."

"Thanks."

Sheriff George looked on like a favorite uncle.

We found out from him that a bridge spanned the creek about a mile north. I asked why the road took such a bend away from the railway.

He said, "You rather build a twenty-foot bridge over water or a fifty-foot bridge to span sand too?"

"The water goes all the way out to the bank there?" Paul asked. His voice sounded like Santa Claus was on his way.

George said, "Yeah, son. Why?"

In answer, Paul pulled a tile of dried sand from the top of one foot.

"Mm-hmm," George said. "You boys could do with a little water, now that you mention it." He took his hat off and wiped his forehead before setting the hat back on. "Tell you what. It's no more than a mile. Put your boots on and walk, and I'll drive your car and keep it clean inside."

Henry shrugged.

I said, "Paul?"

He hesitated, then said, "Okay."

I wondered what was going on behind that mask.

We tried half a dozen ways of fixing the hog feeder lid so it would ride in or on the car, but it was just too big unless somebody held it there. George couldn't do that and drive.

"You all carried it out here," Henry said. "Paul and I can carry it a ways, I figure." He still hadn't gained back all the weight he'd lost when he was sick, and the sight of his ribs served as a reminder of what had set him on the road to good behavior to begin with.

George folded himself in behind the steering wheel and looked the instrument panel over. "What do I do?"

Paul's milky eyes bugged. "You've never *driven?*"

"Heck, no. Only auto in Burlington belongs to Ed Stillwater, and John can fill you in why nobody borrows that. Why'd you think I wasted most of a day to come out here and help?"

"Because you're nice?" I guessed.

He laughed. "Right. Now just give me the low-down. Nothing's going to happen, Paul. Believe me."

Henry and I talked over each other, giving him the shorthand lesson, and he nodded when he was ready. We gathered our clothes from where we'd flung them and dumped them in the backseat to put on after we'd washed. I grabbed the crank and, on second thought, snatched our shirts out of the car. No use burning skin that had never seen sunlight.

It was a whole new sensation, swinging the crank naked, and I was glad the car blocked everyone's view. The engine coughed and spat sandy dirt at us like it was disgusted by what had gone on and it finally had a chance to tell us. Only then did it catch, sputter a little for punctuation, and start chugging. I tossed the crank in the back and saluted.

"See you in the funny papers," George said. A few jerks and catches later, he was gone. I do mean gone. He took off full throttle north and left us with our mouths collecting dust.

We stared after the Ford as it got smaller and smaller, standing there in our boots, holding our shirts and wearing nothing but dried mud for pants. Dirt-crusted peckers. That's what we had, and that's what we were.

"Oh, shit," Henry said.

That about summed it up.

Paul cleared his throat. "How far is it to Burlington?"

My tongue came unstuck. "Twenty miles, give or take."

"Oh, shit," Paul said.

We all agreed on that.

"Let's sit down and think about this." I lowered myself onto the hog feeder lid and thought better of that in no time. I stood up and rubbed my burned butt.

"What's there to think about? We start walkin', don't we?" Henry looked like he wanted to work up an anger at somebody. Anybody. Just like the old days.

"Which way, though?" Paul asked.

"Hell's bells, toward the bridge!" Henry said.

"Or toward the handcar," I said.

Paul nodded.

"Oh." Henry cooled down just that fast.

"What do you think, John?" Paul asked.

There it was—my answer to *How long till you come to me for advice?*—and I was too miserable to enjoy it.

"I don't know. Let's think this out. Stationmaster Ed said the next train goes through here at noon." I looked at the sun and guessed it was about nine o'clock. "We might make it to town before then and we might not. But Ed wasn't exactly happy to see me roll in on railroad property when there was one of me and I had pants on."

Paul looked grim. "So that way, we either get hit by a train or ride into town . . ."

I knew it was too horrible to put into words. "We go the other way, at least we know there's a bridge. And water."

"Dirt's the only britches we got. You wanna wash it off now?" Henry asked.

He had a point.

"But that's also where the road is," I said. "Who knows? Maybe somebody with a good heart and a sense of humor will come along and give us a ride."

"George might be there," Paul said in a quiet voice. "He may not have left us."

"I want to believe you," I told him. "Hell, the man gave me a place to stay last night, rode all the way out here today—"

"And he knew there was a brand-new Model T at the end of *that* rainbow," Henry tossed out.

I whipped around.

But he wasn't blaming me. He just looked sad.

"But what good does it do him?" Paul said. "I mean, one way or the other, we get to town—"

"Where he's the law and nobody within six hundred miles knows us from Adam, Cain, and Abel," I reminded him.

"Oh, shit," he said.

Amen to that.

Henry bent and picked up one side of the hog feeder lid. "Well, if our chances of help are slim and none, I'll take slim. I vote we walk north."

I picked up the other side of the disk. "Good enough."

"Which way's north?" Paul asked.

I turned him by the shoulder, and away we trudged, off to the guillotine with a plate to hold our heads.

CHAPTER EIGHT

IT TAKES ABOUT FIFTEEN MINUTES TO
walk a mile in good weather and a good mood. It
probably takes twenty when it's hot and you're tired.

I'd say it takes thirty when you're down on your
luck, down in the mouth, and you've got no choice
but to wave your dirty wiener in the wind. We were
some sorry souls walking that mile.

Nobody said a word until we saw a speck on the
horizon. Henry and I squinted, looked at each other,
and squinted again.

"Can you tell what it is?" I said.

"What *what* is? What do you see?" Paul came to
like a puppy waking up to a new bone.

"Calm down there, Geronimo," Henry told him.
"It's just *somethin'* right now. Maybe it's a tree. Can't tell."

Even a tree sounded good just then. I hadn't seen
shade anywhere between Goodland and Burlington.

We all walked a little faster.

Another thirty feet and Henry called out, "It's the bridge!"

"Anything else?" Paul said.

I made a scope with my hand and looked through that. "I . . . can't tell. Can you, Henry?" I was afraid to say it.

He dropped his end of the feeder lid and ran a ways ahead. When he whooped, I knew my eyes hadn't been playing tricks.

I turned and saw Paul's eyes were wet.

"Is it there?"

I barely heard him. "It is."

He sobbed one time and then shook his head hard as if to dislodge something. His smile broke out, and it was like seeing it for the first time. With his eyes nearly shut, he looked like anybody, except more like a moving-picture star than most.

"Henry, get back here," I yelled.

But he was already off at a lope.

I picked up his side of the feeder lid. "Paul, can you run with this damn thing?"

He was still smiling. "Nope, I'm feeble." He moved his hand to get a better grip. "Ow! Hot!"

"Feeble, yes, but sharp as a tack."

He laughed out loud.

"Let's go."

George was leaned back in the driver's seat with his hat over his face when we got there.

This time, I had no doubt about waking him. "Get up, you lazy sinner," I hollered.

He jumped and fumbled his hat onto his head and looked all around. "Time for dinner?" He yawned.

"Very funny." I was the one who knew him best, so I led the charge. "You got any idea how scared we were that you up and left us out here?"

"Damn straight I do." He opened the door, got out, and stretched his arms above his head. That made him only fourteen feet tall. "That's why I did it."

I was struck dumb.

Paul said, "You wanted to scare us?"

"Yup. John told me yesterday you all are driving clear from Kansas City or better to Yellowstone and back. Is that right?"

We all nodded.

"Well, you got to be more careful. There's a whole lot of *elements* out there, and you're bound to run into most of them. You could get robbed, even killed, for less than a Model T Ford."

Henry piped up, almost cheerful. "We already been robbed."

George fixed him with a long look. "And yet you let me, somebody you barely met, get in the auto that held all your belongings—even your britches—and drive off."

"But, well, you're, you know," I sputtered. "You're a man of the badge."

He nodded. "That I am. But I've met men wearing

a badge I wouldn't trust to watch my dog. I'm not saying you can't trust anybody. I'm saying keep your eyes open. You there . . . Paul. You had a moment of doubt, right?"

Paul nodded.

"Listen to your gut. Trust in God and everybody else—just keep your hand on your wallet."

Even Paul was staring down at his feet by then.

George nodded toward the bridge. "Great big bathtub over there I'd be in if I was you."

It was like the bell ringing for recess. Henry and I took off, and I'm ashamed it was him that remembered to come back and take Paul by the elbow. We stripped off our shirts and shoes and washed away more than just the dirt that was on us.

We put our clothes on and drove toward town with Paul and me in the backseat holding the hog feeder lid above our heads. George directed Henry to Farmer Pete's place so we could return his Handy Model T Unsticker, and he didn't seem the least bit curious that our handcar had turned into a Ford and there were twice as many of us as before.

Once Burlington came into sight, I started getting a little excited without knowing why. Then we motored past the drugstore with the town council meeting out front. They all cheered and whistled when they saw George.

This was my town. That was what had me going.

I knew the place, and Paul and Henry didn't. Childish, but true.

We stopped in front of the jail, and George got out. We thanked him for helping out, using just about all the words we knew.

He pshawed.

I asked if I should go tell Ed where his handcar was, and he grinned. "Ed will be along asking after it sometime in the next minute or two. I'll tell him." Then he asked if we were staying over or moving on.

We hadn't planned anything past getting the car out of the creek.

Paul said, "I imagine a home-cooked meal or two and a night in a bed might do us some good."

I was glad. I'd have a chance to show them around.

George said, "Well, I can't make you all an offer less than the one I made Handcar Hank here. Spend your money on food and such, and come on back tonight and sleep in the jail for free." He looked up and down the street. "I'm not expecting an uprising before morning." He took his grin inside.

Henry said, "I'm starved."

Paul said, "I want a newspaper."

We left the car in front of the jail and walked back to Main Street. I introduced the other two to the old men on the benches as best I could and made a little extra over Old Man Number Four for his idea of using the hog feeder lid.

We were coming out of the drugstore with Paul's newspaper when Henry spied the saloon across the street. "Beeeer," he yelled.

I grabbed his collar before he could run out into the street in front of a team and wagon.

He turned to me. "You got drunk yesterday, and that's why you didn't come out to get us, isn't it? You left us out there for bobcat bait—"

"I did nothing of the sort. I didn't even go near the place." I don't know why I lied. A little kernel of guilt, I guess.

"Well, hell, men, let's go!" Henry started to step out in front of a rider on a roan quarter horse.

I grabbed him again.

"I want food," Paul said.

"Me too," I said.

"Well, you two go on, then. You know where I'll be." He managed to cross the street without getting run over and then disappeared between the swinging doors.

"Miz Henderson sets a fine table at the hotel," I told Paul.

He nodded but frowned. I had a pretty good idea what his gut instinct was telling him about Henry just then.

If the little colored girl serving in the hotel dining room remembered me from the night before, she kept it to herself. She darted between tables like a dragonfly. Paul and I were barely seated before she set water glasses in front of us and was gone again. I explained to Paul how things worked.

We had pork potpie, no doubt made from left-overs of roast, and pickled beet salad with hard-boiled egg. I unfurled the paper after I'd got my stomach to stop growling. It was a Burlington rag filled mostly with who visited who and what was to be done about electrifying the lights along the main street. I wished I'd hung on to the weekly I'd read the day before.

"We're not far from Denver," I told Paul. "They'll have a decent newspaper."

It's hard not to act like you know it all when you do.

The local paper did carry baseball scores. Both St. Louis teams had reversed their fortunes of the day prior—the Cardinals beat the Pirates and the Browns were trounced by Detroit. Paul was happy—he liked the Cards.

I remembered to tell him I'd read about the two towns in Nevada competing for the championship fight on the Fourth of July.

He thought for a minute. "Reno, if they're smart. It's got better railroad connections. Bring more folks in from all over."

He'd never seen a map, and he still knew the country better than I did. My pride lost a lot of its shine.

"You think people are gonna travel any distance just to see a fight?"

He looked surprised. "Don't you remember read-ing about that man in Wichita? The white man beaten to death, just because he said he thought Jack Johnson would win? This is hardly just a fight. There'll be some who go just to see what happens after."

"Oh, now, I know Henry said some idiotic things and there's some others too, but most don't take it serious about provin' anything, do they?"

Paul shook his head like he was disappointed in me. "Ever hear of the Civil War?"

I guessed he had a point. There were still some back home unhappy about how that turned out.

After we'd finished eating, I said, "Want to go join Henry for a beer?"

"Not yet," he answered. "If we're staying over, I'd like to walk around, see the town a little."

We passed by and nodded again to the Old Men of the Benches. I told Paul about the finery in the window of the dressmaker's shop and the tooling on the saddles in the cobbler's window. We came to a confectionery, went in for ice cream cones, and walked down the sidewalk trying to stay ahead of the drips. Paul told me that putting ice cream into cones instead of dishes had started at the St. Louis World's Fair. That the ice cream man ran out of cups and started using waffles from another stand. I was pretty sure I already knew that.

At the west end of the main drag was a huge elm tree with a horse trough, hitching post, and iron bench underneath. We took advantage of the shade.

I picked up little sticks and broke them into lengths I tossed into the water.

"So how's it going?" I asked Paul.

"Well, last night was a little rough. I know Henry's turned over a new leaf and all, but I don't quite trust that leaf not to fall. I half expected him to sneak off and leave, just to scare me."

"Yeah, I know. I wouldn't have left you, if I'd known it would be overnight. But, hell, what else was there? Send Henry off and depend on him to come back with help?"

Paul gave a chuckle so dark I felt better about my mistrustful ways.

"But that's not what I meant. I mean the trip so far. Is it turning out how you expected?"

He shrugged. "I didn't expect to be robbed our first night out—that's for sure."

"Of course not. But you know what I mean, don't you?"

He sat a long while. "I don't know, John. I guess. Part of me hoped we'd drive into some town along the way that had a big banner at the city limits reading *Welcome, Paul Bricken! Make your home here!* He chuckled. "You'd have told me if one did, wouldn't you?"

I bumped elbows with him.

He went on. "So far, people seem to be about the same everywhere we go. I can't say I expected that."

We had, without a doubt, come across a wide range of personalities, but I thought I understood what he meant. The people who helped us, held a gun on us, slammed the door in our faces, gave us a place to sleep, or couldn't meet our eye—we'd been just as likely to run into any one of them no matter where we were.

"So what do you think?" I asked. "Are we just fooling ourselves? Is every place in the country no different than Wakenda?"

"Most are bigger."

We both laughed. We sat for a moment, lost in our own thoughts.

"Better parents," he finally said.

"Hmm?"

"I don't know about you, but the parents on the road have been a lot better to me than the ones with my last name at home."

"I don't understand."

He ticked them off. "The Heversons. The Williamsons. Sheriff George."

"Those were just nice folks we came across!"

"You think so?" He tilted his head back and smiled into the sunshine. "You think if we'd been three forty-year-old men from the next town over, all those people would've done what they did?"

He had me there. I tried to picture how we came across to the people we met. Wet behind the ears, likely. My face started getting warm, and I changed the subject. "So you didn't have any trouble with Henry last night?"

"Trouble? No . . ."

"But what?"

Paul frowned, like he was weighing something in his mind. "We talked a lot."

"We always talk a lot."

"Yes." Paul went on frowning. "Henry is trying really hard, but he's struggling."

"What do you mean? Struggling how?"

"Trying . . . trying to sort out what he knows from what he thinks he knows." He didn't explain, and it became obvious that Paul was struggling with something too. Either he didn't understand or didn't want to make Henry sound foolish, or they'd made some kind of agreement not to talk about it to me. His expression didn't say.

"Well, hell's bells, aren't we all?" I finally offered.

We both gave out nervous chuckles.

I said, "Wanna go find him?"

"No. But we'd better."

We could hear him half a block away. Paul's mouth pulled into a tight line.

"Here we are," I said and held the door for Paul.

"Here they are," Henry yelped. "Two of the best fellers west of the Mississippi and maybe east too." His face was red underneath the brown of his sunburn. He was standing at the bar. When he took a step toward us, his heel hooked in the brass rail and he fell into my catch.

The men standing around chuckled, but not like they were amused.

One of them looked at me. "You the blind one?"

I propped Henry against the bar while Paul said, "Yes, sir."

The man still kept me in his sights. "Ah, then, you must be the smarty pants." It reminded me of the barman in Lexington our first day out—just before we were robbed. This was probably a good time to remember folks really were the same everywhere.

"I said he was smart, not a smart aleck," Henry complained. He reached for his mug and missed. "Gimme cigarette," he said to me.

"I don't smoke. And you don't either." I wanted to enjoy the idea that he had described me as smart, but it didn't seem like much to celebrate just then. "Come on. Maybe we should leave."

The men around Henry exchanged looks. "Oh. Smart *and* too good for the likes of us?"

"He ain't too good for nothin'," Henry bellowed.

"Thank you. I think."

"Are there tables?" Paul asked.

One of the men mouthed the words in a sarcastic way. That got a laugh from his buddies.

Paul asked, "What?"

The man repeated his hysterical performance.

I had an uneasy feeling about why they wanted us to stay.

"Yes, there are." I took his elbow to guide him

to the farthest corner. Over my shoulder, I said to Henry, "You joining us?"

"Sure."

I got Paul sitting and watched Henry knock over three chairs on his way over.

Paul laid a dollar on the table. "I'll take a beer."

"Me too! Barkeep! Three more for the bestest fellers a feller could—" Henry's train of thought ran off the track.

Over Henry's head, I held up two fingers to the man filling mugs.

He nodded.

"What? *What?*" Henry looked genuinely astonished when only two beers arrived. "Am I invisible? Isn't anybody in the forest and can't hear me when I fall?"

"Don't you think you've had enough?" Paul said.

Henry was flabbergasted. "Enough? *Enough?* Why, I've spent two and a half weeks swallowin' the biggest part of Kansas! I damn near died, and I've got well, and I'm goddamned thirsty is what I am. No, sir, I do not think I have had enough." He stood up, balanced for a second, then jumped up onto his chair and waved his arms over his head. "Barkeep! I say to you—" He included the rest of the room in a sweeping gesture. "To all of you: I! Have! Not! Had! Enough!" And he lost his balance and went crashing through the table next to ours, where two men were playing cards.

I jumped to my feet to pull him up out of the

splintered wood. I sputtered apologies as fast as I could to the men who were now on their feet too.

Henry had a little cut in the middle of his right eyebrow but looked unscratched otherwise.

I said, "Paul?"

He drained his beer in one swallow, stood up, and tripped over a table leg that hadn't been there when he sat down.

I heard, "I'll take him," and wheeled around to see Sheriff George. He had his hands on his hips and did not appear nearly as amused as the audience behind him.

"Geor— Sheriff Windom!" I said. "Look, I'm sorry. We'll pay for it. He can pay, I mean. It's just . . ."

The big man picked Henry up and threw him across one shoulder like a sack of corn. I remembered Henry puking down Jack Williamson's back and hoped he would not repeat that performance.

"Aw, well. He was going to sleep in the jail tonight anyway."

I picked up my mug and drained it.

When he saw me start to follow, the sheriff said, "You two haven't done anything. Stay here awhile, if you want. Enjoy Colorado. Come see me when you're ready to bed down."

I told Paul I'd be right back and went up to the man behind the bar. "Whatever those two were drinking." I nodded to the card players, who'd sat down at a table that was still in one piece. "And how much does . . . he owe you for the table?"

He set two mugs on the bar and waved me away. "Your friend who cannot hold his liquor worth a damn left more than enough to cover that and two more tables besides. He needs somebody sober to go around with him and carry his money."

I nodded and thanked him.

I didn't particularly want more to drink after seeing the spectacle of Henry, and I guess Paul didn't either. But nobody told us to leave, so we sat the rest of the afternoon and talked like we would around a campfire. Nothing much to remember, just friendly talk, keeping company. When the subject turned to family, though, it did remind me I'd intended to send my sister a postcard.

"Well, let's get to the drugstore before they close," Paul said.

We waved our thanks to the barman and headed out.

I blinked against the sun while my eyes adjusted. Paul walked on ahead.

I found a postcard with a photograph of the Rocky Mountains on it and gave the man two pennies for it and a stamp. I licked the back of Benjamin Franklin's head and stuck it in the corner. Paul asked the man if he sold gasoline and bought two gallons in cans he could return for a deposit.

We found the benches out front empty—a sure sign suppertime was close.

I sat down with a pencil I'd borrowed and thought hard. "What would you say if it was your sister, Paul?"

"Hello, Elizabeth."

I waited for the joke.

"Sorry. Long story. What do you want your sister to know?"

"Hmm." I thought some more, then wrote:

Catherine,

We haven't seen mountains yet, but we're close. I'm safe and I miss you.

Love,

John

I read it to Paul, and after·he nodded approval, I put the address on and went to return the pencil.

"I'll take that for you," the man told me. "Postmaster too." My load lightened a little when I handed over the card.

We stopped by the Model T outside the jail and strained gasoline into the tank. We walked the empty cans back to the drugstore and went to the hotel for our fill of ham steaks and potatoes and gravy. They must have made too much beet salad at noon, because we had that again too. My pants felt tight when we left, and I was glad. We might not see home cooking again before Denver, at least two days away.

We knocked at the sheriff's quarters, and I hoped it would be him who answered. No such luck. Wild-Eyed Alma threw open the door, looked from me to

Paul, shrieked, and slammed the door.

Paul jumped a little. "What was *that*?"

"Sheriff's wife." How to explain? He'd never seen Selma Clark back home either. "She's . . . got some problems, I calculate."

"Mmm." He tilted his head. "She get a load of me?"

"Well, yes, but she doesn't—"

"Don't worry. I'm used to it." What a thing to be obliged to say.

The door opened again to the smiling face of Sheriff George. We heard squawking from another room as he stepped outside. "Don't mind the little woman. There's a devil in her tries to scream its way out." Such another thing to be obliged to say.

He unlocked the front door of the jail, and Henry's snoring sliced the evening air. "Well, at least he stopped singing," George said. He led us to the cell farthest from Henry's. "Doors are open. Pick whichever. I'd stay in this one. Or the hotel."

"It's okay," Paul said.

I added, "Somebody probably ought to keep an eye on him anyway."

"Uh-huh, well, there's a job I wouldn't want full-time." George nodded to me. "Just like last night, I'm locking the front door. Try to fight off the urge to shoot him when he wakes you up puking in the morning."

Of course that's just what he did. No food but the sheriff's bread out by the creek had made an empty cask for all that alcohol, and it wouldn't stay put past dawn. Paul and I gave up just as it was getting light. We put on our shoes and went to wait up front. I opened the one window there, and we put our noses up to the bars like bloodhounds.

George showed up a few minutes later. "Need some fresh air?" He stepped through the doorway and lost his smile. "Good Lord." He strode back to Henry's cell and unlocked the door. "Get that slop bucket out back. Now."

Paul and I made a break for the outdoors.

Henry looked three-quarters dead and praying for the rest when we poured him into the shotgun seat of the car and loaded everything up again. We thanked George over and again for coming to our rescue and giving us a bunk. I didn't know what to say about Henry.

When we were in the car and ready to go, the sheriff stepped to the driver's side and leaned on the frame. "Remember what I told you about keeping your eyes open."

We all nodded.

I said, "That's a lesson we'll not soon forget, Geor— sir."

He unbuttoned his shirt pocket and came out with a wad of bills. "Mr. Barleywine here already did. I took this off him last night after I dumped him on the cot. There's over three hundred and fifty dollars there. Fellas get knocked in the head for a whole lot less than that."

I took the money and turned to Henry. "You hear that?"

He moaned in answer.

I stuck the money in my own shirt pocket and told George, "Thank you," with as much heft as I could put into two words.

We headed west parallel to Ed's railroad line on a path that was more ruts than road. Henry bawled like a sick calf every time he was jostled, about every five seconds or so. No more than a mile out, an ungodly stink made my eyes water, and Henry lurched his head over the auto's side and heaved. I glanced back at Paul and met an ornery little grin I'd never seen.

"Paul?" I asked.

"Beet salad. With eggs."

I waited until Henry was sitting, head back, announcing his upcoming demise. Then I let fly. We took turns punishing him until the dry heaves were too painful to hear.

I stopped in the middle of the road—we weren't exactly blocking traffic—and said, "Henry? You really got our backs up yesterday."

He nodded without opening his eyes.

"I mean it. You almost started a fight, you tore up a table—"

"You lost all your money," Paul said.

Henry shot straight up and started patting his pockets. "Oh no, what the—?"

"You didn't even hear the sheriff this morning, did

you? He took it off you last night to teach you a lesson."

"Where is it?" a feeble Henry asked.

I patted my pocket.

He held out his hand.

"I don't think so. Not yet." I put the car in gear and drove on.

More than a week earlier, I had found myself comparing each town we passed through with either Wakenda, Lexington, or Kansas City—small, medium, or large. Eight or ten miles down the road, we came to a little Wakenda kind of town called Bethune.

I said, "Who wants breakfast?"

Paul said, "I do!"

Henry moaned.

I found a general store and looked inside to see that it had a counter with stools. I went back to the Ford and told the others.

Henry just moaned.

Paul and I went inside and sat down.

A fat granny with a bad leg hobbled plates back and forth between the counter and a cookstove in back.

Without asking, she poured us each a cup of coffee. A minute later, she came back, wiping her hands on her apron. "Uh-huh?"

I looked at the two men shoveling in lumberjack helpings of eggs, fried potatoes, and what appeared to be a whole pig dismantled and cooked. "That," I said, nodding.

Paul looked confused. "Same for me."

"Pig's eye sausage and bullfrog pie?"

He blanched.

She laughed. "Just funnin' you, just funnin' you."

Paul smiled as she walked away.

When she was out of earshot, I asked, "Doesn't that bother you?"

"What?" He sipped coffee and felt for the saucer.

"Teasing like that?"

"Good-natured teasing or a woman screaming when I come to the door. Which would you rather have?"

Neither. I scalded my throat with coffee instead of saying it.

We had just dug into platters of homemade bliss when I remembered Henry outside. "Um, ma'am?" I got her attention. "Could you make a hamburger sandwich with cheese that we could take with us?"

Her eyes swept our plates, still mostly full.

"We've got a friend out in our car feelin' poorly. We ought to feed him something."

She came from behind the counter and pulled back a curtain at the front window. Then she hobbled back and made the motion of tipping back a bottle and raised her eyebrows.

I nodded.

She sighed. "Come across Kansas, didn't you?"

I was astonished. "How did you know?"

She laughed her head off and went to put a hamburger patty in a skillet on the stove.

When it was ready, we took it out to Henry and I told him to take it slow.

He seemed grateful for the food and nodded.

We were well out of town and the sandwich was gone before he found his grouse. "It's your fault." He threw a look my way.

"How's that?"

He jammed himself down farther in the seat. "If you hadn't gone off and left us the night before and had your own hullabaloo, I wouldn't'a been so god-awful anxious to—"

Paul let fly with a rip so foul I nearly lost my own breakfast. He must have been saving up. Henry was back over the side, offering his sandwich to the hang-over gods of Colorado, and we never did hear any more about whose fault it was.

Henry humbled, and Paul sickening him with farts: a most curious round of musical chairs.

My pants were even tighter after dinner in a little town called Flagler, and I started thinking maybe I didn't need to be storing up. If this kept up, I was going to have to buy new britches.

Henry paid for dinner out of my pocket and over his protests. He was feeling better and hadn't started in on us again, but I still wasn't ready to hand over the stash of bills. It wasn't his any more than mine anyway, was what I told myself.

There didn't seem to be a lot to do in Flagler unless

you were hungry, so we pushed on. The countryside was starting to rise a little, but not so much you'd notice until you turned around and looked at where you'd been. Other than that was desert. Sandy dirt, scrub brush that wouldn't look any different if it caught fire and was doused later.

I'd read about tumbleweeds in dime novels back home, and I'd seen fake ones in cowboy picture shows at the nickelodeon in Carrollton, but here they were real. We saw some cactuses. Great big green things standing with their arms up in surrender and others that looked like spiny green Ping-Pong paddles tied together in clumps.

There was nothing else that would pass for food in a pinch. And no water at all. I had almost suggested buying an extra canteen when we filled ours back in Flagler but had held Nelly's tongue. It'd be a hell of a note to win that contest by dying of thirst.

If not for the rail line, it would have been downright spooky. Even so, the whole afternoon of June 23 passed without a single train, and I started to pray we wouldn't break down. *Not here, God, please.* Sometimes the ruts we followed were so faint I thought I might be imagining them, but those train tracks spoke of civilization. People had been here. We weren't the first and wouldn't be the last.

Along about four o'clock, we had a flat tire.

"What the hell did you hit out here?" Henry said.

He had me there.

It was the right rear, the only one that hadn't been changed since we started out. That proved to be the problem—the rubber was worn all the way through to the tube.

Paul got out too, and Henry helped me get the jack under the back end.

I was busy with the valve stem and the tire tool when Henry went to the toolbox and announced, "Shit."

"What?" I was in a crouch and didn't look up.

"It's going to be our last outer casing," Paul answered.

Henry bolted upright. "How'd you know that was what I was gonna say?"

Paul just smiled.

"What are we gonna do?" Henry said.

I wrestled the casing off the inner tube and gave that a spin. It seemed to be okay. "Well, lucky for us, one casing is all we need."

"But we're nowhere near Denver! What if we have another flat? Why didn't you buy more in Topeka?"

I stood up. "Why didn't you?"

"It wasn't my job!" He couldn't have looked more astonished if he'd just found out he was pregnant. With twins.

"It's not mine either. You told me so yourself."

"Well, it still was when we was in Topeka!"

I couldn't hold off laughing.

Henry's face got redder. "What?" he demanded.

"If you don't know, I can't explain."

"Huh?"

Paul said, "He's about to die trying not to say, 'I told you so.'"

"But—" Henry's face went through contortions until he finally walked off some distance and sat down with his back to us.

After I wrestled the tire cover on and took the Ford off the jack, I went and sat beside him. "We'll be okay," I told him. "Something's always come along when we needed it so far, hasn't it?"

He was looking straight ahead at the edge of the world. "We're a long way from home, John."

"Well, yeah, but that was kinda the point, wasn't it?"

"Yeah, but—" His face held the light of a bottom-less well. "It made me mad when you was bossin' us around, but I never was scared of nothin' then."

I figured that was his way of saying he was scared now. Henry. Scared. Go figure. "We'll be okay," I told him. "We can all be in charge of lookin' out for one another, without anybody bossin' anybody."

"I guess so," he said, but his voice held all the optimism of a man headed for the gallows.

The sun was low enough in the sky to make driving west an unhappy job when I hit the brakes and said, "Mother of God."

"What?" Henry said, then he followed my line of sight. "Holy shit."

From the backseat came, "Hey! Mother of God holy shit *what*?"

I was too much in awe to laugh.

"Mountains, Paul. Honest-to-God mountains."

"With snow on top," Henry added.

"No kidding. How far?"

"No idea," I told him. "No idea. But it's— My God, it's the likes of which I've never seen before— that's for sure. You've seen postcards—"

"No. No, I haven't. But I know what a god-damned mountain is."

I'd heard Paul say *shit* a few times but that was just about it for swearing.

I turned to see his face knotted as tight as a fist. "What's the matter, Paul?"

His fingers were rubbing that nervous way I hadn't seen since Topeka.

I waited.

"Sometimes it's hard, okay?" More finger rubbing. Then the floodgates busted, and words poured out. "Sometimes it's just hard. I can hear it in your voices. This is special. Goddamn it to hell, this is something I want to be able to *see*."

I looked over at Henry. He stared straight ahead. My eyes wandered forward too, and we got lost in the view again, just like that. The hills back home were nothing like this. We were looking at something right out of a picture book.

Henry started talking like he was in a daze. "It goes all the way across. The top is like a jagged line, all the way north that you can see and as far south as you can see. They're gonna get taller and taller as we drive toward them, and there's no way to tell from here how tall that's gonna be."

I joined in. "I can count . . . ten, twelve . . . I don't know . . . a dozen and a half different peaks, not all the same height but all in the same family. Not all in a straight row, some in front of the others and closer to us."

"Only the tallest few have snow," Henry said.

"From this distance, they look almost blue. And one of them has poked a hole clean through a little cloud. Looks like it's wearing it for a hat."

We were quiet till Paul said, "Purple mountain majesties."

"Uh-huh," I said. "That's it exactly. Just exactly."

We sat in silence for a few more minutes until I could focus on the road in front of us and drive on.

The town of Deer Trail blended in so well with the backdrop of the mountains in the distance that we were nearly upon it before we saw it. It looked to be about the size of Lexington. We motored into town and asked the first person we came across if there was a Ford dealer in town. He looked at us like each of us had three heads and none of them spoke English.

Paul piped up from the back. "What about a smith or a bicycle shop?"

The man studied Paul's face and then pulled back like he had almost stepped in something. He motioned with one hand—up a ways and over a little—and I explained this to Paul. I didn't bother to thank the man before we went on.

We found the bicycle shop and showed the mechanic our worn-out tire casing.

He said, "Well, now, that there's ready for the scrap heap. But I can sell you some patches and rubber cement that might could help if you have any more trouble before Denver."

Paul paid for three patches.

Henry asked for two more. He searched all his pockets and was starting to panic before he remembered I had his money. "Gimme a dollar, John, would ya?"

I pulled the whole wad of bills and handed it over.

He shook his head. "Naw, go on and hang on to it for me."

We eyeballed each other, and I nodded.

That night, we found a place that was half cafe, half tavern, and half music hall. Jake's Roadhouse, it was called, and it was the first time since Topeka we'd seen someplace with almost as many cars as horses parked outside.

Inside, the place jumped. Musicians played fiddle, bass, guitar, and banjo, and you could almost hear them over the foot stomping and hollering going on. Women wove their way through the tables carrying trays of plates and glasses way up over their heads, and most of them looked like they'd been interrupted while they were getting dressed. Three couples twirled and stepped and nearly crashed into the guitar player on the little space set aside for dancing. Everybody looked like they'd gotten a large head start on us. It looked like a fun place.

"Get you boys a beer?" our waitress asked.

I said, "Sure."

Paul said, "Yes, please."

And Henry said, "Milk for me."

She gave him a hard look and grinned. "Sure you don't need a little hair of the dog? Shot of whiskey with a raw egg?"

I was afraid Henry was going to give her his dinner as an answer, but he swallowed and said, "No, ma'am. Just milk."

She came back with mugs in a couple minutes and shouted over the music, asking if we were eatin' or if we had eaten—hard to tell which.

Henry and I squinted at each other.

"Want some ribs?" she hollered.

We all nodded to that.

I looked around some more while we waited. There was a knot of men crouching close to the floor over in one corner, and every once in a while, one would whoop or yell something foul you could hear even over the music. I finally could see through the crowd that they were rolling dice. I noticed three of them were wearing sidearms, and I did a hasty survey around the place looking for holsters. There were lots of them, and those were just on the men who weren't hiding them behind tables. I got Henry's attention and pantomimed a pistol, then jerked my head toward the bigger part of the crowd. He frowned, looked around, then met my eyes with a worried look that I was pretty sure mirrored my own.

I was thinking maybe Jake's was fun more like a picture show is fun. You might want to watch, but you don't necessarily want to be in it. I couldn't imagine this many guns and that much alcohol—and gambling, to boot—without somebody taking a bullet before the night was over. It just seemed unlikely when you added things up.

Then the woman who'd brought us our mugs walked by, and a man at the next table pinched her bottom. She turned around and slapped him, and he stood up and punched her in the face. She went down like a sack of potatoes.

Henry and I both started up out of our chairs, but a quick look around told us nobody else had taken notice. Like it was a regular thing. And before the man sat back down, we saw the Colt revolver strapped to his thigh. Henry and I met eyes again and sank back down in our chairs.

His escapade the day before had reminded us how quick a good time could head south, and it looked like the south covered a whole lot more territory here. And I know I was remembering we didn't have a friendly sheriff to come rescue us this time.

A different woman brought our food. We ate,

then paid and left. Paul didn't ask why we were in such a hurry. Maybe he didn't like the sound of the place.

From the car out front, we could still hear the ruckus. It took on an even worse feel apart from it. The thought came to me it might be some kind of hell in there. Like maybe all of it went on around the clock day after day, month after month, until it wasn't even fun anymore and everyone wanted to leave but couldn't. Maybe we could come back anytime to see the same people trying just as hard to have a good time, when really the whole thing was ugly and sour.

Paul interrupted my thoughts. "This is just a suggestion, mind you, but what do you think about camping out tonight? I could do with some quiet." It was almost like he'd seen what I was thinking.

We headed west out of town about a mile and decided anywhere was the same as another. There was nothing around except about a million stars and those mountains in the distance, their snowcaps showing pale blue in the moonlight. Everything to see was above us.

We built a fire out of a little wood we'd picked up on our way out of town and sat around it. A reflection of the flame flickered in Paul's pale eyes.

"Is it just me," I started, "or was that just about the worst good-time place there could be?"

Henry blew out a breath. "I thought it was just my hangover talking till you pointed out all the guns and that guy took out a couple of that woman's teeth."

"*What*?" Paul sat up straight. We had to explain what had happened, including why we hadn't done anything about it. Doing nothing still seemed like the right decision to have made at the time, but that didn't make it feel good.

"All I knew was it felt a little . . . desperate," Paul said.

My turn. "Yeah. That was part of it too. Like everybody was trying too hard." I glanced at his eyes and shivered. "I don't know how to explain the feeling I got when we left except if we went back right now, I don't know I'd be all that surprised if the place wasn't even there." It was pretty much the opposite of my earlier thought, but either way seemed possible.

"You think we had supper with ghosts?" Henry sniffed. "The food was real. Real good too."

"I think I know what you mean," Paul said. "Kind of like it might have appeared, all of a cloth, just for tonight?"

"Yeah," I told him. "Something like that."

We all sat with our own thoughts until Paul spoke up some minutes later. "Have you ever thought about what you would do if you could drop yourself into another place or another time? Where you'd go?"

I'd never given a second to such a fancy notion. But wide-open desert does provide a lot of room for the imagination to grow.

In no time, I was imagining myself some kind of Revolutionary hero like Paul Revere or riding a raft down the Mississippi with Mark Twain when he was a boy.

"Where would you go, Paul?" Henry asked.

I hadn't gotten around to wondering about either of them.

"I'd go back to the day I was born and trade places with Elizabeth." Paul's voice was flat.

"Who?" Henry asked.

Paul sat so long I thought he'd made up his mind not to answer, and I wondered why he'd brought it up in the first place. But then he shook his head. "My twin sister."

"You got a twin?" Henry sounded as surprised as I was.

"*Had* a twin." Paul started rubbing his fingers, but slow—more preoccupied than nervous. "'Perfect little angel.' That's what my mother always says. 'Perfect.'"

I wanted to know but didn't want to ask.

Henry obliged. "What happened to her?"

"She was born dead. I came out first, and she came out with my cord wrapped around her neck. She never took a breath."

A piece of wood in the fire cracked so loud we all jumped.

My heart was beating like an Indian drum when Henry said, "It wasn't your fault."

Paul snorted. "I've told myself that for nineteen years. But if I could go back, anywhere and anytime? It would be the blind baby who died."

We sat in the quiet until Henry spoke. "I'd go back before I was born too."

Paul said, "You wish you'd never been born? Aren't we a pair?"

"No," Henry said. His face was fierce. "Not that. But I'd be born right. Not hurt my mother like I did. Grow up with her alive and maybe my pa wouldn't'a . . ."

"It wasn't your fault either," Paul said.

The words hung in the air like a song just finished.

I had imagined myself larger than life, some kind of special, while Paul and Henry just imagined themselves being wanted.

All of a sudden, ordinary seemed a lot better than it had before.

CHAPTER NINE

WE HEADED TOWARD THE MOUNTAINS straightaway the next morning and felt the Model T strain for the first time as the hills got a little steeper, like practice for what was ahead. The view changed every foot we moved, the peaks getting taller by the second, and there was a certain charge in the air. Something about making it to Denver felt big. I for sure didn't know anyone who'd been there.

I was in the backseat, studying the map. "Looks like a town called Byers coming up. Maybe we can look for dinner there."

"All we do is look for food and someplace to sleep." Henry had been in a bad mood all morning—got up on the wrong side of the bedroll, I guess.

"Mountains!" Paul bellowed.

Henry slammed on the brake. Good thing he did, because I jumped and the map flew out of my hands and fluttered out behind us. I scrambled over the back door.

Henry laid into Paul. "What the hell was that for?"

Paul was wearing a shit-eating grin when I climbed back in. "Just thought I'd describe the countryside."

"Well, do it without scaring the hell out of the driver, would ya?"

Paul hooted. "What? Afraid you'll steer over into traffic?"

We hadn't met anyone, horse or automobile, outside any town since Burlington.

And I hadn't seen the two of them squabble since before Henry was laid up sick in Junction City. It was comforting in a way. Like stepping out of a new pair of shoes that pinch and into the pair you've worn for a year.

They went on like kid brothers until I determined to drown them out. "Oh, give me a home, where the buffalo roam . . ." It was hollering more than singing and felt twice as good.

Henry turned around and shouted something I couldn't hear over my own "Where the deer and the antelope play . . ."

"I've got your goddamn discouraging word," he said when I took a breath.

It struck me so funny I choked.

Paul joined in laughing.

When we'd caught our air, Paul said, "Henry?"

"What?"

"It is my understanding that the skies are not cloudy *all day*!"

And we set off laughing again.

Henry looked disgusted and put the car back in gear.

In Byers, Henry pouted all through a meat loaf plate while Paul carried on like it was the happiest day of his life. It was almost like the talk around the fire the night before had bound Henry up and set Paul free.

I guess there's not much difference between having nothing and having nothing to lose, except how you look at it. And that view is always subject to change.

After dinner, as bad as I wanted to see Denver, I wasn't ready to jump back into the Ford so soon.

I guess Paul wasn't either. When we stepped outside the May Cafe, he tilted his head back and sniffed the air. Then he licked a pointer finger and held it up like he was checking the wind.

"What?" Henry repeated his last word from an hour earlier.

"Do I detect, somewhere in the area, beer?" Paul tilted his head to the side, considering.

"Kinda early, ain't it?" That was rich, coming from Henry.

Paul pretended to take a watch out of his pocket and study it. "Nope. John? Join me in a spot of barley tea?"

"Sure." I took his elbow and walked down the street and across to a place named Bar.

It was just opening up for the day, and we had the place to ourselves, along with the little man behind the counter. He looked like he was made from one long tendon, more wire than muscle. Cannibals would have passed him up as too tough. He wore a ring of slate-colored hair around a shiny dome and looked like he'd traded beaks with a hawk. "Who are you?" he said.

Byers was a Wakenda-sized town, and I guess he didn't see many strangers.

"Tom, Dick, and Harry," Paul answered, still wearing the grin he'd woken up with.

"Jesus, Joseph, and"—Henry gave Paul a little shove—"Mary."

Oh, shit. I hoped we hadn't happened upon a Bible-thumper.

"Huh. Looks to me like Asshole, Butthole, and Twat."

My shoulders relaxed. Funny thing, being happy to be called Twat. Butthole. Or whichever one I was.

We carried mugs to a table, and when he was through setting up supplies for the day, he brought a cup of coffee over and sat down with us.

"So who wants to tell their life story first?" His features were so sharp, you'd never suspect he was a friendly sort.

None of us answered straightaway.

"How about you?"

When Paul didn't answer, the man elbowed him.

"Oh. I'm blind."

The man squinted. "You deaf too?"

"No, sir, I'm not. But you have to say my name for me to know you're talking to me."

"Ah." The man looked like he was waiting. "Well? You with the movie-picture looks. What's your name?"

I kicked Paul under the table. "He's talking to you."

Paul's ears turned red.

"He don't know he's pretty," Henry explained.

"He thinks he looks like a buffalo," I said.

"He don't know what a buffalo looks like either," Henry argued.

The man's face turned back and forth like he was watching a game of catch. Then he said, "Enough of that. How about your story all together? You got to have one."

So we told him. Between us, we told it all to this stranger, who got up and refilled our mugs whenever they were empty.

Getting wrapped up in telling about yourself will help you forget you've got a case of grumpiness, I guess, or at least that's how it seemed in Henry's case. It's safe to say, too, we were all glad to have someone to talk to other than one another.

When we'd got caught up to the present, Paul asked the man if he'd heard any recent word of the big fight coming up.

He stared at his coffee cup before answering. "Well, it's a subject I've tried my best to keep out of here. Pouring alcohol into a hothead is about like throwing gasoline on a fire, you know. And there don't seem to be any cool heads that can talk on the subject."

"I'm just curious," Paul told him. "I'm not sure we've kept up with all the news."

The man stared at the cup in front of him. "I know there's some preacher out east got up a petition to stop the fight on the grounds it ain't Christian."

Paul said, "Because they're just beating on each other, instead of nailing somebody to a piece of wood?"

The man chuckled deep in his throat. "You got a point there. Then there's some—the governor of California one of them—saying Johnson's planning to throw the fight."

Henry spoke up. "We heard that too. Because somebody's bound to kill him if he wins."

"But if he were afraid of that, why would he sign on in the first place?" Paul said.

The man looked over his shoulder toward the door. "No, like most things in this world, it comes down to filthy lucre. Money. This Governor Gillett claims the moving-picture people out there explained the whole deal to him. Johnson and Jeffries both stand to make a whole hell of a lot more money on the movie of the fight if Jeffries wins."

What a thought. All this talk and the possibility, when all was said and done, it wouldn't amount to any more than what outcome would better line the pockets of two men already rich.

"What do you think, Mr. I-don't-know-your-name?" Paul slurred a little.

"I think . . . I believe . . . it might rain tomorrow.

You boys might want to get on to Denver before it does." He smiled before he stood up and took his coffee cup back behind the bar.

We paid up and moved on.

That afternoon, we got close enough to Denver that the foothills of the mountains, nothing more than overgrown bluffs, blocked the view of the range behind them. I tried to explain to Paul how strange it was, having the giants disappear behind the pretenders. I drove up steeper and steeper hills all the time, and I kept thinking each one we crested would make the mountains reappear, but they didn't.

The Ford was straining and grunting a little harder with each height, slowing to a crawl before rounding the top and picking up speed on the down-hill side. Then came a hill where our crawl ground to a halt, and we stalled two-thirds of the way up. The motor sputtered into silence.

"Now what?" I said.

Paul spoke up, still a little thick in the tongue. "Can you back down and take a run at it?"

"I dunno, Paul. I was goin' pretty much flat out before we started up this time."

"We could get out and push." Henry sounded like a man on the way to his own hanging.

It was plenty hot by that time of day.

"Maybe." I looked behind us. "Or we could try to and get run over instead."

"No way. Don't chance it," Paul said. "No way around it, I suppose. North of here? South?"

I looked around. "Not in this state or the next, from the looks of things." I realized each possibility we said no to was bringing us closer to ending the trip right here. Right on the wrong side of Denver.

"Lemme think." Paul was rubbing his nose like a genie might come out. A man driving a team came up behind and passed us with a curious look but no offer of help. Paul snapped his fingers. "Remember in the manual, John? The ratios of the gears?"

"Well, I remember reading the manual," I said.

"The gear ratio for reverse is lower than that of any of the forward gears. The auto has more pull going backward than it has even in first gear going forward."

Even half drunk, he was smarter than me.

"It's worth a try," he said. "Go back down and try backing up the hill."

I looked at Henry, and he shrugged.

It was easy enough getting down the hill, but turning the auto around was a different proposition. Forward and back, forward and back—it was the first time I'd done it, and it did not come as what you might call second nature. Finally I was situated.

"Ready?" I turned and draped my right arm over the back of the seat. "Get to one side, Paul."

He scooted over.

I opened the throttle and swerved back and forth across the road a few times before I got the hang of steering backward as we started up. Lucky for us, no one was coming in the opposite direction.

We were at the halfway mark before the car started slowing down.

"Give it more gas," Paul called.

"It's wide open," I yelled back.

The Ford started whining a mechanical version of "I don't want to," but it kept going. A little slower, a little farther, slower, slower . . . We passed the point where we'd stalled before, and Henry muttered something.

The engine was working so hard I found myself counting the cylinders as they fired.

Henry heard me, then Paul heard him, and we were all chanting, "One-two-three-four," like a good luck charm.

Then one cylinder missed, and my heart caught along with it.

"*One-two-three-four*," we begged.

And it worked. We popped over the crest of the hill and started cheering even as I hurried to throttle down and brake, fighting gravity that was all too willing now to keep us moving.

Having had the recent practice, I only took half a year to get the Ford turned around this time, and we zipped on, scanning the road ahead. It looked like we'd just climbed the highest of the hills outside Denver. In fact, I could just make out some signs of civilization.

At the bottom, I stopped and killed the motor.

"Now what?" Paul said.

"Pee." I stepped to the side of the road and un-buttoned.

Henry climbed out, and we peed in harmony.

When we buttoned up and turned back to the Model T, Paul was climbing out of the back.

"Now you're going? When we're ready to move on?" Henry said. Another round of musical chairs. This time, the Nagging Nelly verse.

"I wanna drive."

Henry and I laughed, and I saw Paul bristle.

"Paul, you don't mean—"

"Hell I don't," he answered me. His chin came up. "It's my car, isn't it? We're not exactly overrun with traffic, are we? No big ditches to run off into? Why the hell not?"

Neither Henry nor I read anything useful on the other's face. We shrugged at the same time.

"Who's the teacher?" I asked.

Paul was sitting in the driver's seat, feeling the locations of levers and pedals.

"You," Henry said.

I gave him a look.

"No, really. You read the manual with him. You know what to call everything so he'll understand." He had a point.

"All right, but you crank."

When the motor sparked, the Ford crept forward a couple inches, like it sometimes did, and the look

254

on Henry's face indicated it was a good thing he'd just peed. He dove and did a barrel roll out of the way.

Paul went on adjusting and exploring the controls, unaware.

Henry stood up and brushed himself off, then hopped in back.

He was out twice again when Paul killed the engine trying to set out, but then we were flying along. At least that's how it felt—like we were going twice as fast as usual, even though I knew we were only at half throttle.

I kept up a running list of instructions. "Little left, not so much, right there, uh-huh, small hill coming, throttle open a little, left, straight, okay, right, throttle back. You're doing great."

Paul wore a smile as wide as if he owned the world.

I started to let my guard down a little. I'd say left or right, but once he got the hang of the hills, Paul would adjust the throttle and brake when he felt the tilt of the ground. We passed two autos coming our way and my blood pressure went up a little, but Paul held steady. We had one halfway tall hill left, and after that, we should see Denver.

The car strained enough going up that Paul opened up full throttle. We slowed some, but there was no threat we wouldn't make it. We came to the crest and—

"Slow down!"

We were over the top and picking up speed on the way down.

"Brake! Throttle! Brake!"

"Holy shit!" Henry screamed.

I glanced over to see Paul's grin about to split his face in two.

"No, Paul, no! Brake, damn it. Throttle down." I reached over and closed it myself, but I couldn't reach the brake. "Left! Left! *Left!*"

And then I was bracing myself, and there was a boom and the sound of metal scraping against metal. I hit the front panel hard enough to empty my lungs and make me think I would drown out in the open air. Bedrolls came flying over from the backseat, and I heard Henry's "Oof!" right after my own.

Paul had run dead straight into the first tree we'd come close enough to smell in over three hundred miles.

Henry got his breath back before I did. "What the *hell*?" he asked over and again. "What the *hell*, Paul?"

I was taking inventory. No bones broken, no blood, some places that smarted enough to turn black and blue by tomorrow.

Paul looked stunned. His face had hit the steering wheel, and blood dripped from his nose off his chin and onto his shirtfront. "What was it?" he said, barely above a whisper.

Henry leaned over into his ear. "Tree!" he screamed.

Paul didn't flinch. "Anybody hurt?"

"Well, I'm goddamn banged up—I'll tell you that!" Henry snorted.

"Not really," I told him. "You've got a bloody nose."

"So we didn't hit anyone else?" Paul asked. "And we're all okay?"

"Well, I wouldn't speak for our goddamn car," Henry yelped.

And Paul busted out laughing. Just like that. He reached in his pocket for a handkerchief and wiped blood off his face, ha-ha-ing like he'd just heard a corker. He winced a little when he blew his nose. Then I'll be goddamned if he didn't start laughing again.

"What is wrong with you?" Henry hollered.

Paul laughed louder. "Well, for one thing, I'm blind!"

Henry climbed out first and gritted his teeth as he twisted and stretched. I followed suit and found it painful too. We walked around to the front of the Ford together.

We each got a handhold and pushed the auto away from the trunk of the tree.

"Axle's broke," Henry pronounced. "Not just bent. Broke clean through."

"Wheels bent. Tires are history. Headlights too," I said.

He nodded. "Fenders might could be straightened out."

"Yeah," I said. "I don't think the radiator's busted. Wouldn't it be leaking water or steam or something?"

"Seems like." Henry looked up toward Paul, still sitting behind the steering wheel, chuckling. "Hey!

Mr. It's My Car! Come look at what you've done!"

"Right away. Soon as I can see."

"Goddamn it to hell, Paul, this is serious," I said. "We got some major damage here."

"Glad to meet you, Major Damage. General Mayhem here."

Henry stalked around to the driver's side and jerked Paul by his collar out onto the ground.

"Hey!" Paul sat up and brushed off his shirt. "What's that for?"

"What's that for?" Henry looked so close to boiling over I stepped closer in case I needed to grab him. "You just about killed us, you're sitting there laughing like it's a goddamned joke, and we lost our ride *is what that's for.*"

"But we weren't killed," Paul said. His voice was somber. "I'm sorry you were scared. Not seeing what's coming does protect me from that. As for the car . . ." He shrugged.

"What?" Henry demanded. "As for the car, what?"

"It's not a total loss. We'll get it fixed. We must be close to Denver, right?"

"Do you know how long that'll take?" Henry said.

Paul shrugged again. "You on a schedule?"

We walked nearly four miles to the Ford dealer, asking directions along the way. The man there listened to our story, then nodded and told us to wait as he started for a door in the back. I guess he thought again, because he came back and pocketed the key from the lock in his desk drawer. Henry and I exchanged a look.

The dealer came back with a man who was wiping his greasy hands on a rag.

"Where'd you leave it?"

We told him as best we could, and he calculated with his boss without using words. "Meet me around back," he said and disappeared.

He was firing up a big steam engine Holt tractor when we found him, and he motioned us to climb on.

We scrambled for handholds and places to brace our feet when he took off, and the breeze from moving almost made up for adding steam to an already ungodly hot day.

"Yeah, buddy." Roy, as his name turned out to be, whistled through his teeth when we got to the auto. He walked all around it and squinted up the hill. "Brake give out on you?" He was looking between the car and the road, like he was trying to picture it happening.

Paul answered. "No, sir."

Roy nodded and guessed, "Flat tire."

"No, sir." Paul again.

"Throttle stuck?" Roy frowned.

"Nope."

"Well, then, would you mind sayin' what did happen?"

Chin up and no apology in his voice, Paul said, "I was driving, sir. And I'm afraid I'd . . . been drinking."

Roy's mouth dropped open. "You were driving."

Paul nodded.

"And you—" A chuckle broke loose.

Pretty soon we were all laughing. If you could forget the part about how busted up the auto was and how we could have killed somebody, ourselves included, it was pretty damned funny.

Roy hooked on to both broken halves of the axle with a chain and lifted them to pull the Ford behind the tractor with only the back tires touching the ground. "You might as well sit there where it's comfortable. Same weight wherever you are."

So we rode back to the dealership in the Model T with our noses pointed toward the sun. Paul sat in the driver's seat with both hands on the steering wheel. Henry and I took to waving at everybody who gawked.

"Could be five days, could be ten." That was the dealership owner's assessment of the situation after he'd met with Roy out back. "Depends on how long it takes the parts to get here." The shrug of his shoulders said, *And I don't really care.*

I turned to leave.

"You got any sportin' women in this town?" Henry asked the man.

That stopped me.

The man rested his hairy arms on his desk and clasped his hands together.

They'd make a hell of a sledgehammer, I thought.

"Son, I'm a God-fearin' married man. You don't

want to be askin' me that."

"So am I, sir. So am I." Henry stood as straight as a broomstick. "Well, not married, no. But God-fearin', yes. In fact, I've been known to do a little preachin' in my day. I was thinkin', long as we're stuck here, I might use my time to turn some hearts toward God and maybe save some souls. My sister . . . was a harlot before she saw the light. It's kind of a callin' for me, sir."

I very nearly broke into applause.

Paul had turned his back, and I had no idea if he was amused or appalled.

The man bowed his head and closed his eyes. When he opened them, they burned with light. "Well, now, I been told there's women like that who live in that big brick house west edge of town. I wouldn't know, mind you."

Henry nodded, solemn as all get-out. "I'm sure I can find it, sir. And I thank you. God bless."

We were barely outside when he yelled, "Let's go get us some poontang," so loud my ear nearest him started to ring.

"Goddamn it, Henry. Keep it down, would you?"

"Hell, no!" He skipped ahead of Paul and me and turned to walk backward, facing us. "Ain't nothin' gonna keep it down right now!"

We were in front of a saloon. I grabbed Paul's arm and walked in, saying, "Let's go in here and talk about it."

Funny thing about alcohol. It can make a fellow get up a harebrained plan about traveling the country and be too proud to back down from it. It can make a blind man think he can drive. Enough of it will even make a fellow wet behind the ears think he's God's gift to the women of the world.

Henry said, "I know why you two're scared. You ain't never, have you?"

Paul just said, "Nope," like it was no big deal.

But I was wearing whiskey stilts and felt twice as big as life. "Hell, yes, I have. Plenty of times."

Henry loosed his wicked smile. "Well, then, you oughta have a reltney by now."

I was glad Paul asked so I didn't have to. "What's that?"

Henry's smile got even wider. "Why, that's a hard-on so big it stretches your skin out tight enough you can't close your eyes."

Walking three abreast across town, we banged shoulders so many times I started feeling bruised. It's a fine line, being drunk enough to do something stupid and still sober enough to walk there to do it.

A woman my mom's age opened the door, but I had sure never seen Mom painted up like that. The color of the woman's hair didn't look like one God had picked out either.

"Three dollars apiece," she said. "Ya got it? If ya don't, don't bother trackin' in on my good rug."

Henry reached into my shirt pocket and peeled a five and four ones off the roll. "Yes, ma'am, I do," he told her, then nodded to Paul and me. "My treat."

She opened the door wider, and we went in.

It did look like a good rug. All dark reds and blues and greens and so thick I felt each step sinking into it. I was looking all around at the brass light fixtures and polished wood, fancier than any house I'd ever seen, when the woman looked hard at Paul and said, "Wait here." She pulled back a ruby-colored velvet drape and disappeared into another room.

She came back with five girls trailing her like ducklings. They were all painted up like Mama, and none of them looked any too happy. I scanned down the line and, in the course of a glance, full-out lost my heart. Fifth in line was the prettiest girl I'd ever seen—hair like gold and a rosebud of a mouth I could taste just by looking at it. She was wearing a blue dress that brought out the color of her eyes and made them sparkle like she was smiling even if she wasn't. I was ready to propose marriage on the spot.

"Take your pick," the woman said and stepped aside.

Before I could get my tongue untied, Henry guffawed. "Paul, you might as well take the ugliest one, hadn't ya?"

And with that, my angel stepped forward and took both of Paul's hands in hers. "I'll take you," she said. My heart broke a little bit as I watched her lead Paul up the stairs by the hand.

But Henry had paid for all three of us, and I turned to see who might best offer consolation. He had already chosen a black-haired girl by slapping her on the behind, and I wondered if sporting girls ever hauled off and smacked somebody just for acting stupid. I had a feeling I might find out.

I caught the green eye of a redheaded girl and nodded, feeling my face go hot even as I did. Too bashful to speak to a whore—that was me.

I followed her up the stairs and could barely take in enough air with her hips swaying in front of me at eye level like that. She went down the hallway to the third door on the left, opened it, and then we were inside and she'd closed it.

I just stood there and blinked. It seemed like I ought to ask her name or something, but I doubt I could have said *ouch* if somebody had dropped an anvil on my foot. The right side of her mouth went up in a kind of grin, and she turned her back. I heard water pouring, and then she stood in front of me with a washbowl. I stared at it and back up at her.

"Hold this," she said.

I did, and then she unbuttoned me and started washing me with her hands, and that was all it took for part of me to lose its shyness. She took the washbowl away and gave me a gentle push onto the bed. Then she hiked up her skirt and climbed on top.

About a minute later, she climbed off and came back with the washbowl. I washed myself this time while she watched with a smile.

"First time's always quick," she told me. "Next time'll be better."

"How'd you know it was my first time?" I asked.

She threw back her head and laughed.

I fell off my stilts but fast.

Henry showed up in the parlor fifteen minutes after I did with a shit-eating grin. "How long you been done?"

I'd been there long enough to see three more men come in and go upstairs, but I said, "Just got here. Just now. A second ago."

"Uh-huh." He called out, "Ma'am?"

The woman who ran the house appeared as if conjured. "You got somethin' to wet our whistle while we wait for Lover Boy?"

She disappeared and came back with two bottles so cold they were sweating. "Sarsaparilla," she said.

Henry started to protest.

She said, "No liquor. Not in this house. That's all I need."

So we sat and waited. We finished our drinks, and the woman came through to collect the empty bottles. Two men came downstairs, and two more came in and went up.

I was just past admiration and starting to worry about Paul when my darling with the yellow hair appeared at the top of the stairs holding a dressing gown closed at the breast. "Y'all can go on now," she said. "Paul's going to stay awhile."

My jaw dropped, and I turned to see Henry's face mirroring mine.

"Well, what's 'awhile' mean?" Henry said.

She laughed, and it was pure music. "Come back tomorrow about noon. I might let him go by then." And with that, she disappeared again.

Henry and I had no choice but to leave. We found a room at a boarding house nearby for three dollars and settled in for the night.

"What the hell?" Henry asked.

I knew without asking what he meant. "I don't know," I said. "I reckon we'll find out when we go get him tomorrow."

But the girl with the blue eyes didn't let Paul go the next day.

We showed up at the cathouse at noon like she'd said, and we had to wrangle with the boss lady that we weren't there for any six dollars' worth more. Finally, she went up the stairs and came back with a disapproving look and no Paul. "He says come back when the auto is fixed." She sniffed. "He'll stay with Evangeline until then, he says. I do hope he has money."

My eyes went wide. "Oh, he does, ma'am."

"Ain't all he's got is my guess." Henry's voice was filled with marvel.

Over supper that night, we decided we weren't about to wait until the Ford was fixed before we collected him. No telling what all was going on out there, and I for one thought that some of it might not be to Paul's benefit. So we came back yet again the next day around noon, and the lady of the house answered the door and said, "He's not here. Or are you back as paying customers this time?"

"What do you mean, he's not here?" I said at the same time Henry said, "Yes."

I threw him a look.

"What?" he said, all innocence. "It's my money, ain't it?"

I supposed so. I peeled off three ones and handed them to him. He squeezed his way past the woman and went inside.

"He's at Evangeline's place," she told me and started to close the door.

I stuck my foot in the crack. "So he is upstairs?"

"Huh. She works here. She don't live here. She can do as she pleases on her own time, but I told her to get him out of here. Out about a mile that way." She tilted her head to the west. Then she hit my foot with the door hard enough I drew it back, and she was gone.

I sat down on the stoop, took a boot off, and rubbed my foot. I contemplated waiting for Henry. But that made me think about what Henry was doing, and thinking about that made me stand up. I considered going back into the house, after all, but my pulse told me it would be enough just to keep reliving the best sixty seconds of my life for a little while longer. I got my boot on and started moving again.

Henry caught up with me at our rooming house later. "What do you suppose is going on?" he asked.

"I don't know. I thought we'd go out and find something to do after supper."

"That's not what I mean, and you know it."

My face got hot. I couldn't think about where Paul was without picturing him with Evangeline the way I'd been with that red-haired girl, and that made me feel as bad as if I was watching them through a window. "I guess they hit it off," I finally said.

Henry snorted. "I'll say." He whinnied and pawed the ground with one foot.

I looked away, blushing harder.

So he and I didn't have much choice but to explore Denver. We set out from our room on foot to see what we could see. Time and again, I'd tell myself I was going to walk out to Evangeline's to check on Paul, but two steps in that direction, I'd find myself red faced and I'd turn around. He was a big boy, I kept telling myself, older than me. Worry might keep me looking to the west, but it wouldn't move my feet very far in that direction.

It was the first time since the stockyards in Kansas City that Henry and I had been together just the two of us, and getting around without Paul along was so much easier. I felt guilty for noticing. Just being able to say, "Hey, look at that," was a treat.

I offered to get work since we were going to be there a while, but Henry said, "Naw. We can go till the money runs out, and if it does, we can all get work."

I thought, *Hot damn. That's the spirit, Henry.*

We found a woman who took in washing and gave her everything we weren't wearing. The next day we changed in her outhouse and gave her our last dirty clothes to wash. In clean clothes and out of the all-day sun, I felt brand-new. At least until I got around people other than Henry.

Denver was a Kansas City–sized town but a whole lot more cowboy, and that didn't translate into much friendliness. Folks were more or less polite, but their eyes looked wary even when their mouths were smiling. We learned to eavesdrop everywhere we went to learn about the goings-on in town without needing to ask outright.

Maybe folks would have been nicer if we'd come at a different time. But the Jeffries and Johnson fight was less than a week off and had taken over Denver. It seemed like it was something in the very air. Folks took in a breath and came out with an opinion.

Reno had been decided upon for the site, just as Paul had predicted. Both fighters were there and had set up camp by then, and I guess that gave folks solid pictures in their minds to help fire their imaginations. For sure, to fuel their mouths.

Paul had gotten me in the habit of reading the newspaper, and now there was very little but talk of the fight there too. The *Denver Post* had sent one of their reporters to Reno, and his columns and lots of others repeated from other cities' newspapers pretty much covered the front page every day.

Just about everything on the page painted Jeffries as a hero and Johnson as some kind of animal. Jeffries had set up camp in an ivy-covered cottage surrounded by a tall fence with a sign that said Private: Keep Out. Johnson's people had taken over a roadhouse and resort outside of town and were supposed to be whooping it up all day and night, drinking and dancing. There was an armed guard patrolling the grounds at night because Johnson was getting so many death threats in the mail, and some writers in the *Post* even made it sound like any reasonable white person would send him one.

The movie palace in Denver took advantage of people being all fired up and showed boxing pictures every single night. Henry and I went once and saw the 1908 fight between Jack Johnson and Tommy Burns in Australia—the one where Johnson first took the championship away and started this whole firestorm. Watching that put the upcoming Fourth of July fight in a whole new light, seeing the spectacle played out of black skin against white, set to smash and destroy.

Neither Henry nor I had ever seen anything bigger than a fistfight in the schoolyard, and it was a shock to see grown men—any grown men—going at it like roosters, like they'd be happy to fight to the death.

Walking out after the show amid the shoving shoulders and muttered cussing of the crowd, we saw a colored boy get pushed to the ground for the offense of walking by at the wrong time. One man shoved him, and others went out of their way to step on him—his hands, his head, all over. The boy closed his eyes and took it. He never made a sound.

Henry started that way.

I pulled him back and pointed him in another direction.

"Goddamn them to hell," he said low.

I just nodded.

He'd been quick enough to jump on the bandwagon with the Johnson haters back in Kansas City, but back then, he'd put no more thought into anything than a parrot does. Now he was spending a lot of time in our room, staring at his shoes. I didn't ask him what he was thinking, but I was pretty sure what he was thinking about. I figured he'd talk when he was ready.

I'd not been of any opinion at all when the fight was a far-off proposition, but now I was ready to call it a flat-out mistake. The whole thing. You couldn't walk down the street without overhearing snippets of conversation: "Sparred eight rounds yesterday . . . Strong as ever . . . The black ain't even workin' out . . . How much you wanta bet?" I was tired of taking in tension every time I drew breath. It wears you down.

Henry and I wondered out loud behind the closed door of our room what Paul would make of all this and if he was keeping up with the news. Of course, then speculation would turn to what Paul was doing at the moment, and I would change the subject fast as I could.

Tuesday was one day sooner than the dealer had guessed the car might possibly be fixed, but by then I was more than ready to leave Denver.

"Headlights came. Still waitin' on the axle." The man at his desk in the Ford dealership barely glanced up from his newspaper, reading about the fight.

"Are you sure?" Henry asked. I guess he wanted to leave as bad as I did.

The man looked up at him over his half glasses and from under his brow. He didn't blink.

I grabbed Henry's arm. "Come on, pardner. Let's go look in on Paul."

Outside Henry said, "What the hell does that mean? You wanna watch him with that girl?"

That was an image I could have done without. "Aren't you the least bit worried about him?" I said.

"No. Why?"

"Four days, he's been there."

"Yeah. Lucky dog." Henry waggled his eyebrows at me.

I walked faster and didn't answer. No car, no

Paul, anger building to a boil all around us—I was the most unsettled I'd been since we'd left home. If Henry wouldn't go to check on Paul, by God, I'd go alone. All the way this time. Yessiree. One foot in front of the other.

I was about halfway to Evangeline's when it started to rain. It was the first shower I'd seen since early Kansas, and that set me to thinking about the Heverson brothers. Already that seemed like four or five lifetimes ago.

I was plenty warm even once I was soaked, but I could have done with dry shoes by the time I spied a shotgun shack standing all by its lonesome some fifty yards back from the road and nearly hidden by juniper trees.

A little blonde girl about five years old answered my knock at the door, and I was so surprised, I took a step backward. Then I heard Paul's voice ring out. "Who is it, Rae?"

"I don't know. They ain't said." She tilted her head back and smiled up at me—and I saw then that anybody who didn't know better might think she was Paul's little girl. She looked just like him. Same hair, same cheekbones.

She even had his eyes.

CHAPTER TEN

PAUL CAME TO THE DOOR WEARING clothes I'd never seen—a white shirt with no collar and a pair of brown pleated pants, both in fabric that looked as soft as that little girl's skin. "Who's there?" he said.

"Paul?"

His face split into a smile. "John! Come in! Come in! Is Henry here too?"

I stepped into a spotless little room with just a few pieces of furniture. "No, he's"—I looked at the girl—"where Evangeline works."

"Ah." He just nodded. "This is Rae Ann, Evangeline's daughter."

"Hello, Rae Ann," I said, and she curtsied. To Paul, I said, "I was just . . . I mean, we didn't know what . . . You know, I wanted to make sure . . ."

"You wanted to make sure I was okay." Paul smiled.

"Yeah."

"Is the Ford fixed?" He looked so relaxed and natural.

Before I could answer, Rae Ann jumped in with "Does Paul really have a auto, mister?" Her face looked like Easter morning.

"He sure does," I told her and then said, "No, Paul, I'm afraid not."

"Ah." He considered this. "Well, then, more time for Puddin' Pie here to learn how to read."

"Paul's learnin' me how to read!" Rae Ann told me.

"I'm *teaching* you," he corrected her.

"You sure are!"

He and I both laughed.

"So . . . I'd offer you some coffee or something, but Evangeline's about out of everything. She's supposed to go to the store when she leaves work." For all the expression in his voice, she might have had a job as a seamstress.

My head spun with unasked questions. "No, no, that's okay. I need to be going." Lord, we were talking like neighbors our parents' age. "I guess if you're okay—"

"I am," he said and reached out to comb Rae Ann's shoulder-length hair with his fingers. Then he said, "Honey pie, you haven't been to Odessa's since I got here. Why don't you go say hello to her and see if she's got an egg we can borrow?"

Rae Ann twisted the toe of her shoe on the wood floor. "You said Mama's goin' to the store today."

He laughed. "She is, but she doesn't know I used the last egg for your breakfast. Run along, okay?"

It was obvious she didn't want to leave, but she curtsied in my direction again and ran out the door.

When it closed behind her, I half stumbled into a chair. "What the hell, Paul? What the holy hell is goin' on?"

He laughed again, easy as could be. My guess was he hadn't done any nervous finger rubbing at all the last few days. "Where do you want me to start?"

"At the beginning! I mean, not all the . . . details, you know . . ."

He sat there with his movie actor smile. "Well, you were there when Evangeline picked me."

My heart sank the same way it had then. "Yeah?"

"It doesn't take much imagination to think that was because of Rae Ann. Evangeline had never met another blind person. We spent most of that first night talking."

"Talking."

"Yes, is that so hard to believe?" I didn't answer, and he went on. "She wanted to know where I was from, what my life had been like. She'd never heard of the school in St. Louis, and she doesn't have . . . she doesn't have a lot to go on here, as far as knowing what's out there in the world. What the possibilities are for Rae Ann."

"I see," I said, then winced at my choice of words.

He answered as though he'd seen me cringe.

"Figure of speech, John. Drop it."

"Okay. But none of that tells me how you ended up here. At Evangeline's house. Four days ago."

"We hit it off," Paul said with a smile so wide I had to start laughing. He joined me. "And of course I wanted to meet Rae Ann. And then . . . well, isn't she just about the sweetest thing you've ever seen?"

I had to agree. Then I thought of Catherine with a pang that reminded me how long it'd been since I'd thought of her last.

"Okay . . . who's this Odessa she just went to see?"

"Colored woman Rae Ann stays with part of the time while Evangeline's working. Lives near here. Rae Ann adores her."

There it was. "But, Paul. Doesn't it . . . bother you when Evangeline's working?"

He sat for so long, his face a mask, that I felt sorry for asking. But then he cleared his throat and said, "No, John. When I think of the entire spectrum of things that have bothered me in the course of my nineteen years, Evangeline's job barely registers."

Not much I could say to that.

Rae Ann came busting through the door again, radiant as the sun and with an egg in her hand. "Here you go!"

Paul swung her up in his arms and hugged her.

I was having trouble swallowing all of a sudden. "So I'll just . . . come back out when the car's ready?"

"You do that. I'll be here."

I walked the mile back to town. The sun popped out and made me think of what my grandma had said when I asked where I came from. "The buzzards laid you, and the sun hatched you." Could be true, for how I felt.

Henry had as good as made a family with the Heverson brothers. I couldn't imagine him going farther than their place on the way home. And now Paul had moved right into a family of his own here in Denver. Peculiar as the circumstances were, I could see him staying on.

And I was alone. I still had no idea where I wanted to live. Where I belonged. What I was capable of doing, other than a few things I knew wouldn't make me happy. I went back to the room in town, pulled off my rain-damp clothes and climbed under the covers in my drawers and a dry shirt.

I knew something was wrong as soon as I came to. I sat up and puked all over myself and then stared at the mess.

"What'd you do that for?" Henry asked.

I tried to answer and gagged instead.

He grabbed the chamber pot and shoved it under my chin, and the smell of stale piss just about turned me inside out. When there was nothing left to bring up, I laid back on the bed, exhausted.

Henry pawed at the buttons on my shirt.

"What the hell? Get off me!" My voice was so weak I didn't even convince myself.

"I'm not sleepin' in the same room with puke clothes," he said.

And that was it for me until I woke up in the dark.

I looked over and saw Henry sitting at the small table in the corner with a kerosene lamp and a look on his face like he was studying something.

"Hey." I tried to sit and gave up the effort. My ribs were sore and my stomach muscles knotted. "I must've slept a couple hours, huh?"

"Try twenty-four."

That got me up. "Huh? You saying this is Wednesday?" I wobbled over and looked out the window. "Wednesday night?"

"Yep." Henry had some kind of game board spread out and covered with little black and white pieces I couldn't quite make out.

"But"—I felt panicked—"we didn't check on the auto."

"I did. Still no axle."

"But you should've gotten me up anyway. I needed to—"

"What?"

"I don't know. But I sure as hell didn't mean to—"

"Oh, relax." Henry was reading some small print on what looked like the lid of a box. "You slept off a bad belly, and the world kept turnin' without you."

Great. I was alone *and* unnecessary.

Remembering my lonesome walk back from Evangeline's reminded me I hadn't told Henry. So I did. I told him about walking out and about Rae Ann. I told him about Paul and his new clothes and how he looked right at home and like a daddy to Evangeline's little girl. I said I could see him staying on, making his own family here.

"And you got lovesick. That's what happened to you."

"Oh, don't—" I started. Then I thought about everybody belonging somewhere but me.

Lovesick made as much sense as anything else. I shut my mouth. A few minutes later, I shut my eyes.

The next morning, Henry was sitting right where I'd seen him last. He had game pieces all over the table and still looked like he was studying. "Oh, good," he said. "You're awake. Come on."

"What is that?"

A game called Go was what it was. Henry said he'd gone into the drugstore looking for a jigsaw puzzle to work on in our room and found this instead. It was nothing like checkers or cards or anything we were used to. We spent all morning reading the rules and arguing about what they meant.

After dinner, we walked to the Ford dealership to learn nothing new, and when we got back, Henry took such a long time in the outhouse I was able to sit and read the game's instructions again. They made a lot more sense without him helping. By the time he came in, I was raring to play.

I beat him four straight times. Each game, he'd change tactics. One time he'd be on the attack and try to keep me from claiming any territory. The next time, he'd spend the whole game in retreat, trying to run away from my game pieces. All I had to do was the opposite of him to win.

He didn't get mad, though. He seemed to think every time I won was nothing more than dumb luck, and he was always the first to suggest another game. I have to admit I welcomed any opportunity for Henry to make me feel smart. I'd been feeling a little short in that department.

After supper, we walked by the saloon, but angry voices trying to outshout one another made us turn away. The fight. Of course. We went back to the room and picked up our own contest. I was more than happy to stay off the streets.

Friday morning, July 1, we played one game of Go after breakfast and decided to walk out to the Ford place to work up an appetite for another meal. With nothing much to do and nowhere pleasant to go, meals were starting to count for more than fuel. They were a way to parcel out the day.

The man whose name we'd never asked brightened a little when we walked in. "Come in! Come in," he said. "Axle came in yesterday after you were in. Had no way to get ahold of you."

"So the car's ready?" I said.

"No, not quite, not quite. But it should be by closing time."

We both let out war whoops, and the man seemed pretty pleased his own self.

We headed toward the door, and then I had a thought. "How much is it gonna run?"

The man acted like he hadn't thought about it yet, and I figured that was trouble. "Well, let's see." He opened his desk drawer for a pencil, licked the lead, and set in ciphering on a tablet.

"Looks like"—he peered at us and glanced down like he was making sure—"two hundred and sixty-one oughta get it."

Henry whistled through his teeth. "What'd Paul pay for the whole thing? Eight hundred?"

"Nine something," I answered.

"Damn." Henry scratched his head. "Figure he's got that much left?"

"Cash on the barrel head," the dealer leveled at us. "You're not getting near that machine until I'm paid in full."

"You will be. You will be." Henry waved a hand. "Don't get your drawers in a knot."

I yanked him outside.

After discussing our options, we walked out to Evangeline's to tell Paul the good news and the bad. I'm sure Henry wanted to see the house too.

"Damn" was also Paul's assessment. Then he

told the little girl real quick, "Don't repeat that, Rae, okay? Your mama will have my hide."

Henry and I carried on a whole conversation in one look between us.

Paul started pacing. "I don't have it. Not with me, I mean."

"I do," Henry told him. "Don't worry about it, Paul. Like I told Johnson here, we'll all spend till it runs out, and then we can all work."

"No, I won't have that," Paul said. "I set something up with Sam back home just in case. Rae Ann, will you stay here and be a good girl if I go in to the Western Union office for a while?"

"Yes, Paul." She worshipped him, you could tell.

We three were a quarter mile away from the house before I had a thought. "Paul, how long's it gonna take for Sam to get your message and wire money back?"

"I don't know. I'd guess tomorrow."

Henry stopped in his tracks. "Tomorrow," he declared. "But the car's gonna be ready today!"

Paul's expression didn't change. "That doesn't mean we have to leave today, does it?"

"Paul, we been ready to leave for days!" Henry emptied his lungs. "This hasn't been the best place to hang around—not that you'd know it, out there in the hills playin' house."

Paul walked faster, and we stepped to catch up.

"I can't leave without saying good-bye, and Evangeline won't be back until morning."

Henry dropped back a step to look at me, his face asking, *What do we do now?*

I wanted out of Denver too. And I knew that with anybody else, I'd have been raising holy hell, but still and all . . . I just looked at Henry and shrugged.

He said, "Well, I suppose it won't kill us to stay one more night." But he looked like there was an acorn-sized rock in one of his shoes.

I said, "If we stay out of public places, it won't kill us. Probably."

"What are you two talking about?" Paul asked. His mind seemed to come back from somewhere.

"Fights breakin' out all over town," I explained.

"What's going on?"

"*What's goin' on?* The prizefight. Remember?" Henry looked as astonished as I was. "The championship? Fourth of July? Monday?"

"People are all worked up about it. It's all anybody's talkin' about, everywhere we go."

"To tell you the truth," Paul said, "I kind of forgot about it."

"Well, nobody else did," I said. "I can guarantee that. Leastwise, not in Denver. I sure as hell don't want to be here Monday night."

Henry nodded.

Paul nodded too. "It makes sense in a crazy kind of way, though. The more illogical a fool's position, the more passionate he's likely to be about hanging on to it."

Henry said, "I don't know what in Jesus' name

you just said, but people here are ready to beat the hell out of one another."

We'd made it to the heart of town, and we steered Paul toward the Western Union office. He sent a message for Sam, care of Charlie's in Wakenda, and I realized that by nightfall, the whole town would know we needed money. I guessed we'd find out when we got back whether we'd been branded heroes or buffoons.

Outside, Henry and I started out on what felt like our constitutional, walking to the Ford dealership. Paul stopped after a few steps. "Evangeline's is that way." He pointed to the west.

"Yes, Paul." I tried to be patient. "But the Ford dealership is this way, and we at least need to let the man know our plans. Tomorrow's Saturday, and after that comes Sunday. We're gonna have to make some kind of arrangements to get the Ford whether he's open when your money comes or not."

"I can pay today and get the car. Then we can take off as soon as your wire comes," Henry threw in.

"No," Paul said. "I mean, I don't want you paying for it. That's final. I'll pay for it myself." His voice was telling me money wasn't the issue at all.

Henry scuffed his boot on the sidewalk and worked at a splinter. "Paul? It's a loan, okay? We can't go anywhere else till your wire comes now anyway, right? But we may as well get the auto if it's ready."

Paul looked like his gut was twisted, but he said, "Okay."

The scene at the dealership was a distant echo of the day Paul bought the Model T. I counted out two hundred sixty-one dollars and handed it over to Paul. He paid, I put his hand in position to sign the papers, and there were handshakes all around.

The man walked us out back. "Looks brand-new, doesn't she?"

The Ford had been washed and polished after it was fixed, and all traces of Kansas and quicksand were gone. It seemed wrong somehow. I ran my hand over a front fender and could feel slight little pock-marks—so small I couldn't see them—and somehow that was satisfying. The Model T shouldn't be exactly the same after a month away from home either.

We drove Paul out to Evangeline's and told him we'd be back for him noon sharp on Saturday. He gave a glum nod and went inside.

On the way back to town, Henry said, "What do you make of him stayin' out there all week? I mean, it'd be one thing if she was there with him all the time, but Jesus . . ."

"I expect it's the closest he's ever come to family."

"Well, yeah, but . . ." I knew he was picturing Evangeline the same way I was.

"I know. I expect that complicates things." I didn't want to repeat what Paul had said to me about how Evangeline's work barely registered on the spectrum of his troubles. It seemed like we'd talked about him enough behind his back already. We were quiet the rest of the ride.

Back in our room, we were halfway through a game of Go when we heard loud voices in the street outside. *Pow! pow! pow!* came a sound like when the Model T expressed an opinion. We bumped into each other, pulling back the curtain to look.

A man the color of chocolate laid facedown with his head in a pool of blood still spreading. Four white men stood some ten feet away, one of them holding a pistol. A colored woman stepped off the sidewalk to go to the man shot, and the one with the gun shouted. When she looked, he aimed at her, then pointed the gun up and fired into the air. She gathered her skirts and ran without ever making a noise. We watched as the four men milled around talking and finally walked off in pairs. The black man laid there, bleeding.

"Christ." I'm not sure which of us said it.

We stumbled over to our chairs, and I wiped my hands over my face.

Henry knee-walked back to the window and looked out again. "I can't believe it. Gone. Already. Nothin' but a big stain." He turned, and we looked at one another a long time.

We tried, but we never could pick up the thread of the game again. "I don't understand," Henry finally said. He pushed his chair back from the table. "I mean, not just tonight, but that boy outside the picture show. People walkin' on him like he was sawdust instead of a human being."

I snorted. "You're the one who drove the colored man and his wife off the sidewalk in Waverly. Scared the hell out of those two men in Topeka too. What do you call that?"

He waved a hand. "Aw, hell, I was just havin' fun. Plus, I didn't know any better."

"Well, I expect that's your answer," I said. "A lot of people don't seem to know any better."

He went on like I hadn't said anything. "You know, I keep thinkin' about the Heversons. When I asked them what they thought about the fight and had to explain to them it was a chance to prove white over black and all that, all they kept saying was 'Why?' I didn't understand then at all what they meant, but now I do. They meant, why does anybody have to prove anything? Why can't everybody just treat other people the way they want to be treated their own self?" He was so serious, like it was something new he'd made up on his own.

"Well," I said, "I believe that's just exactly what's known as the Golden Rule. Preachers talk about it all the time, Henry. And those who want to listen, do. Those who don't, well—"

He shook his head. "But that's wrappin' it up in God and hidin' it inside a church. All I'm talkin' about is, why do people keep harpin' on all the ways we're different instead of payin' attention to everything that's the same?"

Henry had been surprising me just about every day. He was like some kind of bush that had lived in the shade all these years and finally found sunlight or something. I couldn't help thinking that if he'd had a different situation growing up, he might have become a great man.

Hell, he still might, I thought. I should have told him that. I didn't.

The rooming house we were staying in wasn't fancy enough to have a dining room. But the owner, Mrs. Stockwell, lived there all the time, so I knew there'd be a kitchen. I went down and knocked on her door and ended up paying twice what it would have cost anywhere else for enough food to get us through supper and breakfast. It was worth it.

The next morning, the street was filled with people going about their Saturday business. You couldn't even see anymore where the black man had died.

Close to noon, we told Mrs. Stockwell we wouldn't be back and we headed out with our stuff to pick up Paul, sticking to little side streets as much as possible.

He was as happy to see us as he would have been to see the undertaker, but he came along. On the trip into town, he only spoke once. "Rae Ann's got a fever."

I guess Henry didn't know what to say to that either.

The Western Union man counted out three hundred dollars in twenties and tens and laid them on the counter. Henry picked up the pile and counted out two hundred sixty, handed that to me, and put the rest in Paul's hand. I shrugged and ignored the man's raised eyebrows.

We walked out into the noonday heat, and Henry said, "So that's that. Eight days, and we can finally leave this hole."

"Rae Ann's got a fever," Paul said again.

Henry looked off somewhere like he was counting to ten.

I cleared my throat. "Paul? Are you fixin' to stay?"

"No! Well, I mean, not . . . I can't—"

"Yes, you can." My heart picked up its pace. "I can't say I want you to, but that's for selfish reasons. Henry and I can take the train back home, if that's what you really want to do."

Paul wrestled with this.

Henry said, "Hell, for that matter, we can take the Ford on to Yellowstone and bring it back and *then* take the train home."

"No! You can't." Paul didn't have to think that one over.

I said, "Why not?"

Henry asked, "You don't trust us? After everything?"

"Of course I do, but Yellowstone . . . I mean, that

was the goal, that was the whole purpose—"

"No, it wasn't." I recognized it as truth when I said it.

Paul turned toward the west. "Yes, but giving that up . . . Well, it would feel like giving up, period."

A man on a strawberry roan galloped by whipping its hindquarters like he was on the lam or going to be soon.

Henry's face was so hard it looked brittle.

"So. What do you wanna do, Paul?" I asked.

"Rae Ann's got a fever."

"Yeah, we know," Henry said. "Can we go now?"

Paul sounded dazed. "One more night."

"Holy shit!"

"I don't believe you!"

"What the hell!"

"Paul, we gotta get outta here! Now!"

We came at him from both sides.

He held up a hand. "Just one more, I swear. Let me take care of Rae tonight, and I promise tomorrow . . . Well, Evangeline doesn't work on Sundays. She can take care of her then."

Henry's eyes went wide. "Paul, what's gonna happen when she gets sick next week? Next month? Next year?"

Paul swallowed. "I won't know about it. I won't know to worry about her. I won't feel like I'm leaving when she needs me."

"Paul, we gave up our room," I tried. "Saturday

night, I doubt we can get it back."

"Come camp out. It's nice weather," Paul said. "Look, you want to get out of town, right? But you got no place in particular you want to get to, do you? You keep saying Denver's ready to boil over. You think Cheyenne's going to be any better right now?"

He had us there.

"One more night, fellows. Please. For a little girl who spends too much time alone as it is."

Damn. He knew how to heap on the guilt.

But what really got to me was his face—usually stone and now pure torture.

So we drove out to Evangeline's house and had supper, the three of us, at her table. Paul got up and ministered to Rae several times when she called him. He acted like it was second nature. Then Henry and I went outside to make a campsite.

"I feel like we've been sent to the colored help's quarters," he complained.

"Not tonight, you don't. I imagine we'll rest easier than any colored people in America."

"Well, at least it'll be over soon." Henry yawned. "One way or the other. If Jeffries wins, whites get what they wanted and can shut up. If Johnson wins—" He looked like he'd been kicked.

"There's gonna be hell to pay, no matter what happens. Look." I pointed toward town, where a two-story building was in flames. "Think somebody left the chimney flue closed?"

No fire of our own, we stared at the one a mile away until it burned down to a glow and we fell asleep.

The air was still gray and thick when I heard a noise and opened my eyes to see Evangeline slip inside her front door. Henry was sleeping, and I tried to get back to that thoughtless land myself.

The best I could manage was a daydream, though, with Evangeline rising from her bath all rosy and flushed, her hair curling around her face as she reached for a towel. I watched her dry her dainty little feet and her soft rounded knees and make it up to her damp thighs—

I felt a nudge and found Paul standing over me.

I jumped up like he knew. "Oh, hey." I raked my fingers through my hair.

"Let's get going. What needs to be done?"

I looked around. "Well, nothing. Roll up our bedding and take a leak. After we get Henry moving, that is." I poked him with one big toe, and he roused. I looked toward the house with its smoke coming out the chimney. "I don't suppose there's any chance of breakfast—"

Paul held out a cloth-covered package. "For the road."

Less than five minutes later, we were standing next to the Model T with our belongings stashed inside.

I said, "Do you need to—?"

"Done."

We headed north, and once we'd put Denver behind us, we were in high desert land again and the real mountains popped up into our view to the west like they were rewarding us for leaving that godforsaken place. The land directly around us wasn't pretty, to say the least, unless sagebrush and tumbleweeds count for something I don't know about. But the air was cleaner and easier to breathe.

That's how I felt anyway. Paul rode shotgun, still as a statue. I told him what the world looked like around us, and he didn't even nod. My guess was he saw something different.

We had dinner and bought some gasoline for our spare can in Loveland, a little town about halfway between Denver and Cheyenne. I was all for making Cheyenne and passing through so we could camp somewhere the other side, but when I suggested it, Paul came back to life.

"No! We can't do that."

I nearly veered off the road. Like that would matter much. We were following a trail cut by wagon wheels, and it looked like those had been following cow paths.

"Sure we can" came from the backseat. "Pick up some provisions, say thank you, and get the hell out."

"But that defeats the purpose," Paul argued.

"All this time you been hidin' the fact you got a *purpose*?"

I glanced back to see Henry smiling, and it struck

me as a sight I hadn't seen in nearly a week. We could have done with a lot less Denver.

"Four major cities along our route," Paul recited. He ticked them off on his fingers. "Kansas City, Topeka, Denver, Cheyenne. We can't just skip one."

"Paul," I said, "how about we sightsee in Cheyenne on our way back? A week or so from now?"

"I thought we'd take a different route back."

I snorted. "You want roads worse than these?" Right on cue, I hit a deep rut that rain had sluiced across the trail. We bounced down, then up, then started on with a limp I recognized as another flat tire.

All the while Henry and I worked to change the casing and patch the tube, we argued. Henry reminded Paul he'd been away from the ugliness of town the past week and didn't know what he was asking for. Paul said we'd made our point, but observing didn't mean you had to get caught in the fray. That's what he said: *caught in the fray*. By the time we were ready to push on, it was clear that the ugliness leading up to the fight was something Paul would just have to see for himself. So to speak.

The sand of northern Colorado and southern Wyoming, it turns out, isn't at all good for making mud. Instead, when rain falls, it runs and cuts miniature Grand Canyons across the countryside. There were dozens of them in our path, and they ran as far east and west as the eye could see. There was no way we could go around them. We had another flat before Cheyenne, and the travel in between was the slowest going we'd had the entire trip.

I was so starved by the time we hit civilization I couldn't have argued with Paul any more anyway. We drove down a dark main street with Henry and me squinting at signs.

"Tavern, saloon, bar," Henry muttered. "Don't these people eat?"

"What are you lookin' at?" a cowboy on the sidewalk yelled.

Thunk! The business end of his bullwhip cracked on the Ford's front fender.

Paul jumped. "What was that?"

"Welcome to Cheyenne," I told him.

We settled on a tavern not too much in the thick of things and walked into what you might call a lively debate.

As we were getting situated at a table, a man wearing full cowboy gear right up to the hat pounded his glass on the bar and said, "What I wanna know is, he thinks he's all-powerful and better than white people, then how come he only goes around with white women?"

The crowd seemed to agree.

There was no question who he was talking about.

"He's forgot his place is what," someone shouted.

A man wearing a bloody apron came through a back door and over to our table. "You havin' food or just gettin' drunk?"

"Food," Henry answered. "What you got?"

"Steak," the man said.

"What else?" Paul asked.

The man frowned at him. "Another steak," he growled.

"I meant, what comes with it?"

"Beer or whiskey, your choice."

"What kind of steak is it?" Paul asked.

Couldn't he hear the annoyance in the man's voice?

"Coon steak."

Paul blanched.

"What the hell you think? Beef." He used his apron to wipe his nose and dropped it again. "You want one or not?"

We all nodded.

"Drink," he said.

"Beers all around," I answered, and he was gone.

Paul clasped his hands on the table, and they were shaking a little. Every time someone yelled, he flinched. It was a hell of a way for Henry and me to earn an *I told you so*.

Once our beers and bloody-rare steaks came, we didn't say much except "Salt" and "Pepper." There was enough being said. We didn't hear anything new and, for sure, nothing smart, but that didn't slow down the flow of words any. And not a word spoken was about any subject other than the fight.

When we were almost finished, a bowlegged man with a Santa Claus belly staggered into our table and bumped Paul's shoulder. "Sorry," he mumbled.

Paul tilted his head back and said, "Sure."

That stopped the man dead. He bent over until his nose was three inches from Paul's. "This is what I'm goddamn talkin' about," he bellowed.

I started to my feet and saw Henry coil like a spring.

"If we'd take all the retards and the other defects and drown 'em when they're born, the goddamn spooks wouldn't look around and get such a high opinion of theirselves. We need to start cullin' and sortin', I tell you. Cullin' and sortin'."

"Let's go," I said. "Paul. Two steps to the left and forward." Paul and Henry stood, I threw two bills on the table, and we lockstepped out with Paul in the middle.

Our bowlegged friend couldn't let go. "Long way to a river," he yelled at our backs. "Jes' throw him down a well!"

We walked out to a chorus of drunken laughing.

My hands were shaking on the lever and throttle, and it took Henry three tries to crank the Ford started.

"Where to now?" I said once he was in the backseat.

"Out of town. Camp. You were right." Paul's teeth clacked together.

"Wait." Henry leaned over between us. "Drive on down the road and get away from here and then stop." When I had done that, he went on, "I say we find someplace here to stay tonight."

"Here in Cheyenne?" I thought I must have heard wrong.

"Listen," Henry said, "you want to be out in the middle of nowhere, just the three of us, if that asshole back there and some of his buddies happen by on their way home later?"

He had a point.

I drove almost to the edge of the city and stopped in front of a hotel that didn't look any worse than the others we passed. We all got out and walked up to the door together.

A man unlocked the door and pointed a shotgun at us. "Try anything and I'll shoot."

We raised our hands like we'd seen in moving pictures. For Paul, it must have been instinct.

"We're not trying anything, sir," I said. "We need a room. Someplace safe."

His eyes narrowed. "Who you runnin' from?"

Henry stepped forward. "Sir, have you heard of Motherlode Jones, the biggest miner to strike gold in Idaho?"

"I . . . guess so," the man said.

Thank God I was in no mood for anything to strike me funny.

"Well, this is him," Henry hissed and tossed his head my direction. "We're accompanyin' him back east and, well, there's all sorts would like to know what he's carryin', if you know what I mean." Henry nodded toward his own metal safe box, tucked under his arm.

The hotel owner looked us up and down. "You don't look like you got a pot to piss in."

Henry winked. "Well, now, wouldn't do to tip

our hand, would it? Too much at stake to be showy about it."

The man still looked suspicious. "One at a time, then, and I'm gonna have to pat you down. I don't need no trouble."

"Of course." Henry stepped through the doorway first. He handed me the metal box, and I felt his gun slide and hit one side. He grinned. "Can't be too careful."

Upstairs, Paul threw himself on the bed. "I don't want to talk about it," he told the pillow.

"We need to talk some," I said. "About tomorrow."

Henry was nodding. "You got the map?" I took it out of my pocket and handed it to him. "I dunno. Whaddaya think? Laramie?"

I looked over his shoulder. "We can make it a little farther, don't you think? Wheatland, maybe?"

Paul rolled over. His face looked like a shirt that had been slept in. "What? What in God's name are you planning?"

"Where to be for the fight tomorrow," Henry said.

"How about someplace they've never heard of it?"

I smiled a hair. "Don't think we can get to the moon by tomorrow afternoon."

Paul sat up. "No. I mean why don't we camp out miles from any town and stay as far away as possible until it's over?"

Henry and I looked at each other and shook our heads.

"Same reason as tonight," Henry said.

"Who knows who might come along and what kind of tear they might be on?"

Henry said, "We don't want to be here—"

"But there's some safety that numbers can offer," I finished. "We want to be—"

"In a small town," Paul said. "We want to be in Wakenda."

CHAPTER ELEVEN

JULY 4, 1910, DAWNED OVERCAST WITH clouds that looked none too friendly. We slipped out of town early and as quiet as we could. After we left the hotel, the only stop we made was at a baker's shop—open before everything else—for enough bread and sweet rolls to get us through the day if need be.

We had settled on Wheatland as where we'd stop driving that day. It looked to be a little over sixty miles from Cheyenne, and the way the map was keyed, you could tell it was no major town. We thought there was plenty of time to get there, until we started crossing more gullies washed out across the road. Henry and I took turns driving and reminded each other there was only one patch left to get us to our next stop.

None of us mentioned the two Ford dealerships in Cheyenne that could have supplied us with any parts we wanted. We weren't going back.

I was driving when Henry turned around and

called, "And there it goes. Gentlemen, we have just lost sight of Cheyenne." At that second, the sun broke through the clouds, and we all busted out laughing.

Along about noon, we came into a town called Chugwater that wasn't shown on our map. It was a Wakenda-sized town, and we were almost out the other side before we turned around and came back to the dry goods store. We all got out to stretch, and I went in. There was a lunch counter with stools back in a corner, and I came out to get the other two.

We took the last three seats and ordered fried chicken with mashed potatoes and gravy, the only things written on the menu slate up on the wall. The men sitting at the counter gnawing on chicken bones nodded and gave us a friendly howdy. The man and his wife who ran the store and the kitchen turned out to be just as nice.

Once somebody asked where we were from, we became star entertainment for the whole group. The three of us took turns telling stories, and the locals all took turns going out to look at the Model T.

"Nobody here got a automobile yet?" Henry asked.

The missus reared back her shoulders. "Russell Horsch has got one. Brings it to town every month or so. It's not like we've never seen one." She rubbed at the counter with a rag, just a little too hard.

Not one of them mentioned Paul's blindness. Even better, nobody mentioned the fight coming up that afternoon. It was like we'd driven into a bubble, with all the meanness left on the outside. After we'd finished eating and gathered the well wishes of our fellow diners, we went over to the cash register to pay and get toothpicks.

Under my breath, I asked Paul, "Want a newspaper?"

He just about broke his neck shaking his head.

I asked the woman as she handed me change, "Are there any hotels or rooming houses here in town?"

"Nearest is Wheatland."

"Any place at all we could stay over? We don't need anything fancy."

"Nope. Sorry."

So staying in this friendly little town until the brouhaha blew over wasn't an option. If we did stay, we'd have to camp. Exposed. Open to all the elements, natural and otherwise.

And looking over your shoulder is worse than facing whatever happens. Probably.

As we got closer to Wheatland, I realized neither of the other two had spoken since we'd got out of Chugwater and I was driving even slower than I needed to.

"We've got to be somewhere," Paul finally said.

Henry nodded.

I gave the Model T a little more gas.

"It was almost one o'clock when we left there," Henry said. "Fight's at one thirty. Take our time, it may all be over before we get to Wheatland. We might miss the whole thing."

"It's not the during-the-fight part I'm worried about," I said.

We got to Wheatland, a Lexington-sized town, around two o'clock. Main Street was easy to find, and from the crowd milling around talking, it seemed like maybe we really had dodged the whole event. The crowd was divided, all the white people in a group on one side and half as many coloreds on the other, but voices were quiet and postures were normal. Maybe we'd been afraid for nothing.

I stopped the Ford next to a fellow who looked to be about our age.

"Who won?" I asked him.

He snorted. "Ain't started yet. Rumor has it that coon's turned out to have a whole lot of chicken in him." He spat in the street.

"Why's everybody out here?" Henry asked.

"'Cause we won't all fit in the telegraph office—that's why." The man threw a look toward Paul. "You got any stupid questions?"

Of course Paul didn't answer.

"Oh, I see. Deaf, dumb, and blind. Ain't you three pretty."

Henry started out of his seat, and I motioned him down.

"Just traveling through—that's all," I said. "Just thought we'd ask, in case the fight was over."

"Over before it's started, far as I'm concerned.

'Bout time somebody shut that big, black mouth. I hope he kills him."

Paul must have flinched or frowned—I didn't see.

The fellow let out a laugh that sounded like a donkey braying. "Gotta darkie lover here, do you? Or don't he know what colored is?"

Henry's face was getting red.

I said, "Thanks for the information."

Henry muttered something, and I put the auto in gear and moved down the block before I stopped again.

"Let's just keep driving," I said. "Do we really need to listen?"

Paul spoke up for the first time since we'd hit town. "And go where? You said it yourself last night. Where can we go to avoid whatever's going to happen?"

"We can just keep driving."

But I didn't put the Ford back into gear. We sat there with the motor putt-putting and none of us saying anything more. Finally, Henry craned his neck to turn around and scan the crowd behind us, and I couldn't help doing the same.

I didn't want to know. I had to know. Goddamn it to hell.

"We stayin' till it's over, then?" I asked.

A good long minute passed.

Then Paul said, "I think we have to."

No words would explain it in a way that made sense, but I understood.

Three blocks from the crowd was a sheriff's office with a jail attached, and I figured that was as safe a place as any to leave the Model T. When we started to get out, I saw Henry shove something into his waistband under his shirt.

"No. Henry, no. Do not take that with you."

"What?" he said, all innocence. "My wallet? I'm puttin' it someplace safe. Didn't you hear those fellers last night talkin' about all the pickpockets in Reno right now? You think they're *all* there?"

I took his measure and could tell there was no leeway for changing his mind. "Okay, then, but be careful. Let's all of us be real careful."

We walked back to the main street and saw the mouthy man from before on the far side of the white crowd, almost where the black group started. Henry headed straight for him, and I saw them exchange looks. I took Paul's sleeve to hold him back just as the announcement came that the fight was about to start.

A man in a suit fit for a funeral was the one who said so from the doorway at the top step of the telegraph office.

"Who's he?" I mumbled, more to myself than anybody.

"The mayor," a man next to me said with a glance. Then he looked again like he was memorizing the stranger who'd come to town.

I looked away.

"Harry shall read the telegraph tape as it comes

through," the mayor was telling us. "And I'll pass along each and every word. I promise. I won't even make the fight come out the way I want it to."

Most of the white people laughed. There were some murmurings from the colored side of the crowd, and the mayor raised an eyebrow in that direction.

Then something inside caught his attention. He turned back to us. "The battle of the century has begun," he proclaimed.

I wondered if he'd ever been a patent medicine peddler. He'd have made a good one.

The description of the fight was stutter step at best— a sentence would come over the wire, the telegraph operator would tell the mayor, and he would shout it out with great urgency and importance, and then we'd all stand and wait. A few minutes later, the next sentence would come.

The first part of the fight sounded more like a dance, the two big men locked in a clinch more often than not.

A man standing near me nodded. "That's the way, Jim. Use your weight."

Out of habit, I started to turn to Paul and describe what was going on, then realized he was experiencing the fight exactly as we all were.

In the third round, Johnson landed four upper-cuts in a row. The crowd in the street fell so quiet you could hear a fat man wheeze from twenty feet away.

Then in the fourth, the first blood was drawn,

and it was Johnson's. A cheer erupted from the white crowd, and it looked like the black people shuffled a little farther away.

But Jeffries was bleeding by the middle of the fifth and seemed to take the brunt of the punches all the way through the seventh. The part of the crowd I was in started getting restless.

I looked over at Paul and couldn't read his face. I tried to look through the crowd at Henry, but there were taller men and women with hats in the way.

After the seventh round, the teletype fell silent. We waited. An ambitious tavern owner from down the street made a circuit under the broiling hot sun through the crowd—the white crowd, anyway—selling glasses of beer and lemonade from a tray.

The mayor asked the telegraph operator if he was sure the machine was still working. He was.

Ten minutes had passed. The tavern owner came back with more drinks, this time trailed by a black girl who looked to be about fourteen. She carried a second tray and commenced selling beverages on the other side of the crowd.

"Hope he washes his glasses real good," a man near me muttered.

Fifteen minutes had passed. Still we waited. The crowd on both sides of the color line was getting impatient, milling around, the murmur getting louder.

After twenty minutes had passed, the mayor's head whipped around and we heard him ask the telegraph operator, "What? Are you sure?"

He looked dazed when he turned to face us, and his voice was only half as loud as earlier when he said, "Johnson wins in the fifteenth."

There were two seconds of stunned silence, and then the colored side of the crowd went crazy. They were whooping and yelling and crying. I saw tears among the white folk too.

Most of the whites hung their heads for a long moment and then started shuffling off in various directions. A few, five or six of the younger men, drew into a tight little knot and talked right up in one another's faces.

The teenaged colored girl walked by the bunch with her tray of empty glasses shoulder high. One overgrown boy stuck out his foot and tripped her. The whole group laughed as she fell and glass shattered all around her on the hard-packed dirt.

"Hard to be uppity on the ground, ain't it?" one of them said, and the rest roared.

The girl got to her knees and looked at her bloody palms.

"Oh, lookie," said another from the group, "the white part of her's bleedin'. Well, if that ain't fittin'."

The rest of the group liked his comedy too.

The girl didn't even look up. She started crawling around picking up shards of glass and collecting them on the tray. One of the men who had yet to join in gave her a hard kick in the rump that laid her out flat on top of the field of glittering glass.

"What's going on?" Paul said close to my ear.

"They're tormenting a colored girl."

"Well, let's *do* something," Paul said.

I opened my mouth to answer him, but nothing came out.

The girl rolled over and sat up. There was blood on her face, on her dress, and all down the length of her arms. She looked dazed.

"Get outta there, Lucinda," a woman's voice rang out. I looked to see the colored people huddled together like sheep in a storm. "Get up!"

"Yeah, get up!" It was the guy our age—the one who'd called us deaf, dumb, and blind. The toe of his boot caught Lucinda under the chin and sent her flying backward. She landed flat on her back and didn't move. The same fellow took another step toward her.

Henry stepped between them and put up a hand that said, *Stop.*

"Henry!" I yelled. *No, no, no, no.*

"What? What's he doing?" Paul pulled at my sleeve.

Henry and the other fellow were shouting. I couldn't pick their words apart, but it was clear what they were saying. Then the other fellow shoved Henry hard, and Henry's right hand reached inside his shirt. I wanted to run to him, but my feet felt like they were mired in quicksand.

"No!" It was so loud I couldn't have been the only one. The sound echoed in my ears while my leg muscles still wouldn't budge.

Henry's hand came out of his shirt with a glint of metal in the sunlight. I strained forward, still without taking a step, as he pointed the barrel of the gun in the air.

Had the next second not stretched to seem like a minute, the four shots that rang out would have sounded as one. As it was, they were set apart by the motion each one spawned.

First, a puff of smoke issued from Henry's pistol as he fired a warning shot.

Second, a hole opened in the right side of his chest and knocked him back a step.

Third, a force bent him forward like he'd been kicked in the stomach. He started to straighten up, and I thought our eyes met. They couldn't have. That far, that fast, they couldn't have. But there was no question about the start of a smile on his face.

Then fourth, his head blew apart like a pumpkin, showering bits of Henry onto everyone within six feet. My mouth was still shaped in an *O* from saying "No."

He hit the ground, and I heard a loud cry that may have come out of me.

"What's going on?" Paul was clawing at my arm. "What happened?"

I took a step backward to make sure of my balance. Things were starting to go around me in circles.

Whatever I said was going to make it real.

"He saved her life," I said, and then the day went dark.

I opened my eyes a few seconds later, sooner than I would have wished. Paul was kneeling over me, looking terrified. "John? John! Don't leave me!"

"I'm right here."

"Are you shot?" He was patting me down.

"No." I sat up. I didn't want to look. I didn't want to say.

Paul was shaking like he had the ague. "What do you mean, he saved her life?" In the background, there was a chorus of wailing women and the thunder of cowboy boots. Men with guns still in their hands ran past. I watched them untie their horses, roll up into the saddles, and gallop off like the cowards they were. Still, I didn't look behind me.

"John! Say something!"

"Henry's dead." There. It was true, whether I turned to look or not.

"No!" Paul stood up and wailed. "Go for help. Get a doctor!"

"Paul." I hoisted myself to my feet and put my arms across his shoulders so we were face-to-face. "It's too late for that. God himself couldn't put him back together."

Paul's face crumpled, and tears streamed from his cloudy eyes. Eyes I had never imagined I could envy. But I did. I would have been willing to give up sight if it meant not to have seen what had just happened to Henry.

Then I felt myself go numb, and it seemed like I

was watching the whole scene from a distance. Looking down from the top of a mountain, maybe. There were two white men holding each other up, one of them crying.

There was a group of black folks, some running away and some paired up just like the two men were, arms tangled and tears running free.

There was the girl Lucinda still bleeding, now on her knees by the dead boy and wrapping his shattered head in her apron while she cried. There was the sheriff, walking up to the two white men and saying something that caused them to walk away with him.

I came back to myself, sitting in a chair in the sheriff's office, holding a cup of coffee I didn't want. Paul sat nearby, his face a pale mask.

The sheriff sat behind his desk with a look on his face that said he'd just asked a question. It was a face that had seen its share of trouble—a face older than the body it went with.

"I'm sorry. What did you say?"

He scratched the back of his head. "I asked if you saw which ones of them shot."

I shook my head. "I wouldn't know them to tell you even if I had." I told him how we were travelers from Missouri, on the road five weeks with nobody around we knew but each other. "Three of them shot. That's all I know."

"Four!" Paul spoke up. "There were four shots."

The sheriff looked at me.

"The first one was Henry," I told him. "He . . . he fired a shot in the air to try and warn them off."

"Henry had a *gun* with him?"

The sheriff took in Paul's astonishment and looked back to me.

I shrugged. "He didn't have a wallet, Paul."

"Oh."

The sheriff frowned and rearranged some papers on his desk. "Well, I guess the next order of business is asking you boys what your plans are now."

Our plans. I wanted to say our plans were for all three of us to go to Yellowstone. To make it home again, all of us alive. I said, "I don't know, sir."

He nodded. "What about . . . What arrangements should be made for your friend? For the body, I mean. Does he have family back in Missouri that should be notified?"

I thought about the father who hadn't been sober since his wife died. The one who blamed Henry for that loss. "Not really. His sister, I suppose. Ellen." Surely at least she'd want to know.

The sheriff nodded. "Well, then, how about we all walk over to the telegraph office together and send a wire? Then I'd suggest you two be my guests here at the jail until you're ready to leave town."

"You're arresting us?" Paul cried out.

"No, son." The sheriff's voice got gentle. "I'm tryin' to protect you."

Paul's Adam's apple bobbed at the same time mine did.

I walked with them to the office, writing and rewriting telegrams in my head. Then the circle of bloodstained dirt where Henry had fallen came into view, and I nearly went to my knees. *It will be gone tomorrow*, I thought. *Just like that man they killed in Denver. People will walk over that spot like nothing worth noticing ever happened there.*

The sheriff took my elbow, and we went up the steps like we were entering chapel.

The telegraph operator sat in a bramble of ticker tape. It was all around him on the floor, left over from the fight. Had it really been that short a time?

I cleared my throat and said, "Her name is Ellen McCombs." The little man scribbled on a pad of paper. "Wakenda, Missouri." I spelled it for him. Then I looked to Paul, but he said nothing. "Let's see. Um, 'Sorry to report Henry dead stop.'" At least telegraph language made the message seem more official, less personal. "Um, 'Please advise stop.'" The operator wrote this down, and everyone looked at me. "That's all, I guess."

Paul spoke up. "Died a hero stop. Be proud stop."

The operator looked at me, and after a couple seconds, I nodded.

The sheriff waved away my offer of money for the wire and walked us back to the jail, promising to lock the front door and come back for us as soon as a reply came through.

For the third time since leaving home, we laid back on

bunks in a jail cell and tried to get some rest. Every time I closed my eyes, I watched Henry's head explode. I saw his face disappear over and over in a spray of blood and flesh until I thought I would be sick. I sat up to let my stomach settle. Paul was laying as still as a corpse himself, and there was no way to tell if he was sleeping. I laid back down and tried again.

This time the whole sequence repeated itself again and again. The first shot up in the air, the shot in the chest that stood him up tall, the one in the stomach that had him bow to the crowd, the straightening up and the smile . . .

"He was smiling," I blurted out.

"Huh?" Paul sat up fast. He hadn't been close to sleep either.

"Right before— Right before the last shot, Henry straightened up and looked our way. I swear he was starting to smile."

Paul's head cocked, and then he nodded. "He'd gotten his answer."

"His answer? What are you talking about?" I was too exhausted for riddles.

"That night you spent in Burlington and we were out in the desert with the car stuck in the creek."

I nodded and waited. Then I prodded him, "Yes?"

"We talked about a lot of things that night, and somehow we got around to talking about things that scared us. I had a lot more than he did, but that probably doesn't come as a surprise." Paul grimaced. "He told me the thing he was most afraid of was dying without ever doing anything worthwhile. That when he was gone, the time he'd spent here wouldn't count for anything or have made any difference." Paul's eyes welled up. "He died knowing it did. That's why he smiled. He knew he was saving someone else's life."

I wanted to argue that it happened too fast for all that to go through Henry's mind. I wanted to admit I didn't know if he really saved the girl's life or not, that I'd said so just to keep from saying what I'd seen. That it was stupidity, not bravery, that killed Henry.

I wanted Paul to have to share the weight of knowing exactly what it looked like when Henry met his death. But looking at his face, I couldn't tell him.

And it came to me: This is how heroes are made—in the memories of those left behind. Henry was a hero, could be one for all eternity, just because Paul said he was.

And that was enough said.

We heard the front door open, and we froze. The sheriff came back where we were with a piece of paper in his hand. "Either of you know a Jonas Hartmann?"

Somebody else might have felt some relief knowing his dad had taken charge. "Yeah," I said.

The sheriff handed me the telegram, and I read it out loud for Paul. "'Ellen says no money for funeral stop. Do your best stop. John come home stop. Wiring money for train stop. Urgent stop.'" I crumpled the paper into a ball and closed my fist around it.

The sheriff's face held a question.

"My father," I told him.

He hesitated, then nodded.

He walked us down the street to the undertaker's. Paul and I tried to pay for a coffin, but the man there told us the colored people in town had already taken up a collection. I didn't know what to say to that, and there weren't any other arrangements to be made, so we went back to the jail and spent the night not sleeping there.

Sometime past midnight, Paul spoke up as though we'd been talking all along. "I keep thinking it was written in the big book."

I was glad to break up the quiet but didn't know what to make of that. "What do you mean? What was written where?"

"Henry dying."

I thought about that for a minute. "You talkin' about *God's* big book?"

"Yes. Fate."

I turned this over a few times. "You think everything's already planned out for us? You don't think we have any say over what happens in our lives?"

"No, no, no. I believe in free will. But truth be told, I never could picture Henry as an old man. Could you?"

It was another reminder that Paul had a lot more experience making pictures in his head. I stared into the darkness to see what I could call forth. There was Paul with white hair. There I was, with grandkids crawling all over me—and a woman nearby whose face I couldn't quite see. But when I thought about Henry, all I saw was red hair. Freckles. Seventeen years old.

"I guess not," I admitted. "But what you're saying doesn't make any sense to me, Paul. How can you believe in destiny and free will both? Seems to me like you got to pick one or the other."

"It was written in the book," he said, "but Henry's the one who turned the page."

I thought about that until the sun came up.

The next morning, we had a little service at the grave-yard on the edge of town. There were twenty or so black folks gathered around the hole in the ground, and I nodded to as many as met my eye. Paul and I and the sheriff standing guard with his gun drawn were the only white faces there. We hadn't thought to ask for a preacher, but I was pretty sure that was okay. If I understood anything at all about the person Henry had turned into, this group came closer to his idea of what God was about.

Someone said a few words and some sang a spiritual, but I don't remember yet what it was. I was concentrating as hard as I could to freeze the whole scene. Make it something like a crystal I could take out later and thaw when it was safe. When I was somewhere by myself.

When there was nothing left to do but fill in the dirt, I nodded a few times more in the general direction of the colored people. Then I took Paul's elbow and walked straight to the telegraph office.

The operator perked up when he saw us. "There you are. Your money's here. Fifty dollars."

Fifty dollars was more money than I'd ever seen in one place before Paul bought the Model T. Dad laying out that kind of cash, without me asking for so much as a nickel, was a fair indication of just how worried he was.

I understood. I'd found out for myself how hard it is to let go when you think you're the only one who can take care of everything.

But I'd also had to face the fact that the only story I could ever write was my own. I couldn't take over for somebody else any more than I could erase a single thing they wrote. No matter how much I wanted to.

And I hoped Dad would come to accept that fact too.

"Send the money back," I told the telegraph operator.

He looked confused.

"Send it back with this message: 'Going on to Yellowstone stop. Do not need money stop.'" I paused.

The operator looked up when he was finished writing. "Is that all?"

"No," I told him. "Add this to the end: 'Thank you stop.'" I turned to Paul and saw him smile for the first time in days. I smiled back, sure he could feel it.

"Are you sure?" The operator wore a frown and tapped on the paper with his pencil.

I took Henry's money out of my pocket and peeled off a bill. "Yep."

CHAPTER TWELVE

TWO DAYS LATER, THE SEVENTH DAY of the seventh month and our thirty-seventh day away from home, Paul and I stood elbow to elbow at a wood railing and watched a geyser spew water a hundred and fifty feet into the air above Yellowstone National Park. I knew we both saw it, just in different ways.

All around us, steam rose from cracks in the earth. I counted twenty-five separate plumes before I gave up. The big one in front of us, Old Faithful it was called, ended its show and sprinkled our faces with moisture as it went back to sleep for another hour or so.

We stood and kept company with our own thoughts for a while.

Then Paul said, "I'm going to teach."

It came from so far out of the blue I wasn't sure I'd heard right. "Say what?"

"I'm going to teach. If they'll still have me—and

I think they will—I'm going to go back to St. Louis and teach at the school."

He'd said before that would be like giving up, like going back to the only place other than Wakenda where he knew his way around.

"I know what I said." He nodded like I'd reminded him out loud. "But that was before Denver. Before Rae Ann." I waited for him to mention Evangeline. "I really enjoyed working with her, John. Teaching her to read. It felt so worthwhile. Like it really counted for something. I've thought about it a lot since then."

I nodded. I could see him doing that—working with blind kids, teaching them there was a world out there waiting for them to do whatever they wanted with it. Showing them how big their lives could be.

What I couldn't see was him back in Wakenda, living with his parents. Treated like a liability by people who had no idea who he was or who he could become. People with no idea what he could accomplish.

Then it came to me that I was describing myself as much as Paul. A jolt went through me and lodged someplace I'd never felt before.

And while we stood there, an idea that had first sprouted at the telegraph office in Wheatland took hold and grew wings. I drew in a deep breath, held it a second, and said it. "They've got colleges in St. Louis, right, Paul?"

He said, "Sure. There's Washington University and Saint Louis University and—" He turned to me with a wide smile. "I thought you couldn't pay for college."

I grinned back. "So what? If I'm smart enough to go to college, surely I can figure out something."

"So what?" he echoed, and then we were both laughing and yelling.

"So what? So what? *So what*?"

I put my hand on his shoulder, and we turned our backs on one of the biggest wonders known to mankind—a miracle of nature that would repeat itself as long as there was a world around it. Like the great comet and all the other clockworks of the universe, it would tell its story without needing us or any other mere mortals there to turn the page.

We walked out to the road and, in a ritual second nature to us, cranked the Model T back to life.

ACKNOWLEDGMENTS

I started the research for this book in 1990. Louis Tutt, then superintendent of the Missouri School for the Blind, was a kind and patient resource. A wonderful group of women volunteered at a Ford library within the Dearborn, Michigan, Central Library in that era, and I called them many times. They always set me on the path to the information I needed.

Several authors unknowingly contributed to this book as their works became resources. Geoffrey C. Ward's *Unforgivable Blackness: The Rise and Fall of Jack Johnson* was invaluable. The Ken Burns film based on that book, as well as his documentary *Horatio's Drive: America's First Road Trip*, offered more insights. I read and reread Floyd Clymer's *Model T Memories*, and the publishing arm of the Ford Motor Co. itself—Books About Ford—made it possible for me to own a replica of the original Model T instruction book, an official account of "The Story of the [First Transcontinental] Race," and many other documents. About.com provided a trove of archived newspapers from small towns in Missouri that put me right there in 1910.

You people! You know what you did and why I thank you: Dan Roettger, Phil Freshman, Ron Kidd, Barbara Felt, Peter Barber, Neil Ross, Paul Fey, Kimberly Finch, the other eight Six Chix, George Clipner,

Lu Oros, Bill Wilkins, and Duane Daugherty.

To the people at Medallion Media Group: you have been nothing short of wonderful. Ali DeGray, Emily Steele, Helen Macdonald, James Tampa, Arturo Delgado, Brigitte Shepard, and others who have contributed behind the scenes—thank you.

Alec Shane at Writers House: you continue to amaze me. In a good way.

Most of all, I thank my grandfather for the story and my dad for teaching me how to tell one. I know you're both still there, just not where I can see you.